EVERY LITTLE THING

BUTLER, VERMONT SERIES, BOOK 1

BY: MARIE FORCE

Every Little Thing
The Butler, Vermont Series, Book 1
By: Marie Force

Published by HTJB, Inc.
Copyright 2017. HTJB, Inc.
Cover designer: Kristina Brinton
Interior Layout: Isabel Sullivan, E-book Formatting Fairies

ISBN: 978-1946136060

www.marieforce.com

AUTHOR'S NOTE

Welcome to book one in my new Butler, Vermont Series! Some of you might be wondering about the change in direction and the new series name. Last year, I decided to part company with the publisher of the Green Mountain Series and to self-publish the rest of what I hope will be a long series. To make things easier behind the scenes, I decided to give the series a new name—the Butler, Vermont Series—but *Every Little Thing* picks right up where we left off in *Ain't She Sweet* with all the characters you've come to love from the Green Mountain Series. The only difference readers will notice is the series name and the numbering sequence of the books. I appreciate readers rolling with me as I continue into this next phase of the series.

Because it's been nearly a year since you read *Ain't She Sweet*, I've included a prologue taken from that book to set up Grayson and Emma's romance in *Every Little Thing*. I hope you'll enjoy their story and the others I have planned for the remaining Abbott and Coleman siblings.

Thanks for sticking with me through this transition! I hope you love *Every Little Thing*!

xoxo

Marie

PROLOGUE

Grayson Coleman poured three fingers of his uncle's best scotch and took a seat in the corner, away from the fray of Hunter and Megan's wedding. The first sip traveled through him like liquid fire, heating him from the inside and giving him something to think about other than the rage that had been resurrected by the decision his cousin Max's ex-girlfriend, Chloe, made about their baby son.

It had been twenty long years since Grayson's father walked away from his wife and children, leaving Grayson and his mom to pick up the pieces for the others. He'd loved being the oldest in his family and had wallowed in the privileges that went along with being the eldest. Until he became the man of the family overnight, responsible for his distraught mother and seven younger siblings who were looking to him to make sense of something that still didn't make sense all these years later.

Here he was now, a man of thirty-six, an accomplished lawyer, and the scene with Chloe and Max in his aunt Molly's kitchen had taken him back to the long-ago night that marked the official end of his childhood. He could still remember the panic, the despair, the fear, the rage… all of it congealing into a hot knot of anxiety in his gut that he'd carried with him ever since.

How anyone could walk away from their own kid, let alone eight of them, was beyond him. He actively resented Chloe, a woman he barely knew, for what she'd done to her son tonight. For someday, in the not-too-distant future, Caden would find out that his mother had rejected him, and he'd never be the same.

Grayson had never been the same. He took another deep sip of the scotch, letting the searing heat soothe him.

"What's that stuff?" a little voice next to him asked.

He looked over at the girl with the red curls who'd sat next to him in his quiet corner that wasn't so quiet anymore. "It's scotch. You ever had it?"

She wrinkled her adorable nose. "Of course not. I'm a kid. Kids don't drink scotch. My Pop likes it, though, so that's how I know what it is."

"What do you drink?"

"I like apple juice, but Mommy says it has too much sugar, so it's a special treat."

"Your mommy is very wise."

"She's very pretty, too." Pointing, the girl said, "That's her right there."

He followed her finger to the blonde he'd met the night before, and had to agree that Lucy's sister, Emma, was indeed gorgeous. Her daughter took after her aunt Lucy with her red hair, green eyes and pale skin, whereas her mom was a willowy blonde with big blue eyes.

"Do you have a girlfriend?"

"Who wants to know?" he asked, amused by the girl's blatant matchmaking.

"I do."

"And what's your name?"

"Simone."

"That's a pretty name. Do you have a boyfriend?"

"No! I'm nine. Nine-year-olds don't have boyfriends. You're like Colton," she said of his cousin, who was engaged to Lucy. "He knows *nothing* about kids."

Grayson knew more about kids than any childless man his age, but he didn't share that information with the girl. "What kind of stuff should I know?"

"Well, you should know that nine-year-old girls don't drink scotch and have boyfriends."

"I guess you don't smoke, then, either, do you?"

She dissolved into giggles, and he lost a tiny piece of his heart to her. What a cutie. "*No!* I don't smoke. Smoking is gross, and it kills you."

"That's exactly right. Stay away from that stuff."

"What do you want for Christmas this year?" she asked.

God, what a sweet question. What did he want anyway? How about some peace and a whole new life? That'd be a great place to start. "I want a pair of socks. What about you?"

"Socks? Who wants socks for Christmas?"

"I do, and it's my Christmas list, so you don't get to make fun of it."

"That's true. Sorry."

He nudged her with his elbow. "I was only kidding. You can make fun of me. Socks are a dumb thing to want for Christmas. What's on your list?"

"I asked for a new American Girl doll, but they're kind of expensive. Not sure that'll happen. But it's okay if it doesn't. I always get lots of cool stuff."

"I'm sure you're spoiled rotten."

"Not really. It's just me and Mommy, so we have to watch our pennies. That's what she says anyway."

Grayson wanted to buy her the doll and any other damned thing she wanted to make up for the fact that her father wasn't in her life. He was drawn out of that thought by the arrival of Emma, who'd come to claim her daughter.

"Are you bothering Grayson?" Emma asked.

"Your name is *Grayson*?" Simone asked, giggling. "What kind of name is that?"

"Simone!"

"It's a smart, distinguished name, I'll have you know."

Simone covered her mouth, as if that could contain her laughter, and he was utterly beguiled by the glee in her mischievous eyes.

"I'm sorry about her," Emma said. "The charm school wouldn't have her, so I'm doing the best I can on my own."

"I'd say you're doing a pretty great job," Grayson said, looking up at her. She had a body that wouldn't quit and absolutely stunning blue eyes.

"You should ask my mom to dance," Simone said. "She loves to dance, and she doesn't get to very often cuz of me."

"Simone, honestly."

For Grayson, however, the thought of dancing with Simone's sexy, embarrassed mother was far better than sitting in the corner drinking scotch alone while old memories resurfaced to prove they could still hurt him all these years later. "That's about the best idea anyone's had all day," Grayson said.

Simone's expressive eyes widened with joyful pleasure. "Really?"

Grayson stood and extended his hand to Emma, who blushed madly. "Really."

"Oh, um, you don't have to," Emma said haltingly.

"I'd love to. Shall we?"

As she looked up at him and took hold of his hand, Grayson felt like he'd been struck by lightning or gut punched or something equally unpleasant, except there was nothing at all unpleasant about it. In fact, it was the best feeling he'd had in a long, long time.

Hours after everyone else had gone to bed on Christmas night, five days after the wedding, Grayson lingered at his aunt Molly's because he'd yet to run out of things to talk about with the beautiful, shy and funny Emma Mulvaney. They sat in the den on the sofa closest to the fire that he'd kept stoked for hours while they chatted about their lives in Boston and New York, her adorable daughter, her sister's romance with his cousin and their jobs.

He learned that she worked as the office manager for dentists, and the rest of her life was devoted to Simone. Until recently, his had been devoted to work. That had led to their current conversation about balance and how to find it.

"So what made you decide to make the move now?" she asked.

He'd discovered she was an excellent listener, which made him want to tell her things he normally kept private. Most of the people in this world were accomplished talkers. Few were as good at listening. Emma was a true exception.

"I had this case assigned to me... We have these A-list clients, you know? The ones we pander to, no matter what disgusting thing they might've done. The senior partner calls them the 'gravy' clients. So this guy, a bigwig in the local business community, beat the shit out of his wife, and it was my job to get him off even though we all knew he did it. He put her in the hospital with broken ribs and a broken jaw—and it wasn't the first time."

Emma gasped, and her hand covered her heart. "Dear God."

"I couldn't do it. I couldn't make myself defend him when I knew he was guilty. All the money in the world just isn't worth it. I submitted my resignation, my partners bought me out, and here I am."

"You did the right thing."

"This time. There've been other times when I successfully defended the scumbags, and I'm not proud of that. But after a while, it gets harder to wash off the scum. It stays with you. I made a lot of money in that job. The kind of money I used to dream about having back when we were scrambling to make ends meet after my dad left. But when I saw the police photos of the injured wife, something in me just said, *Enough of this crazy shit. I can't do it anymore.*"

Her hand on his arm was intended to comfort, but it stirred something else he hadn't experienced in ages—pure desire.

"I'm sure you'll make a very nice living here, without having to sell your soul to the devil to do it."

"I hope so. It won't be the living I was making in Boston, but I worked so much, I didn't have time to spend half of what I made there. It'll be okay. Anything is better than what I was doing there."

"What did your partners say when you told them you were leaving?"

"They tried to talk me out of it. A few said I was making a huge mistake, committing career suicide by moving home to the boonies." He shrugged. "Nothing they said convinced me to change my mind."

"Your gut was telling you it was the right move at the right time. I'm a big believer in following my gut."

"What kind of things has your gut told you to do?"

She thought about that for a second, which gave him time to study her sweet face and cheeks made rosy by the heat of the fire as well as several glasses of chardonnay. "It told me not to marry Simone's father or allow him to be in her life."

Grayson immediately sensed from her hesitation that this was not something she talked about often. "How come?"

"He wasn't always nice to me."

"Did he… Did he hurt you?"

"Once."

How was it possible, when he'd only just met her, that he wanted to find the guy and kill him for hurting her even once?

"When I told him it was over between us, he… he didn't take it well."

"What happened?"

"It was a long time ago. A lifetime ago."

"But you've never forgotten it."

She stared into the fire, the sparkle in her eyes dulled by memories. "No, I haven't."

Grayson didn't think before he reached for her, wishing he could take away the pain of someone he barely knew. That was certainly a first. She flinched, ever so slightly, but he saw it and realized the damage ran deep from the one time the man she'd loved hurt her.

"Do you want to talk about it?"

"I never talk about it," she said with a shaky laugh. "Are you sure you're a lawyer and not a shrink?"

"Quite sure," he said with a chuckle, "although sometimes I think the two professions aren't all that different."

Emma took a drink of her wine and continued to stare at the fire. "When I told him we were done, he flipped out. He… He held me down and forced me to…" She blew out a deep breath.

"When it was over, I told him to leave or I'd call the police. I said if I ever saw him again, I'd report what he'd done to me."

"Christ, Emma. You've never told *anyone* that? Not even Lucy?"

Shaking her head, she said, "No one knows how Simone came to be. Except for you now."

"Emma," Grayson said on a long exhale. Though he had no right, he drew her in closer to him, needing to hold her.

"My dad was so mad when he found out I was pregnant. He didn't speak to me for the longest time. I hated that he was so disappointed."

"Why didn't you tell him, sweetheart?"

"Because I didn't want Simone's life to be colored by how she was conceived. I couldn't bear that for her. As soon as I knew she was coming, I was in love with her. I didn't care how she came to be. Somehow I've managed to keep those two things very separate in my mind. There's him and what he did, and then there's her—perfect in every way and no reflection whatsoever of the man who fathered her. In fact, she's a perfect reflection of my sister. I love that." Emma wiped away a tear that had slid down her cheek. "I love that she looks like Lucy. I thank God every day that she doesn't look like him." She released another of those shaky laughs. "What is it about you that has me spilling my guts to a total stranger?"

"I'm not a stranger. Not anymore. I'm a friend, and I'm glad you finally told someone. What he did to you, Emma… It was a crime. You know that, right?"

Nodding, she said, "I've had counseling, and I've come to terms with what happened that night. As much as one ever accepts such things."

"And he doesn't know about her?"

She shook her head. "I've never seen him again, thank God. I used to be so afraid of him coming back and doing the math… But she looks nothing like him, and she's always looked young for her age. There would be no reason for him to suspect she's his."

If he were thinking like a lawyer, Grayson might have something to say to that. But he was thinking as a man who'd been profoundly moved by a woman for the first time in his thirty-six years. "You're amazing."

"Don't say that. I did what any mother would've done to protect her child."

"At tremendous personal expense."

"The payoff has been the most wonderful little girl that anyone could hope for. I'll never regret a thing because I have her."

"She's very lucky to have you, too."

"We're both lucky. We've made a nice life for ourselves, and I never think about this stuff anymore."

Grayson didn't know if he totally believed that, but he wasn't about to question her. "You must be beating the men away with a stick."

"Right," she said, laughing. "Between work and homework and dance class and birthday parties and soccer, I'm a regular dating machine."

"So there's no one special in your life?"

"Just Simone, my dad, Lucy, Colton and a few very good friends, including Cameron."

"Do you ever want more for yourself?"

She shrugged. "I've learned to be very satisfied and thankful for what I have."

"I want to see you again, Emma. I want to spend more time together." The words were out of his mouth before he decided to say them, because the thought of her getting away, of never seeing her or Simone again except at family events, was unacceptable to him. Here he'd just taken steps to simplify his life, and one night with her had made everything complicated again. And that was fine with him.

"Oh, um, you do?"

"I really do. I haven't talked to a woman the way I've talked to you tonight in, well, ever. I don't want to stop talking to you, even though I should let you get to bed so you're not exhausted tomorrow. Something tells me Miss Simone won't be too forgiving of an exhausted mother."

"You're right. She'll take full advantage. But I'm not quite ready to go to bed just yet."

"No?"

She shook her head as she returned his gaze, never blinking as they drank each other in. Once again, Grayson acted before thinking, leaning in to kiss her. He was careful not to move too fast or take too much, but he couldn't let this night end without tasting her. As soon as he processed that first taste, he knew it wasn't going to be anywhere near enough.

The slight mewling sound that came from her throat made him instantly hard. He drew back to look at her, slightly stunned by his reaction. Her eyes were closed, her lips parted and damp. He dragged his fingertip over her bottom lip.

"You're beautiful, Emma."

Her eyes opened slowly, and she took a long look at him, as if trying to gauge his sincerity. He'd never been more sincere.

"How long are you here?" he asked.

She cleared her throat. "Molly invited us to spend the week since Simone is on vacation."

"Could Lucy watch Simone so I could take you to dinner tomorrow night?"

"I... I think they'd both love that."

"How about you? Would you love it if Simone went with Lucy so you can go out with me?"

"Yes, Grayson, I believe I'd love that, too."

CHAPTER 1

*I love you the more in that I believe you had liked me for my own
sake and for nothing else.*
—John Keats

How was it possible to *forget* to breathe? Emma was going to pass
out if she didn't remember to breathe. All day, she'd relived the
magical few hours in the Abbotts' den, sitting by the fire sharing
confidences with the supremely handsome, sexy and successful
Grayson Coleman.

Emma had told him things she'd never told another living
soul, even Lucy, her sister and closest confidant. Waiting for the
clock to move forward today, Emma had expected to feel regrets,
recriminations or something negative for spilling the biggest secret
of her life, a nearly ten-year-old secret that involved the most
precious person in the world—her daughter, Simone.

Something about the way Grayson had paid such close attention to her, listening to every word she said as if they were the
most important words he'd ever heard, had her telling him things
she never talked about—and rarely thought about anymore. It
had been such a long time ago, and Emma was a big believer in

looking ahead rather than back. Nothing good ever came from looking back.

The Abbotts had graciously invited her and Simone to spend the week with them so they could attend Hunter and Megan's wedding and then have Christmas with Lucy and her fiancé, Colton, in Vermont. And what an incredible visit it had been so far, complete with sledding and snowman building and even a ride for Simone on the back of Lucas Abbott's snowmobile.

Her daughter would talk about this week for months.

Simone was spending today and tonight with Colton and Lucy at their home on the mountain. She was so excited to have alone time with Auntie Lu and Uncle Colton and their dogs, Sarah and Elmer. When she left with Lucy earlier, Emma heard her asking if they might see Fred the moose, and Lucy said you never knew when he might come by for a visit.

Emma had felt sort of aimless as she whiled away an unusually quiet afternoon at the Abbotts' lovely restored barn. Her dad had driven home to New York that morning, Lincoln Abbott was in town at a lunch meeting, and his wife, Molly, was at their daughter Hannah's.

Emma finally settled on the same sofa where she'd sat with Grayson last night and tried to lose herself in a book she'd been enjoying. But her mind kept wandering to silly things—like the way the fire had turned his dark blond hair to a burnished gold, the twinkle in his eyes when he was amused, the furrow of his brow when he was concentrating or listening to her, and how he'd shown just the right amount of empathy and outrage when she told him about how Simone's father had attacked her at the end of their relationship.

Grayson was now the only other person on earth who knew Simone had come from a violent attack. She hadn't even told the therapist who'd counseled her afterward about the baby. Perhaps she should regret having shared something so deeply personal with someone she'd only just met, but they'd been wrapped up in a bubble all their own, sharing confidences, and she didn't regret telling him.

She'd learned how he had been forced to step up for his seven younger siblings when he was sixteen, after their father left, but he spoke of his brothers and sisters only with love and affection. None of the burden he must've felt at having so much responsibility at such a young age was apparent in the way he talked about them.

She'd never been as intrigued by a man as she was by him, thus the breathing trouble. And after he asked her to have dinner with him tonight, she'd been left breathless, winded—and nervous. Really, really *nervous*. She hadn't been out on a proper date in, well… years. Unless she counted her good friend Troy Kennedy, who'd been her plus one in the city while she served as his. But Troy didn't count. There'd never been anything other than platonic friendship between them, despite the desire of Lucy and their friend Cameron Abbott to see them together.

It wasn't happening with Troy, but something had definitely happened last night with Grayson.

Emma touched her fingers to her lips, reliving the soft, sweet kiss he'd given her before suggesting they call it a night. If it'd been up to her, he'd still be here and they'd still be talking—and maybe kissing, too.

She'd been so wrapped up in taking care of Simone, working and handling all the parenting and household duties alone that there hadn't been anyone serious since her relationship with Simone's father ended in spectacular—and violent—fashion.

"Don't think about that," she whispered. "Not today when you have a handsome guy taking you out for dinner." Her mind wandered once again to that fleeting kiss and how it had made her yearn for so much more. Another of her deep, dark secrets was one she hadn't told Grayson. She hadn't had sex since the night she conceived Simone.

"Ugh." She dropped her head into her hands, disgusted with herself for hiding behind the cloak of motherhood as an excuse to keep her distance from men. One year had become two, and two became three, and three had become a decade while she was busy raising her daughter, who would be ten in February.

She hadn't planned to put her own life on hold when she had Simone. It had just worked out that way. A single mother of a young child didn't spend her evenings out at bars or clubs or any of the other places women her age met men.

After her sister finally accepted that Emma was never going to think of Troy in a romantic way, Lucy had urged her to try online dating. But there was something so inherently frightening about the anonymity of the Internet, especially living as she did in New York City. She had a child to think about, so even if the idea of meeting a guy interested her, online dating did not.

Grayson Coleman interested her.

George and Ringo jumped up from their dog beds by the fire and bolted for the kitchen. Emma heard Molly talking to the dogs, who barked happily at the return of their loved one. Molly came to find Emma a few minutes later.

"Hi there."

"Hey. How's Hannah?"

"Feeling ungainly, but that's pregnancy for you."

"I remember that stage. I could've been one of the hot-air balloons in the Thanksgiving parade."

Molly laughed and threw some wood on the fire before taking a seat in an easy chair. She put her feet up on the ottoman. The woman was a dynamo. She'd given birth to ten children, but you'd never know it to look at her slender frame and unlined face. The only sign of her age was the mane of gorgeous gray hair that she wore mostly in a braid, but even that did nothing to detract from her otherwise youthful appearance.

"I love the day after Christmas. Back when the kids were little, I used to take to my bed for the entire day, and one of Linc's gifts to me was handling child care while I lolled about, being lazy."

"That's a brilliant idea."

"I thought so, too, and the best part? Linc bowed down to me, *every year*, after one day alone with the hellions."

Emma laughed at the picture she painted of ten unruly kids running roughshod over their dear old dad.

"Christmas is one heck of a production for the moms," Molly said. "Still is, and my kids are all grown. But I do love having the whole family here—the noise, the presents, the bickering, the chaos. And I love today when they all go home and leave me to my wallowing."

"Sorry to intrude on your peace and quiet."

"Oh please! You're no trouble at all, and Linc and I are *in love* with Simone. We want you to come back every year."

"That'd be lovely. Christmas in Vermont is my new favorite thing."

"I'm so happy to hear that. Look at this big empty barn we're rattling around in. We've got plenty of room, and we'd love to have you."

"Simone would never speak to me again if I didn't say we'd love to."

"Then it's settled. Please think of our home as your home, Emma. You and Simone and your dad are family to us now that

Lucy and Colton are engaged. There'll never be a time when you won't be welcome here."

"That's so nice of you. Thank you."

"Linc and I are going to our favorite Italian place in St. Johnsbury tonight if you'd like to come along."

"Oh, um…" She and Grayson hadn't spoken about what, if anything, they would tell other people about their plans for the evening. Would he not want her to tell his aunt they were going out? She made a split-second decision. "Thanks for the invite, but I'm going to stick around here tonight and take advantage of my night off."

"I don't blame you at all. There's a huge tub in our room that you're welcome to if you'd like to take a bath."

"That sounds great."

"Go ahead. Indulge. I'm going to sit right here and have a little nap until Linc gets home. Enjoy."

"You, too."

"Oh, I will."

As she went upstairs, Emma decided she wanted to *be* Molly Abbott when she grew up. What an amazing woman—and mother. Her kids were all great people, even the mischievous identical twins, Lucas and Landon, who'd flirted shamelessly with Emma at Will and Hunter's weddings until Colton told them to back off or deal with him—and his ax. They were adorable and hilarious, but far too young for her. Their attention, however, had not been unwelcome. It had served as a reminder that despite how she felt sometimes, she was still only twenty-nine, not sixty.

Molly had handled a wedding in her living room five days before Christmas and a mob scene for the holiday with nothing but grace and humor and mad skill that had left Emma dazzled. It was official. Emma had a full-fledged girl crush on the woman, and being invited back for next year was the second-best thing to happen this week.

By the time Grayson drove to his aunt's house to pick up Emma, he'd already had a full day. His cousin Ella had taken him to see the apartment she'd recently vacated, and he'd immediately snapped it up, along with the bed and sofa she'd given him. She was moving in with her fiancé, Gavin, and didn't need either item. Grayson was happy to check three things off his to-do list. She'd even suggested turning over her landline number to him. He hadn't had a landline in Boston in years, but in Butler, Vermont, the place where cell service was nonexistent, it was a necessity.

Even though he'd been busy apartment hunting, shoveling snow and doing odd jobs around his mother's house, Grayson had kept a close eye on the clock, which seemed to move in reverse today.

Emma.

His first thought that morning had been of her, of the secrets they'd shared, the stories they'd told and the spark that had burned so brightly between them. That spark had him more intrigued than he'd ever been by a woman. Sure, he'd heard about the spark and had even seen it happen to some of his cousins and friends, but it had never happened to him, until Emma.

And Simone... For it was not possible to consider one without the other. He already knew Emma well enough to understand that there would be no such thing as a relationship that included only her. For a guy who'd never had the urge for a family because he'd already helped to raise his younger siblings, it surprised him to realize he was glad the adorable, smart, funny, sweet, respectful Simone was part of the package.

Pulling up to the big red barn his aunt and uncle called home, Grayson cut the engine in his Audi SUV but left the headlights on so he could get to the door without falling on the ice. His uncle's Range Rover was gone, so they must've been out for their usual Friday night dinner. He was secretly glad that he wouldn't encounter his beloved aunt and uncle when he picked up Emma.

Grayson was nervous enough without adding a family inquisition to the agenda for the evening—and it would be an inquisition with his uncle Linc involved. Serving as a surrogate dad to the fatherless Colemans, Linc was always interested in whatever they were up to. Normally, Grayson welcomed his uncle's interest. Tonight, he was grateful for a little privacy. The light over the back door helped to guide him as he made his way, carefully, to the door.

He let himself in and greeted George and Ringo, who gave him a thorough sniffing before allowing him to proceed into the mudroom, as if to say, *He's one of us.* This had been his second home growing up, and he felt every bit at home here as he did at his own mother's house.

"Hello?"

"Hi there," Emma called from upstairs. "I'll be down in a minute."

"Take your time." As Grayson leaned against the counter in his aunt's tidy kitchen, he thought about his last first date, his good mood souring at the memories of his ex-girlfriend, Heather. He'd been so blown away by her beauty and captivated by her charm as well as the best sex of his life that he hadn't realized she was actually a stone-cold bitch until he'd already been completely sucked into her web. Extricating himself had been nasty, and he hadn't been with anyone in the year since he ended it with her.

Hearing Emma's footsteps on the stairs, he shook off those memories to put himself in the right frame of mind to spend this evening with her. It was high time he got back to the land of the living after the debacle with Heather.

Emma came into the room, and Grayson could only stare at how lovely she looked in a simple black turtleneck sweater that she'd paired with sexy jeans and boots. Her hair was down around her shoulders, and she'd done something to her big blue eyes with makeup that made them stand out. "You said casual, right?"

"I did, and you look great."

"So do you," she said with a shy smile.

He liked that she was shy, that she hadn't dated in years, that nothing about her was fake or fabricated. And he really liked when the spark of attraction from last night flared between them once again, still vibrant and vivid after they'd both had a day to reconsider. He hadn't changed his mind, and judging from the way she looked at him, she hadn't either.

"I should leave a note for Molly so she doesn't worry," Emma said. "I didn't know what to say to her about my plans for tonight, so I didn't say anything."

"You could've told her where you were going."

"I didn't know if you'd want me to."

"One thing you'll quickly learn about this family—and this town—is there're very few secrets."

Emma smiled and dashed off a quick note to Molly, leaving it on the counter where his aunt was sure to see it.

Over her shoulder, he saw that she'd written, *Went to get dinner with Grayson. See you in the morning. Emma.*

"You're planning on an all-nighter?" he asked.

"What?" He hated that she looked and sounded stricken by his comment. "No, of course not. I was just assuming they'll be asleep when we get home."

"I was teasing, Emma. Sorry."

She laughed. "Wow, call me out of practice. I missed that completely."

He chuckled at her adorable befuddlement, also loving that she was out of practice when it came to men and dating. What a breath of fresh air she was. In the mudroom, he held her coat and waited for her to zip up and put on gloves. "Ready?" he asked, extending his hand to her.

She took hold of his hand. "Ready."

He led her out into the night, excited to spend time with her, to simply *be* with her.

CHAPTER 2

Let us always meet each other with smile, for the smile is the
beginning of love.
—Mother Teresa

As they pulled out of Lincoln and Molly's driveway, it began to
snow, going from a light dusting to a steady snowfall in the few
minutes it took to warm up the car.

"I'd hoped that the snow predicted for tonight wouldn't
materialize," Grayson said.

"It's so pretty here," Emma said. "In the city, it's a mess. But
here, there's something magical about it."

"It may be magical, but it's also a menace. If it's going to
come down hard, I don't think we ought to go too far. How do
you feel about pizza?"

"I love pizza."

"I'd planned to do better than that tonight, but I assume you
prefer safety to five-star cuisine."

"You assume correctly." Emma looked out the window,
bending her head so she could see Butler Mountain in the
distance. "Do you think Simone will be okay on the mountain
in a snowstorm?"

"She'll be totally fine. Colton has been living up there for years. Snow is nothing new to him."

"I suppose you're right."

"I bet she's having a blast."

"She probably is. She loves it here. Way more than she loves the city."

"What's not to love about Butler? We have everything you could ever need, including brick-oven pizza." Ten minutes after they left Molly and Linc's, Grayson pulled into the parking lot at Kingdom Pizza and killed the engine. "Wait for me. It's slippery. I don't want you to fall." He got out and went around to open the door and offered a hand to help her out.

"Thank you," she said with the shy smile that made his heart flutter.

Gorgeous and sweet and so incredibly strong... He'd thought all day about the things she'd told him last night. Her courage humbled him and made him want to be the best thing to ever happen to her and her daughter. But that might be putting the sleigh before the horse on a first date. *Dial it down a notch*, he told himself as he held the door to the pizza place to let her go in ahead of him.

Much to his dismay, he immediately spotted his cousins Hannah and Will sitting at a table with their spouses, Nolan and Cameron. They waved them over.

"Hey," Will said. "Want to join us?"

No, he didn't want to, but he also didn't want to be rude to his cousins. Grayson glanced at Emma, who shrugged. "Sure," he said.

"Wait," Hannah said. "Are you guys on a date?"

"Something like that," Grayson said, wondering if he'd missed the time-travel train back to high school.

"We take back our offer to sit with us, then," Hannah said. "Go over there and get your own table. Leave us alone."

Emma laughed at Hannah's trademark bossiness.

With an exasperated smile for his cousins, Grayson took hold of Emma's arm. "Nice to see you, too." He guided her to a table on the other side of the dining room, held the chair for her and then recalled how Heather had hated when he did things like that for her. *"I can get my own damned chair,"* she would say.

Seated across from Emma, he wondered how she felt about a man holding her chair. "Sorry about my cousin."

"I think she's funny."

"Pregnancy has made her extra bossy, and she was already pretty bossy to begin with."

"When is she due?"

"February or March, I think."

A waitress stopped by the table with menus and offered to take their drink order. Grayson asked for a beer, and Emma ordered a glass of white wine.

"Lucy told me about Hannah and how she lost her first husband in Iraq."

"One of the roughest things our family ever went through. We all grew up together. Caleb Guthrie was one of us."

"I'm sorry you lost him the way you did."

"Thanks. I was so glad to hear she'd started seeing Nolan. They're good together." He leaned in closer to her and lowered his voice. "Tell me the truth. Is she looking over here?"

Emma shifted her gaze to the right and then back to him. "They all are."

"For God's sake. This town… I'd forgotten how ridiculous it can be here. That was never an issue in Boston. I could blend into the masses."

"Welcome home," she said with a smile, raising her wineglass in a toast to him.

He returned her smile and touched his bottle to her glass. "It's not *all* bad."

"No?"

"Definitely not." He loved the way her cheeks flushed to a light pink and how she lowered her eyes when embarrassed. "I couldn't stop thinking about you today."

She looked up at him. "Me, too. Last night was very special to me."

"I haven't talked like that to anyone in years."

"Same here. I told you things…" Her eyes dropped again.

He reached across the table for her hand, not caring in the least who might be watching. "I will never tell anyone what you told me. I swear. No matter what."

"Thank you," she said, releasing a deep breath. "I wasn't really worried that you would, but…"

"Someone else knows now, and that makes you feel vulnerable."

"Yes. Exactly."

"I keep secrets for a living, sweetheart. You don't need to be worried about that, and I'd never do anything to cause harm to your adorable daughter."

"That means a lot to me. Thank you."

The waitress approached the table, ready to take their order.

Grayson reluctantly released Emma's hand and asked for a few minutes so she could look at a menu he knew by heart after growing up in Butler.

"Be right back," the waitress said.

"What do you suggest?"

"Their thin-crust pizza is the best I've had anywhere."

"That sounds good to me. You want to split one and maybe a salad, too?"

"Perfect."

They settled on pepperoni and green peppers for toppings and placed the order when the waitress returned.

"What did you do today?" he asked.

"I had a very lazy day. Simone was content to play with her new doll, and I was able to relax and read until Lucy and Colton came to pick her up."

"She got the doll she wanted?"

"She got a doll she's happy with, even if it wasn't the ridiculously expensive one she wanted. How about you? What did you do?"

"I lucked into a place to live thanks to my cousin Ella, who's moving in with her fiancé, Gavin. I'm glad to get that taken care of. I can't live with my mother indefinitely."

"I'm sure she enjoys having you around."

"She enjoys it a little too much. I have a honey-do list that could choke a horse."

Emma laughed at the face he made. "Awww, that's sweet."

"What would be sweet is if my brother Noah, the contractor, who lives down the street from her, would install the new bookcase in her office and stock up her firewood. But, no, he's too busy. Good old Grayson will take care of it because he always does." He paused and then looked at her, immediately regretting the rant. "Sorry. I don't mean to sound bitter. Of course, I'm happy to help my mom with anything she needs."

"You just wish the others would pitch in."

"Something like that."

Emma's phone rang, and she excused herself to check her phone. "That's odd. I thought I couldn't get calls here."

"We're right on the line on this side of town to pick up cell towers in St. Johnsbury."

"It's from a New York number, but I don't know who it is. Hello?"

Grayson watched as her face lit up with joy that only added to her stunning beauty.

"Hi, honey. Wait, say that again?" Emma laughed, and the warm, rich sound washed over him. "Auntie Lu is very sneaky." This was said with a smile that lit up her pretty blue eyes. "Yes, you can keep it, but there will be rules. She told you I'd say that, didn't she?" Emma laughed again. "Are you guys having fun?"

Grayson could hear Simone's excited chatter but couldn't make out what she was saying.

"I'm fine," Emma said. "Yes, I miss you terribly. I'll see you tomorrow. Sleep tight, and be good for Lucy and Colton. Love you, too."

"Big news from the mountain?" Grayson asked when she ended the call.

"Huge news. Lucy and Colton got her a cell phone so she and Lucy can FaceTime every night."

"That's awesome."

"Simone is *so* excited. She's been bugging me for a phone for ages. Auntie Lu to the rescue."

The waitress delivered their salad and pizza, along with another round of drinks.

Grayson served them both slices of pizza and took a bite of his. *So good.* No pizza he'd tried anywhere could compete with this. "Did you know about the phone?"

Emma nodded. "Lucy talked to me about it beforehand, and even though I still feel she's too young, most of her friends already have them. Like I said to Simone, there'll be rules."

"Block the Internet for a couple more years. That's key."

"Oh, don't worry. Lucy already did that."

"Another thing I heard my colleagues in Boston talk about is making her think she has a limit on texts, like two-fifty a month or something reasonable like that."

"Even though she has unlimited texting?"

"Yeah, because then she learns to control herself and work within her limits."

"That's a great idea."

"I had a work friend whose teenage daughter sent a hundred thousand texts in a month—before he realized they should've gotten unlimited texting. That cost something like two thousand bucks. Talk about a shocker."

"Yikes. Can you imagine sending a hundred thousand texts in one month?"

"The dad said she had to be texting every second of her day, even when she was in the shower, to get to that total."

"That's funny—but not funny, too. This pizza is amazing, by the way."

"I'm glad you like it. It's my favorite."

"I can see why."

Grayson glanced out the window to a total whiteout. "Damn, look at the snow."

"Wow, it's really coming down."

"Should we take the rest to go?"

"Probably," she said with visible reluctance.

Grayson was glad to know she was in no rush to end their date either.

Hannah, Nolan, Cameron and Will stopped by to say goodbye as they headed out.

"Drive carefully, you guys," Grayson said.

"Do you still remember how to drive in this crap, city boy?" Will asked, grinning at his cousin.

Grayson flipped him off.

The four of them went out the door laughing.

"Don't listen to him," Grayson said. "I'll get you home safely."

"I never doubted you for a minute."

Pleased by her faith in him, he paid their check and held her coat, watching as she scooped up her blonde hair and let it fall in silky waves down her back. He had to resist the urge to run his fingers through it—at least for now. Then she pulled a knit cap from her pocket and plopped it on her head. When she turned to smile at him, he felt like he'd been sucker-punched. She was gorgeous, sweet, funny, sexy as all hell—and she lived six hours from him.

That last one had him sagging under the weight of the impossibility of this situation.

She pulled on mittens that matched the hat. "Are you okay?"

Grayson zipped his coat and picked up the pizza box. "I'm good. Ready?"

"Let's do it."

What should've been a ten-minute ride from town to Molly and Linc's took close to thirty. Emma held on tight to her seat the entire way as they crept through a white wall of snow. "How do you even know where you're going?"

"I know these roads as well as I know anything."

The SUV fishtailed, and Emma gasped.

He reached for her hand.

She tried to shake him off. "You need that to drive."

"I don't want you to be afraid."

"I'm okay."

"We've got four-wheel drive, so we're totally fine. I promise."

Emma clung to his hand and assurances until she saw the mailbox that was a miniature replica of the red barn the Abbotts called home. She released a deep sigh of relief.

Grayson pulled up next to his uncle's Range Rover and cut the engine. "That was all kinds of fun."

"You were great. Calm and cool under pressure."

"Let me walk you in."

"Maybe you should just stay here tonight rather than driving anymore."

"Are you inviting me?" he asked in a teasing tone.

Heat flooded her entire body at the thought of spending the night with him. Thankfully, he couldn't see that in the dark. "Your aunt would surely agree that you'd be safer here than on the roads in this."

"If I stay, would that mean I'd get more time with you?"

"Only if you want more time with me."

"I want it."

"That's good, because so do I. So you'll stay?"

"I'll stay."

CHAPTER 3

You can't blame gravity for people falling in love.
—Albert Einstein

Realizing their date wasn't over yet had Emma's heart doing gymnastics. She felt breathless and overheated even though the icy air leached into the car now that the engine was off.

"Wait for me," he said as he got out and came around for her.

He carried the pizza box and kept an arm around her as they walked toward the light over the back door that had been left on for Emma.

They stepped into the mudroom, shook the snow off their coats and hung them on hooks that bore the names of Grayson's cousins. She followed him into the kitchen, where he stashed the pizza in the fridge and helped himself to one of his uncle's beers. "Want one?"

"Sure, why not? I can sleep in tomorrow for the first time in ten years."

He laughed and twisted the caps off, handing one bottle to her. "I need to call my mom like the good boy I am and tell her not to expect me." Grayson used the landline in the kitchen to make the call. "Yes, Mother," he said, rolling his eyes at Emma.

"I thought you might agree it's better if I stay put. You've got enough firewood to get you through tonight and tomorrow. Call Noah if you need anything. All right. I will." He put down the phone. "There. My duty is done."

Seeing no sign of Molly and Linc, Emma said, "Let's go in the den." Back to the place where they had connected so completely the night before, she thought, looking forward to more time alone with him.

He followed her, lit the fire that had been laid in the hearth and then turned off the lamp so the only light was from the fire and the twinkling white lights on the Christmas tree. Outside, the wind howled and the snow pinged against the window. "Is it okay to say I'm sort of glad it snowed tonight?" he asked.

"Why's that?"

"Because if it hadn't, I'd still be wishing I could do this." He raised his arm, inviting her to move closer.

Emma smiled at him and leaned into him so he could put his arm around her. "This is nice," she said, resting her head on his chest.

He ran his fingers through her hair. "It certainly is."

Emma closed her eyes and tried to lose herself in the romantic moment while not thinking about the many reasons it was a supremely bad idea to get involved with a man who lived so far from her. *Cameron and Lucy did it*, she thought, *and made it work.* But they hadn't had a child to think about. Simone made everything more complicated for her, not that she minded. There was nothing she wouldn't do for her child, and that included stopping herself from getting too involved with a man she couldn't have.

That didn't mean, however, that she couldn't enjoy the time they had together this week.

"What're you thinking about?" he asked.

"Too many things."

"Care to share?"

She lifted her head from his chest so she could see his face. "I'm thinking about how much I enjoy being with you and how sorry I am that you live so far from me."

He raised his hand to caress her cheek. "Your thoughts are amazingly similar to mine."

"Maybe it would be better if… if we didn't."

"Is that what you want?"

She shook her head.

He gazed into her eyes for a long moment, seeming to commit her features to memory. Then he shifted his gaze to her lips in the seconds before he kissed her.

The moment his lips connected with hers, she stopped worrying about the many reasons this was a bad idea and lost herself in a kiss that made her forget everything other than how incredible it felt to be held and kissed by a smart, sexy, handsome man.

Kisses that had been sweet and tentative the night before were hotter now, sexier, more desperate.

Emma had never been kissed the way Grayson kissed her, as if he wanted to devour her, and oh dear God, she wanted to be devoured by him. A libido that had been dormant for ten years roared back to life with an intensity that made her shiver from wanting him so desperately.

He seemed to want her just as badly, judging from the way he kissed her and how he drew her closer to him, until they were stretched out on the sofa, arms and legs entwined, lips joined and his erection hard against her belly.

Emma had to remind herself where they were and what could and *couldn't* happen here. Worries about getting caught had her withdrawing, reluctantly, from the kiss.

"What?" he whispered gruffly.

"I'm trying to remember where we are."

"I can't remember my own name right now."

She laughed softly, and then sighed when his lips moved to her neck as his hand dipped under her sweater. The heat of his palm on her back seared her skin, making her want so much more. She moved against him, hoping he'd touch her everywhere, regardless of where they were and who might catch them.

Groaning softly, he took the hint, moving his hand from back to front and up to cup her breast through her bra.

Emma was glad she'd worn one of the few truly sexy bras she owned.

His thumb slid back and forth over her nipple, setting off a firestorm inside her.

She went on her own exploration, sliding her hand under his sweater.

He gasped from the feel of her skin against his and captured her lips in another heated kiss. His tongue rubbed against hers as their bodies rocked together. Then he pinched her bare nipple between his fingers, and Emma nearly launched off the sofa. She broke the kiss and took a deep breath. "Grayson…"

"Hmm?"

"We have to stop. We can't do this here."

He made an inarticulate noise. "Let's go to your room."

"This is your aunt's house. We can't."

"They won't know, and they wouldn't care."

Emma was so incredibly tempted. "I care. I'm their guest, and it doesn't feel right to…"

"Shag their nephew in the guest room?"

She laughed at his bluntly spoken words. "Yes, that."

He sighed, deeply, then adjusted her bra to cover her breast and removed his hand from under her sweater. "For the record, I'm withdrawing under protest."

"Duly noted," she said, smiling as she kissed him.

"Tomorrow, I could show you my new apartment if you'd like to see it."

His meaning wasn't lost on her. "I'll have to see what's going on with Simone."

He rested his forehead on hers and took another deep breath. "I haven't felt like this in... well... ever."

Touched by his confession, Emma ran her hand over his back. "Neither have I."

He raised his head to look down at her. "How'd this happen?"

"I believe you put your arm around me, and next thing I knew, here we were."

"I don't mean just this." He kissed her to make his point. "I mean how did *this* happen? All of it."

"It's your fault for being so easy to talk to."

"No, that's your fault," he said, smiling.

"I should probably go upstairs."

"Not yet," he whispered, kissing her again.

"Grayson..."

"Ten more minutes."

Could she handle ten more minutes of the kind of pleasure she'd never experienced before? "Okay."

Grayson woke to whispered voices in the kitchen and a warm, sweet body tucked in close to him under a blanket he vaguely remembered pulling over them in the middle of the night.

His aunt and uncle were up, and Emma was asleep in his arms, which was no big deal to him, but it would be to her. He kissed her awake.

Her eyes fluttered open, and a sweet smile curved her lips when she saw him there. Then she realized where they were, and the smile disappeared. "I..."

"Shhh. They're up. Go on upstairs, and I'll be back to get you at noon."

"Get me to go where?"

"You'll see." He kissed her again and released her, patting her ass as she got up from the sofa.

Emma looked over her shoulder and caught him checking her out as she left the room to sneak up the stairs like a naughty teenager trying to avoid her parents.

He fell back against the sofa, missing her already, and she'd only just left him. A few minutes later, he got up, ran his fingers through his hair and put on his shoes. Then he went into the kitchen to face the music with his aunt and uncle.

"Morning," Molly said from her perch at the stove where she was standing watch over a pan of eggs. "Coffee?"

"I wouldn't say no to that."

She poured him a cup. "Cream is in the fridge. Sugar is on the table."

"Thanks. Hope you don't mind me crashing on your sofa. The snow was pretty intense."

"Of course we don't mind," Molly said. "Our home is your home. You know that."

"And I appreciate it."

"So," Linc said, holding his newspaper to the side so he could see Grayson, "did you and Emma have a nice time last night?"

"We did." Avoiding his uncle's obvious curiosity, Grayson stirred cream into his coffee. "Our evening was cut short by the snow, but we had fun. We saw Hannah, Nolan, Will and Cameron at Kingdom Pizza." Ten minutes later, he heard footsteps on the stairs, and his heart raced, knowing it would be Emma coming down to join them.

"Morning," she said, hair damp from the shower and lips swollen from kissing him.

The sight of her made him hard as a rock. His reaction to her was unprecedented. He'd wanted other women, but not the way he wanted her, and he'd known her only a few days. It didn't make sense to him. How could they have gone from perfect strangers to this level of desperate need in the scope of a couple of evenings? Albeit amazing, monumental evenings.

"Morning, honey," Molly said. "Did you sleep well?"

Grayson noticed that Emma went out of her way not to look at him. "Like a rock."

He found her choice of words comical in light of his condition.

"Morning," she said to him as she slid into the chair next to his, bringing a cup of coffee and a cloud of fragrance with her.

He wanted to lean in closer to fully experience her scent as much as her soft skin and swollen lips. "Morning."

"How much snow did we get?" Emma asked.

"Only about fourteen inches," Linc said.

Emma's eyes went wide. "*Seriously?*"

"Welcome to Vermont, sweetheart," Grayson said, amused by her reaction.

She glanced at him, and he took note of the flush in her cheeks. "That would shut down New York City for two days."

"Just a dusting to us," Linc said.

"How many such dustings do you get in an average winter?" Emma asked.

"We lose count," Molly said.

"Wow." Emma glanced out the big sliding glass door that led to the deck and yard. "It sure is pretty."

"Yes, it is," Grayson said, looking at her, not the snow.

When she realized his meaning, she smiled and brought her coffee to her lips. Even the way she drank her coffee was sexy to him.

The house phone rang, and Molly took the call. "Emma? It's for you. A little girl calling from the mountain."

Emma jumped up and went to take the call from her daughter. "Hey, how's it going?"

Grayson once again noticed the way her face lit up when she spoke to her child, and her joy touched him profoundly. He caught his uncle watching him. "What?"

"I could ask you the same thing."

"I… um…"

Linc snorted. "It's like that, is it?"

"Might be."

"Proceed with caution, my boy," Linc said in a low tone intended for Grayson's ears only. "She's not a woman you trifle with."

"I know that," Grayson said, mildly insulted that his uncle thought he needed to be told.

"No offense intended."

"I know that, too," he said with a sigh.

"She's special, and so is that little girl of hers."

"Yes, they are."

"Okay, baby," Emma said into the phone. "Have a great time, and be good for Colton and Lucy." She hung up the phone.

"Apparently, Uncle Colton has offered to teach Simone how to ski today."

Grayson knew a moment of pure elation at realizing Emma was free to hang out with him. If she wanted to, that was.

"She couldn't get a better teacher," Molly said. "Except for Will maybe. But Colton is a fantastic skier."

"I certainly can't compete with her fun aunt and uncle," Emma said.

"She's in a new place with new things to try," Molly said.

"She's not going to want to go home," Emma said. "It's way more fun here than it is there." She turned her potent gaze Grayson's way as she said that, and his heart skipped a beat.

"What're you doing today?" he asked as casually as possible.

"I have no idea. I've been ditched by my kid, so I'm at loose ends."

"You can help me move into my new place, if you want."

"Um, sure, I can do that."

"Great."

They ate breakfast with Molly and Lincoln, and then went outside to dig out the cars, which took well over an hour. Thankfully, Linc had a snowblower for the long driveway. He took care of that while Emma and Grayson focused on the cars.

"This is hard work," she said.

"Vermont in the winter isn't for sissies."

"Are you calling me a sissy?"

"Would I do that?"

"I think you would."

Grayson was heaving a heavy load of snow to the pile they'd created next to the driveway when something cold and wet hit him square in the face. She did not! Her squeal of laughter indicated that she had.

"This is war." He threw down his shovel and ran around his uncle's Land Rover, nearly falling on his ass when he slid on icy snow.

Seeing him coming, she took off screaming, heading away from the house down the driveway.

Grayson caught up to her, hooked his arm around her waist and hoisted her right off her feet.

She screamed with laughter as they landed in a snowbank. Her face was red from the cold, and their breath formed clouds around them.

He kissed her right there in the snow, mindless of his uncle a few hundred yards from them or Ringo and George frolicking in the snow nearby. The whole world could've been watching, for all he cared. He kissed her until he felt her surrender—and then he smashed a handful of snow in her face.

She sputtered and smacked at his arm and shoulder. "That was a dirty trick!"

"You started it."

Raising her arm as if to put it around him, she stuffed a handful of snow down the back of his neck.

"Holy shit!" He jumped up and shook the snow out of his clothes while she lost it laughing.

"Hey, you two," Linc called. "No playing until the work is done."

"It's him." Emma pointed a gloved thumb at Grayson. "He started it."

Glowering at her even as he delighted in her playfulness, he said, "You'll pay for that later."

"Promises, promises."

The comment, the look she gave him and the meaning in her words made him hard—again. Had shoveling snow ever been so fun?

CHAPTER 4

Love is our true destiny. We do not find the meaning of life by ourselves alone—we find it with another.
—Thomas Merton

They left Lincoln and Molly's a short time later and headed for Grayson's mother's home to dig her out. When he pulled up to his mother's house, he saw that Noah had used the plow on his truck to do the driveway.

"Noah was here with the plow," Grayson said, parking behind his mother's sedan. "That makes things easier."

"I've never seen this much snow except during a blizzard."

"Wait till you see a blizzard in Vermont. That's some real snow."

"What's this? Fake snow?"

"This is a whimper. That's a roar."

"It's kind of exciting," she said.

"What is?"

"The snow."

Rolling his eyes, he said, "There's nothing exciting about snow when you have to deal with it as much as we did growing up."

"I like the way it interferes with plans and forces us to slow down. Life is so busy and rushed, but when it snows, everything stops for a little while."

"I guess that's true." He ushered her into his mother's mudroom ahead of him. They removed their boots and coats before proceeding into the kitchen, where his mom was drinking coffee and watching the news on the small TV Grayson had given her for Christmas. "I would've set that up for you," he said of the TV.

"I'm perfectly capable of doing it myself," she said. "Hi there, Emma. There's more coffee if you're interested."

"Thank you, Mrs. Coleman. I had my daily quota at Molly's."

"Call me Hannah, please. I'm the old Hannah in this family. My niece is the young pretty one." She tipped her face up to receive a kiss from Grayson. "You sleep okay at your aunt's house?"

"Like a rock," he said, echoing what Emma had said earlier. "I need to go change my clothes. Somehow I managed to get wet shoveling snow this morning. Be right back."

Emma giggled, and he rushed upstairs to take a quick shower and change. He didn't want to waste a minute of this day with her.

Emma took a seat at the table with Hannah. Though she and Molly were sisters, they were quite different. While Molly wore her gray hair in a pretty braid, Hannah's was cut short, and while Molly smiled all the time, Hannah was less animated and more serious. Now that Emma knew more about the Coleman family, she also understood the tinge of bitterness she'd seen in Hannah.

"How cold is it out there?" Hannah asked.

"Not too bad."

"Is your daughter enjoying her visit to Vermont?"

"She is. She spent last night with Lucy and Colton, and today they're teaching her to ski. I'm afraid she won't want to go home."

"Surely the city is more exciting than what goes on here."

"Simone would disagree. She loves it here."

Hannah eyed her with obvious curiosity. "You're cozy with my son."

Whoa… "I like him."

"He's a good man. Maybe the best man I know."

Emma wasn't sure where this was leading, so she took the cautious route. "I agree."

They watched TV in uncomfortable silence for long enough that Emma was relieved to hear Grayson's heavy footsteps on the stairs.

"Ready?" he asked.

"Whenever you are." Emma stood and pushed in the chair. "It was nice to see you, Hannah."

"You, too."

"See you later, Mom." Grayson guided Emma from the kitchen with a hand on her lower back. He held her coat for her and then put on his own.

His hair was damp, he'd shaved and he smelled delicious. "What'd she say to you?" he asked the second they were out the door.

"Nothing."

"*At all?*"

"No," she said, laughing, "nothing to be concerned about. She told me you're a good man, maybe the best man she knows."

"Hmm, is that right?"

"Yep. I told her I agreed."

"Did you now?"

"I did."

He held the car door for her. "And you already know that?"

"I knew that the first time we talked."

Grayson smiled at her and closed her door.

After he got in the car, she said, "Was she warning me off you?"

"I'm not sure why she would."

"Maybe because I live in New York and you live here?"

"Possibly."

"Where're we going?"

"I want to show you my new place."

Emma wondered if that was code for "pick up where we left off last night," which would be fine with her. He made her feel young again, and with Simone off having fun with Lucy, Emma was free to do something for herself for a change—and she felt a sense of urgency with their time in Vermont limited to only a few more days. "I'd like to see it."

Grayson held her hand as they drove through town, a small thing that was exciting to her after being alone for so long. The sense of connection she felt to him after such a short time both frightened and exhilarated her. With her better judgment warning caution, her hormones had a whole other agenda. Her very own civil war.

"You're quiet," he said. "What're you thinking about?"

"Civil war."

When he shifted his gaze to her, she could see his confusion. "My brain is telling me one thing about what's happening here. The rest of me has a whole other opinion."

"Talk to me about the rest of you. I think I'll like that opinion better than what your reasonable brain is telling you."

"You're right about that. If I were to listen to reason, I'd get out of this car at the next intersection and walk away."

"But…"

"I don't want to do that."

"Which is good, because I'd follow you."

She looked over at him, taking in the handsome face and smooth jaw. He took her breath away. "Even if I asked you not to?"

"If you asked me not to, I'd let you walk away, but I'd always be sorry I didn't try harder to convince you to stay."

"I have to go home on Friday." Three more days. That's all they had. Simone had a birthday party to go to on Saturday that she'd been looking forward to for weeks. As much as Emma might want to extend their time in Vermont by a few days, she couldn't and wouldn't disappoint her daughter. Not to mention she had to work on Saturday.

"I know."

"Maybe we shouldn't…" Her throat tightened, and tears filled her eyes. The idea of missing out on something she wanted so badly devastated her. But the thought of being flattened in the aftermath was worse.

Grayson pulled into the driveway at a three-story Victorian. He left the engine running so they'd have heat but turned in his seat to face her, keeping his grip on her hand. "I want you to know I'm as surprised by this as you are, and I understand the many reasons why it's a seriously bad idea to allow this to become even more complicated than it already is."

Emma waited breathlessly to hear what else he would say.

"But, even knowing all the reasons why it's a bad idea, I want you." He brought her hand to his lips and set her on fire by brushing his lips over her skin. "I want to hold you and kiss you and make love to you and talk to you and laugh with you and tell you things I've never told anyone else and spend time with you and your sweet daughter. And I can honestly tell you that I've never said anything even remotely close to that to any other woman. Ever."

She tried to breathe, as if that could possibly slow the wild beat of her heart.

"It's entirely up to you, Emma. I'll totally understand if you ask me to take you back to Molly and Lincoln's."

"You would?"

He nodded, but his eyes gave away his sadness.

"I don't want that. I want you, as much as you want me. I want to take this time with you and to feel the way I do when I'm with you, even if there's no chance of it being more than what it is right now."

"How do you feel when you're with me?"

"Happy, safe, adored, edgy, nervous, exhilarated, hopeful."

"That's a whole lot of feeling going on."

She nodded.

"I feel the same way. All of it, even the concern about what next week will bring and how I'll ever stand to let you go when it's time for you to leave."

It helped, somewhat, to know he shared her concerns.

"So what now?" she asked.

"Do you want to come in, or do you want to go back to Molly's? I'll respect whatever you decide."

"I'd like to see your new home," she said, feeling shy and excited at the same time. If they went inside, she knew exactly what would happen, and was going into it with her eyes—and her heart—wide open.

"Come on, then." He killed the engine and got out of the car.

Emma met him and followed him into the house and up the two flights of stairs to his third-floor apartment.

He unlocked the door and guided her in ahead of him.

Her heart beat so hard and so fast that she feared she'd hyperventilate. Ten years was a long time to go without. What if she'd forgotten how? Maybe it would turn out to be a disaster, and that would make it easier to put it—and him—behind her after this week.

Now there's a cheery thought.

Annoyed with herself, Emma tried to shake off the worries and focus on the apartment and the man who'd so totally captivated her.

"So I told you my cousin Ella is moving in with her fiancé, Gavin," he said. "She's leaving the sofa and the bed because she doesn't need either of them at his place."

"That makes it easier for you," Emma said, taking in the small but cozy space.

"She said it took six guys to get the sofa up the stairs, so I'm glad not to have to deal with that." He took her coat and hung it next to his on a rack by the door. "She's going to turn over her landline number to me, too."

"I haven't had a landline in years."

"Me either, but you've got to have one in the cell phone dead zone known as Butler." He held out his hand. "Come see the bedroom."

Here it was. The moment of truth. She could still say no. She could still walk away with her heart intact. She stared at his outstretched hand, feeling as if her entire life had come down to this man and this moment. Did she dare take the leap and say to hell with the painful consequences? How could she not?

She took his hand and saw as much as felt his relief.

Knowing he wanted this as badly as she did made it easier to take the first step and then the second.

He stopped next to the big bed Ella had left behind and drew Emma into his arms, looking down at her with affection and desire. "I'm glad you decided to stay."

"So am I. For now, anyway."

His lips curved into a small smile. "If this is meant to be, we'll find a way to make it happen. And if it's not, we'll enjoy it while it lasts."

It was the exact perfect thing for him to say, and it gave her the courage to curl her hand around the back of his neck and bring him down to her for a kiss in which all the usual preliminaries were skipped. Her mouth opened to accept his tongue and her body arched into his, wanting to be as close as she could possibly get to him. The time for questions and hesitation was over. This was the time for pleasure, for taking what she wanted for a change and not denying herself.

She tucked her hands under his sweater and flattened them on his back, loving the way he shuddered with desire that she could feel in the hard press of his erection against her belly. She pushed the sweater up and broke the kiss to remove it. Then she reached for the hem of her own sweater and pulled it up and over her head. Underneath, she wore a formfitting tank with a built-in bra.

"You're so beautiful, Emma," he said gruffly, running his hands over her arms and then up to frame her face. "I thought so the first time I ever saw you. Who, I wondered, is *that*? She's *stunning*." He kissed her neck, making her knees go weak. "And then I got to talk to you and found out that you're as beautiful on the inside as you are on the outside."

She wanted to touch him everywhere, beginning with the muscular hills and valleys of his chest and well-defined abdomen. "You're rather beautifully put together yourself."

"I got nothing on you."

"We can agree to disagree on that."

"I want to ask you something, and if you don't want to tell me, you don't have to."

The statement cut through her buzz of arousal, bringing her back to reality. "Okay…"

"Have you done this since Simone was conceived?"

Mortified to have to admit that she hadn't been with a man in so long, she tried to pull free of his embrace.

Grayson held her close. "There's no shame in it, Emma. I only asked because I want to be careful with you."

She trembled from the strength of her desire for him. "I haven't."

"If you want to stop, all you have to do is say so, okay?"

Nodding, she forced herself to look up at him, to meet the gaze that was looking at her with only care and concern, and not judgment.

He lifted the tank, watching her as he skimmed his fingertips over the skin he revealed.

Emma held her breath until the shirt cleared her head and her naked breasts were crushed against his chest.

"Ah, God," he whispered. "Feels so good."

"Mmm." She couldn't talk or think or do anything other than feel—*everything*.

He unbuttoned and unzipped her jeans and dropped to his knees to help her out of them, his hands gliding over bare legs that quivered in response to his touch. Then he cupped her bottom and drew her even closer to him so he could press his mouth against her silk-covered core.

Emma cried out from the shock and the heat that zipped through her body.

He turned her so she could back up to the bed, but before she sat on the edge where he wanted her, he removed her panties, leaving her bared to him in every possible way.

She wanted to memorize the hungry way he looked at her, but then he demanded her full attention when he dropped to his knees and made himself at home between her legs. Emma didn't have a chance to tell him she'd never... Not like this...

He used his fingers to open her to his tongue.

Oh my God. This must be what it was like to have a heart attack, she thought in the seconds after his tongue stroked her clit for the first time. *Dear God...*

He rested one arm on her lower abdomen to keep her still and used the fingers of his other hand to drive her crazy. No other word could possibly describe the way he made her feel as he stroked her with his tongue while pressing his fingers inside her. Then he sucked on her clit as he drove his fingers into her, and she exploded, coming so hard, she saw stars.

Still in the throes of the most epic release of her life, Emma had the sense to realize she'd probably made a huge mistake letting this happen.

If only she could find the wherewithal to care.

CHAPTER 5

Being deeply loved by someone gives you strength, while loving someone deeply gives you courage.
—Lao Tzu

Grayson couldn't wait to be inside her the next time that happened. Keeping up the gentle strokes of his fingers, he kissed his way up the front of her, noting the rosy glow of her soft skin. He drew her nipple into his mouth and felt her internal muscles clamp down on his fingers.

His cock wanted in on this party in the worst way, but he couldn't stop kissing her and sucking on her sweet nipples long enough to free himself from his pants, to roll on a condom, to do anything but keep kissing her. She made the sexiest noises—little whimpers and mewls and moans. Every one of them made him more determined to bring her the ultimate pleasure.

"Grayson…"

"What, honey?"

She reached for his pants, fumbling with the button and groaning with frustration when she couldn't get it free.

Chuckling softly, he helped her out. "Something you want?"

She looked up at him with those clear blue eyes and nodded.

He withdrew from her only long enough to get rid of his pants and boxers and to roll on one of the condoms he'd brought in case this happened.

The whole time, she watched him as he watched her, which was how he noticed her trepidation at the size of his cock.

"I… um…" She scooted back on the bed, landing on the pillows and curling up on her side. "That's not going to fit."

Did she have any idea how damned cute she was or how sweet or how sexy? She shivered, and that was when he realized he'd forgotten to turn up the heat.

He left her long enough to see to that and pulled the blanket Ella had left at the foot of the bed over them as he joined her. "Come here." With his hand on her hip, he brought her into his embrace. "Relax, honey." He caressed her back in soothing circles. "We'll take it nice and easy, and I promise it'll feel so good."

"I… It's been so long."

"I know, sweetheart."

"There was never anyone I wanted to be with, and it just sort of happened that way."

"You were busy raising your wonderful daughter."

"You don't have to sugarcoat it. My sister has been telling me for years that I needed to get back in the saddle."

"If this is too much too soon—"

She laughed. "It's definitely too much." To make her point, she wrapped her hand around his cock and stroked him until he feared this would be over before it started. "And it's also long overdue."

"If you want to wait, we can."

"I don't want to wait." She moved onto her back and urged him to come with her.

Propped on his elbows, he gazed down at her as she looked up at him. He felt the punch of their connection deep inside, making him ache for her in a way he never had for anyone else.

She wrapped her arms and legs around him, opening herself to him in every possible way.

He rocked against her, his cock sliding through the slickness between her legs and making her gasp every time the head nudged against her clit. Waiting until he was sure she was ready, he reached down to take himself in hand to enter her in the smallest possible increments.

The fit was impossibly tight, and he had to remind himself to keep breathing as he worked his way into her.

She clung to him, her fingers digging into the dense muscles on his back and her body arching into each stroke.

"Talk to me," he said, kissing her neck and then her lips. "Tell me how it feels."

"Big."

He nearly lost his composure when he laughed. "Is that right?"

"So big." Then she groaned because her commentary only made him harder than he already was.

"For me, the key words are tight and hot," he whispered against her ear, making her shudder from the heat of his breath. Bending his head, he drew her nipple into his mouth, sucking and tugging as she squirmed beneath him. He sent a hand down the front of her, teased her clit with his fingers and pressed the rest of the way into her tight channel. Christ have mercy, this was already the hottest sex of his life, and they were only getting started.

Every stroke of his fingers had her internal muscles gripping him so tightly, he had to fight the need to come the entire time he was inside her. He withdrew as slowly as he'd gone in and sank back into her.

"Do it again," she said, her eyes closed and her lips parted.

He did it again and again, picking up the pace when he was sure she could handle more, and continued to stroke her clit. His muscles burned from the effort to hold off and wait for her, but she made it well worth the wait when she exploded, holding on to him for dear life as her entire body shuddered and trembled.

Grayson pressed deep into her one more time and let go, losing himself in her sweetness and heat while breathing in the scent that would remind him always of her. This, he thought as his body cooled and twitched with aftershocks, is the kind of thing that changes plans and lives. And he'd thought he'd had great sex with Heather. That was nothing compared to what'd just happened with Emma.

"Am I crushing you?" he said after a long silence.

"Not at all." Her hands continued to move on his back, soothing as much as arousing him.

"Are you okay?"

"Uh-huh. You?"

"Never been better."

"Never?" she asked in a small voice that tugged at his every emotion.

He raised his head to look down at her. "Never," he said, kissing her. "Not even close."

She beamed with pleasure at hearing that. "Glad to know I've still got it."

"Oh, you've got it, all right. In fact, I can't wait to have more of what you've got."

"You were worth waiting for, Grayson."

Her softly spoken words touched him deep inside. "So were you."

Lucy stood at the bottom of the bunny hill and watched as Colton patiently taught Simone how to ski. She could see him talking with his hands and pointing to the skis as well as demonstrating what he was trying to convey to the little girl who hung on his every word. Simone loved Colton almost as much as Lucy did.

Colton pointed to the bottom of the hill, and Simone nodded.

Lucy was too far away to see for sure, but she suspected Simone was biting her lower lip in concentration as she tried to put it all together—skis and poles and body positioning.

Colton stayed close, ready to intervene in case of disaster.

Wearing the helmet Colton had insisted on to protect her head, Simone moved slowly, carefully and with determination as she started down the little hill.

"You're doing great," Colton called to her. "Keep it up!"

Lucy used her phone to video Simone's descent as well as her triumphant smile at safely reaching the bottom of the hill. "Great job! You did it!"

"I want to do it again. Can we go again, Uncle Colton?"

"You bet." Winking at Lucy, he steered Simone toward the towrope that would take them back up the hill.

Every time they were with Simone, he was endlessly patient and creative in thinking up ways to entertain an active, bright nine-year-old. He'd even gotten Simone interested in the making of maple syrup, and now she wanted to come back to Vermont in the spring to help during the sugaring season.

They waved from the top of the hill, and Lucy began recording again, following Simone as she made the tight little turns that Colton had taught her.

He was going to be such a wonderful father someday. Lucy wished she knew when that someday might be. They didn't talk about getting married or having a family. Over the last year, they'd fallen into a routine that split their time between his home in Vermont and hers in New York, although lately they seemed to spend much more time in Vermont.

Not that she minded. She loved it here as much as he did and enjoyed being surrounded by his family. Having her best friend, Cameron, nearby made Lucy even happier. She'd met Colton through Cameron, after she got together with his brother Will. Now they were married with a baby on the way, while Lucy and Colton were... stuck.

Not that things weren't good with them. Everything was great, and that was the problem, or so she'd decided. What reason did they have to take the next step if everything was perfect the way it was? Her dad used to tell her and Emma that no man would buy the cow if he was getting the milk for free. Such a stupid saying, but Lucy was beginning to wonder if that was why Colton wasn't looking to buy the cow. She certainly gave away plenty of free milk to her insatiable fiancé.

"She's a natural," Colton said after their third trip down the hill.

"You're doing great, Simone," Lucy called to the red-faced girl with the great big smile. She was thrilled with herself for having learned something new and basked in the glow of Colton's praise.

Lucy watched Simone slide smoothly into position on the towrope, which carried her up the hill.

Colton was right behind her, ready to step in if need be.

Lucy didn't know why she felt so down today about her relationship with Colton. Well, yes, she did... She'd been hoping since their engagement months ago that he might bring up the subject of their wedding, but he never mentioned it. As far as she knew, he wasn't even thinking about actually getting married, despite the matrimonial outbreak going on around them.

In the last year alone, Will and Cameron, Hannah and Nolan, and Hunter and Megan had gotten married, while Ella and Gavin had gotten engaged and Charley had fallen—literally—for Tyler. He'd nursed Charley back to health after she messed up her knee while running in the snow. The two of them were now moving in together. They'd probably be married before she and Colton at the rate things were going.

The worst part about this situation for Lucy was that she couldn't bring herself to broach the subject of next steps with her beloved. They talked about everything. They had the kind of relationship she used to dream about before she met him and knew what was possible. So why couldn't she ask him about their future and what he saw happening for them? She didn't know, and that made her feel like a spineless, wimpy, ridiculous excuse for a modern woman who ran her own business but couldn't seem to manage her relationship.

Lucy was descending into a full-on pity party when a shout from the hill had her snapping out of it in time to see Simone mid-fall.

She landed hard on the packed surface and let out a scream that made Lucy's blood go cold. She took off running toward her niece and Colton, who was on his knees next to her.

Simone's shrieks had the attention of everyone in the area.

Her heart pounding, Lucy tried to walk up the small hill, but the snow and ice were so slippery, she kept stumbling.

The snow patrol team had spikes in their boots that made it possible for them to rush by her in their haste to get to Simone.

Lucy stopped and looked up at Colton, hoping for info.

He held his arm up and pointed to the elbow.

"Please let her be okay," Lucy whispered as she watched the snow patrol remove Simone's skis and load her onto a sled-litter thing to bring her down. "Please, please, please."

As soon as they started down the mountain with Simone, who was still screaming, Colton came down to where Lucy stood at the foot of the hill, feeling useless and frightened.

He kicked up a wall of snow as he came to a stop beside her. "I think her elbow is dislocated."

"Oh no."

"The good news is it can be fixed pretty easily. The bad news is it hurts like hell."

At the thought of Simone in so much pain, Lucy felt like she was going to be sick.

"Hey," Colton said. "Look at me. Breathe. She's okay. It sounds worse than it is."

Lucy watched as the snow patrol headed for a building with a big red cross on the outside. "If you say so."

"Hop on."

"What?"

"Jump on, and I'll give you a ride to the first aid building."

"Um, I..." Visions of calamity danced through her brain, making her hesitate.

"Lucy, come on! She needs us."

His urgent tone got her attention. She jumped onto his back and held on for dear life as he pointed his skis toward the building while she tried not to scream her head off. Colton brought them to a swift stop right by the door.

Simone's shrieks could be heard from outside.

Lucy dropped down from Colton's back, landing on unsteady legs.

He had his skis off and his arm around her within seconds, guiding her through the door. "We're her aunt and uncle," he said to the nurse who met them. "What can we do?"

She thrust a clipboard in their direction. "Sign for authorization to treat her."

Lucy took the clipboard and signed where directed, her hand shaking so hard, she could barely hold the pen.

"What's the plan?" Colton asked.

"The doctor would like to do what's called a reduction. We'll need to take some X-rays and she'll be mildly sedated."

"Wh-what's a reduction?" Lucy asked.

"They're going to snap the bone back into place," Colton said. "Which hurts like a mother-effer. That's why they want to sedate her."

"We do them almost every day around here," the nurse assured her.

Lucy's vision began to swim, and she was overly warm all of a sudden.

"Lucy," Colton said, giving her a little shake. "Breathe."

"Would you like to be in with her when they do it?" the nurse asked.

"I will," Colton said. To Lucy, he said, "Go sit and keep breathing. I'll be in there with her, and she'll be fine. I promise." He kissed her forehead and directed her to the waiting area. Then he took off with the nurse.

Feeling like a total wimp, she landed in a chair and dropped her head between her knees the way she'd seen done on TV medical shows. Breathe, Lucy. Breathe. Tears filled her eyes at the thought of her precious Simone in such terrible pain. Emma.

I need to find Emma. She took a chance and tried her sister's cell phone, but the call went directly to voice mail, which meant Emma was somewhere in Butler without service. After leaving a message for Emma to call her, Lucy stood on her shaky legs and walked to the reception desk. "Is there a phone I could use?"

"Of course. Come around the counter."

Lucy did as directed and tried to summon the number to the Abbott home from a memory that had gone blank. She closed her eyes, took a couple of deep breaths and tried to concentrate. Simone needs you, Lucy. This is no time to go stupid. She was about to ask for a phonebook when the number came to her. Her hands were still shaking as she punched in the numbers.

Molly answered on the third ring.

"Hi, it's Lucy."

"Hey, what's up?"

"So, um, Simone fell while skiing and dislocated her elbow."

"Oh no! The poor thing! That's so painful."

"Yes, it is. I'm looking for Emma. Is she there?"

"No, honey, she went off somewhere with Grayson a couple of hours ago. I have no idea where they are, but I'll call my sister to see if she knows."

"If you're able to find her, we're at the clinic on the mountain."

"I'll tell her. Keep me posted."

"I will."

"She'll be fine, Lucy."

"Keep telling me that. All I can hear are her screams. It's horrible."

"It'll be okay. I promise."

"Thank you, Molly."

"Any time."

Lucy ended the call and thanked the receptionist. She was on her way back to the chairs when she heard Simone's screams reach a whole new level. That was the last thing Lucy heard before everything went dark.

CHAPTER 6

Love recognizes no barriers. It jumps hurdles, leaps fences,
penetrates walls to arrive at its destination full of hope.
—Maya Angelou

This has to be a dream, Emma thought as she woke from a short nap to Grayson's warm body snug against her back, his arm around her waist and his legs intertwined with hers. *If it's a dream, I never want to wake up.*

She'd read about sex like they'd had in romance novels, but she'd never expected to experience it. And it wasn't just the sex, but the connection she'd felt with him from the beginning. How would she ever go back to her regular life after this? Even though she loved her life with Simone in the city, it would seem so boring and mundane after this exciting week in Vermont.

She already ached for him, and she hadn't even left him yet.

Sighing, she reached the hand he'd tucked under her breasts and smiled when his fingers curled around hers.

"What's with the deep sigh?" he asked in a gruff, sleepy-sounding voice.

"Just thinking."

"Don't do that. Not yet anyway."

"Easier said than done."

"I know, but for right now, today, everything is perfect, and I'd like to wallow in the perfection for a little while longer before we let reality intrude. Would that be okay?"

Smiling, she said, "That sounds like a good plan. What does this wallowing consist of?"

He pushed his reawakened erection against her back. "More of this. Lots more of this."

"Mmm, I could be talked into more of that." When she would've turned over to face him, he stopped her.

"Like this," he said. "Just like this."

Emma had never done anything other than good old-fashioned missionary, so she waited breathlessly to see what he had in mind.

Grayson released her hand and cupped her breast, rolling her tender nipple between his fingers and making her squirm. His lips brushed against the back of her neck, and she gasped from the sensations that zinged through her body. "Your skin is so soft," he whispered, his warm breath giving her goose bumps. "I love how responsive you are to me."

His hand moved from her breast to her belly and then to her core. He drew her leg up and over his hip, opening her to his fingers.

Emma trembled as she anticipated his touch.

He teased her, running his fingertips over her inner thighs and tracing the outer lips of her sex, making her crave his touch. "Grayson. *Please.*"

His low chuckle had her groaning in frustration. "Patience, sweetheart. You'll get everything you want."

"*When?*"

"Soon."

Not soon enough for her. "You're enjoying this a little too much."

"No such thing." He took mercy on her, sliding his fingers through the dampness between her legs and caressing her clit.

Emma gripped his forearm and bit her lip to keep from screaming from the pleasure. Then he turned her, and she was facedown on the bed, his lips skimming over her back as he continued to stroke between her legs. She was drowning in a sea of sensation with her every sense on high alert. Even the rub of her nipples against the sheet added to the overload. She grasped the pillow, needing something to hold on to as he continued to kiss her back. And when he reached her bottom, he added some gentle nibbles to flesh that had never been so sensitive.

He kept her on the razor's edge of release for so long that by the time he finally began to enter her from behind, she was more than ready to let go, coming harder than she had before.

Groaning, he grasped her hips and drove into her, triggering a second wave that was stronger than the first. She came down from the incredible high to discover he wasn't finished with her yet. Not even close.

He arranged her on her knees, spreading her legs farther apart, and started the climb all over again with deep strokes of his cock while still caressing her clit.

The bed creaked and the headboard banged against the wall, which was, fortunately, on the outside of the house where no one was apt to hear it. Not that she could be bothered to care about who might hear them while being taken on the ride of her life.

"Emma, God, you feel so good. So, so good." His fingers dug into her hips.

She would feel his fierce possession in every muscle she owned tomorrow. But in this moment, she couldn't be bothered with caring about anything beyond right here and right now.

He surged deep into her and held still for a long moment before she felt the heat of his release. His head dropped to her back as he took a series of deep breaths. "Christ have mercy."

Emma laughed. "Someone needs to have mercy on me."

He withdrew from her and arranged them so they were facing each other. "I was rough. I'm sorry."

She laid a finger over his lips. "Please don't apologize. That was… I have no words."

"Is that a good thing?"

Moved by his obvious concern, she said, "The best thing ever. It was incredible. I didn't know… I had no idea…"

He leaned in to kiss her. "Me either."

She felt better knowing they were equally stunned. When she'd come to Vermont for Christmas with her sister's new family, she'd had no idea she'd be having wild sex with her sister's fiancé's cousin. Emma reached for him, and he came into her embrace, capturing her lips in another heated kiss that quickly had her wanting him all over again.

Apparently, he felt the same way, because before she knew it, he was on top of her and inside her once again, moving slowly this time, slaying her with tenderness that was in stark contrast to the earlier frantic pace. *This*, she thought as her gaze collided with his, *is what it must be like to make love.*

Then he was turning them so she was on top of him.

"You're so beautiful, Emma," he whispered gruffly as he cupped her breasts and toyed with her nipples.

She'd never felt more beautiful than she did right then with him gazing up at her with such blatant desire and affection etched into his expression. "Tell me how… I haven't… Not like this."

"Easy, baby." His hands fell to her hips to guide her. "Nice and easy." A huge shiver went through her as she tried to process the new position and how it made her feel. He urged her to move and helped her find a rhythm that had them both gasping. Then he sat up and gathered her in close to him as they continued to move. "How does it feel?"

"So good." The word *good* seemed so inadequate, but with every brain cell focused on other things, it was the best she could do.

"God, Emma…"

The desperate tone of his voice had her moving faster, her every thought focused on the almost unbearable pleasure. He captured her lips in a desperate, carnal kiss at the same time he reached down to where they were joined to coax her to an explosive finish that left her reeling in the aftermath.

She collapsed into his embrace, holding on tight to him through the emotional firestorm that followed the epic release.

He held on just as tightly to her. "Holy shit, that was hot," he said after a long silence punctuated only by the sound of heavy breathing.

"Mmm."

"Are you all right?"

Had she ever been more all right? "Mmm-hmm."

He reclined against the pillows, bringing her with him. His lips brushed against her forehead as his fingers combed through her hair. Happy, sated, warm and cozy in his arms, Emma drifted on a wave of contentment. She should check on Simone and Lucy. She should get up, take a shower, get back to her real life. But she couldn't bring herself to move, to burst the delightful bubble that surrounded her and Grayson.

Real life would still be there in an hour or two. For right now, while her daughter was safely occupied with the aunt and uncle who adored her, Emma decided to take a little more time for herself.

Simone was released from the clinic two hours after the procedure, with the good news that there were no broken bones. Her arm was in a splint and a sling. The pain medication she'd been given had Simone fighting to stay awake.

Lucy had wanted to ask for something for the aunt's shredded nerves to go along with the pain meds for Simone.

As they drove to the barn with Simone sacked out in the backseat, Colton reached over the center console for her hand. "How you holding up, babe?"

"Great. Never better."

"She's fine, and in a couple of days, she'll be good as new."

"It might take longer than a couple of days for the aunt to recover."

He squeezed her hand. "You were a trouper, Luce."

"No, *you* were a trouper. *I* was a disaster."

"You were not. You were understandably freaked out by the way she was screaming. So was I."

"You'd never know it. You were Mr. Cool Under Pressure."

"Not on the inside I wasn't."

"I wonder where Emma is. It's not like her to be out of touch for so long. Usually she calls to check on us when I have Simone."

"She's probably off having fun with Grayson and lost track of time."

"Probably."

"How's your head?"

"It's fine." She had smacked it on a chair when she fainted in the waiting room. "I feel like a fool for being so wimpy."

"You were upset. I'm just glad you're both okay."

"Bet you can't wait to spend another day with the two of us."

"You'd win that bet. I love every minute I get to spend with you guys. Don't be too hard on yourself, Luce."

Darkness came early to northern Vermont this time of year, and by the time they pulled into the Abbotts' driveway, it might've been midnight rather than ten after five.

Colton carried the sleeping Simone inside while Lucy got the doors for him.

"How is she?" Molly asked when they stepped into the family room, where she and Linc were reading and the dogs were sacked out in front of a roaring fire.

"Better now," Lucy said. "They gave her something for the pain that knocked her out."

"Poor thing," Molly said, standing to caress Simone's hair and kiss her forehead before Colton settled her on the sofa.

"No word from Emma?" Lucy asked.

"Nothing yet."

"I wonder where she is." Lucy tried Emma's cell phone again, and like before, the call went straight to voice mail. "Did you try Grayson's phone?"

"Earlier," Molly said, "but I got his message."

"Wherever they are," Linc said, "they're out of cell range, which means they could be anywhere around here."

"Why don't you two get something to eat?" Molly said. "The fridge is full of leftovers. We'll keep an eye on Simone for you."

"Thanks, Mom," Colton said. "I'm starving. Come on, Luce. Have something to eat. You'll feel better if you do."

Though she wasn't sure she could eat, she followed him into the kitchen and took a seat at the table while he made sandwiches for both of them. He wolfed his down while she picked at hers.

"Eat, Lucy. She's fine. Everything is fine."

"My stomach is still a mess. I'm not sure it'll stay down."

"I'm an expert at holding your hair when you're sick. I'll take care of you."

His reminder of the time he'd come to her rescue when she had food poisoning made her smile. "I'd rather skip the whole being-sick part of the program."

"You need to eat, babe."

She made an effort for his sake, even if she really didn't want the food. "I'm so bummed this happened today of all days, when Emma was off doing something fun for a change. She never gets a break, and the one day she does…"

"Shit happens. She knows that."

"I wish I could be more like you. Nothing ever gets to you or rattles you."

"Lucy, honey, I was as rattled today as I've ever been. Your beautiful niece was entrusted to me to teach her to ski, and she got hurt on my watch. Trust me when I tell you it was upsetting for me, too."

"It wasn't your fault. Like you said, shit happens. I'm just thankful she only hurt her arm." Lucy tried not to think about how much worse it could've been.

"Now you know why I insist on the helmet. Skiing is dangerous. People get hurt. It happens. Ask Will about the crash that ended his Olympic dreams."

Lucy cringed, imagining a crash bad enough to end a skiing career.

"This was a fall on the bunny slope, babe. As bad as it was for us, knowing our intrepid Simone, she'll want to get right back on skis again as soon as she possibly can."

"I like the way you say that, our intrepid Simone…"

"She is nothing if not intrepid."

"I like the *our* part, too."

"You know I love her like she's my own niece. What's not to love about her? She's adorable and sweet and curious and so polite and funny. And she's incredibly smart. I've never met a smarter nine-year-old."

His kind words about Simone invoked an emotional reaction in Lucy that had her brushing at tears.

"Aww, baby, don't cry." He tugged her hand to bring her onto his lap, wrapping his strong arms around her as he buried his face in her hair. "You know I can't take it when you cry."

"I'm sorry."

"Don't be sorry. It was a scary thing. It'll be a long time before I stop hearing her screams."

"That was the worst part." She took a deep sigh. "I'm probably better off not having kids of my own if this is the kind of mother I'd be."

"You'd be a great mom. Our kids would be so lucky to have you."

"You really think so?" She wanted to ask if he might have a timetable as to when that might happen, but after the day they'd already had, she didn't have the courage to open that door. Not now, anyway.

"I know so." He held her and kissed her and made her feel better, the way he always did, but she couldn't help but wonder if he ever thought about getting married and having those kids he thought she'd be such a good mother to.

CHAPTER 7

There is only one happiness in this life, to love and be loved.
—George Sand

Emma came to slowly, languidly, after the best nap she'd had in longer than she could recall. Grayson's chest made for a comfortable pillow, and sleeping in his arms was delightful. Then she opened her eyes to total darkness and let out a squeak of distress that woke him, too.

"What's wrong?"

"It's totally dark. What time is it?"

He lit up the face of his watch. "A little after five."

"I need to go." Like Cinderella after the ball, the party was over, and soon she'd turn into a pumpkin if she didn't get home to her little pumpkin. Surely they were back from skiing by now and probably wondering where she was. "Would it be possible to take a quick shower?"

Grayson turned on the bedside lamp. "Of course."

Emma closed her eyes against the light and the jarring return to reality. It was foolish, she knew, to feel shy about being naked in front of him after the afternoon they'd spent together, but she grasped the sheet to her breasts nonetheless.

"Let me see if Ella's packed the towels yet." He got out of bed and went into the bathroom.

Emma watched him go, taking a good long look at the tight muscular ass that made her mouth water when she remembered the flex of those muscles as he pounded into her. A tingle between her legs caught her by surprise. After what they'd just done, how could she still want more?

"We're in luck." Grayson returned to the bedroom with a stack of towels in hand. "Ella hasn't packed up the bathroom yet." He dropped the pile on the bed and held up one of the towels for her, seeming to sense her shyness.

As she released the sheet and wrapped the towel around her body, Emma appreciated the gesture.

He placed his hands on her shoulders and kissed her cheek. "You're not having regrets, are you?"

"What? No, not at all. Are you?"

"Not even kinda. This was the best day I've ever had."

"Same here."

"You want some company in the shower?"

"Oh, I, um… I haven't done that before."

"First time for everything?"

"I really ought to get back to the house. I don't want to take advantage of my sister."

"Of course." He kissed her forehead and released her.

As Emma rushed through a quick shower, using bath soap his cousin had left behind, she wished she'd taken him up on the offer to shower together. Now she'd have to wonder what might've happened if she'd invited him to join her. It was probably just as well that she hadn't, because one thing might've led to another, and judging by the soreness between her legs, she'd already had too much of a good thing.

Emma was careful not to let her hair get wet so she wouldn't have to explain wet hair to her hosts or sister. She felt like a teenager who'd been up to no good sneaking back into her parents' house. Wrapped in the towel, she left the bathroom and found Grayson sitting on the bed, waiting for her.

"I'll be quick," he said, kissing her as he went by her to take a turn in the bathroom.

She heard the shower go on and tried to find her clothes, which were scattered about the floor, a reminder of how eager they'd been. By the time he came out, towel wrapped around his waist, she was fully dressed and becoming more anxious by the minute to check on her daughter.

She's fine. Of course she's fine. She's with Lucy, which is the next best thing to being with me. Still, even knowing that, Emma wanted to see her if for no other reason than she missed her. Except for the time they spent at school and work, the two of them were nearly constant companions. Rarely did they spend more than twenty-four hours apart.

Grayson got dressed and helped her into her coat. In silence, they left the apartment where everything had changed between them in such dramatic fashion. She'd had so much to say to him earlier, but now she had no idea what to say. Was this a vacation fling never to be repeated or the start of something more significant? She couldn't say, and that left her feeling unsettled.

She'd never been a one-night-stand kind of girl. Hell, she hadn't had the time to be, what with getting pregnant at eighteen and becoming a mother at nineteen. Her experience with situations like this was nearly nonexistent.

"You're sure you're okay?" he asked after a long silence.

"I'm sure. It's just a long time for me to be out of touch with Simone. I'm getting twitchy."

"I totally understand. Sorry to keep you so long."

"Don't be sorry," she said, smiling at him. "I'm not."

They arrived at the Abbott home a few minutes later. Colton's truck was parked behind Lincoln's Range Rover. Emma wondered how long they'd been back and whether she'd kept Lucy and Colton from plans by being gone so long.

Aware of Grayson following her into the house, Emma hurried through the removal of her coat and boots and rushed into the kitchen, stopping short when she saw Lucy sitting on Colton's lap as he wiping away her sister's tears.

A cold feeling of dread overcame Emma, making her stagger. "Simone."

"Oh hey," Lucy said as she stood. "You're back."

"What's wrong? Where's Simone?"

"She hurt her arm while skiing, but she's okay," Lucy said. "They gave her something for the pain, and she's out cold."

Grayson's hand on her shoulder offered comfort Emma didn't want after hearing her baby had been hurt while she'd been off having sex.

"Where is she?"

"On the sofa," Colton said.

Emma all but ran into the family room, where Simone was asleep on the sofa, her arm in a sling and her face the ghostly shade of pale it became whenever she was unwell. She dropped to her knees next to the sofa and bent to kiss her cheek. "Mama's here, sweet girl." Smoothing the hair back from Simone's sweaty forehead, Emma battled through the emotional firestorm of realizing her child had needed her while she was in bed with Grayson. This was what she got for being selfish and taking some time for herself. "I'm so sorry, baby. I'm here now, and I'm not going anywhere."

"She's fine, Emma," Colton said from behind her. "She dislocated her elbow, but there was no sign of a fracture or anything more serious. She'll be sore for a couple of days, but no harm done."

Emma blinked back tears. "That's a huge relief. Thank you for taking such good care of her."

"These things happen when kids are learning to ski," Lincoln said. "How many dislocations, sprains, concussions and other maladies did we have, Mol?"

"Too many to count," his wife replied.

Emma knew they were trying to make her feel better, but she still felt guilty for not being available when Simone needed her.

"You want me to carry her up to bed?" Colton asked. "They said she'll be out of it until the morning."

"If you don't mind." Simone was too heavy for Emma to carry anymore. "That would help. Thank you."

Emma and Lucy followed Colton upstairs to the room where Simone had been sleeping. She'd been told it was Colton's sister Charley's old room. He laid her gently on the bed, pulled the covers up and over her and kissed the girl's forehead. "Sleep tight, sweetheart."

Moved by Colton's tenderness toward her daughter, Emma perched on the edge of the bed, trying not to wince from her own soreness. She wished Simone would wake up and fill the room with the usual chatter about everything that'd happened since they last saw each other.

"I'll be right downstairs if you ladies need me," Colton said.

"Thanks, Colton," Emma said. To Lucy, she added, "Did you try to get me?"

"All afternoon."

"I'm really sorry. We were… We went for a ride in the mountains."

"Is that a metaphor?" Lucy asked, giving her sister a knowing look.

Emma should've known that her older sister would see right through her ruse. "I feel sick that she was hurt and you couldn't reach me. What kind of mother—"

"You are the best mother I've ever known in my entire life. Taking a day off doesn't make you a bad mother."

"Not being reachable when my child is hurt makes me a bad mother."

"No, it makes you someone who has now officially visited the cell phone wasteland known as Butler, Vermont. It's not your fault, Em." Lucy sat next to her on the bed. "So you had a nice time?"

"You could say that."

Lucy nudged her shoulder. "Come on. This is me. You can do better than that."

To her utter mortification, Emma began to cry.

Lucy put her arm around her. "What's wrong?"

"Nothing is wrong. Other than Simone getting hurt, today was one of the best days of my entire life."

"So then why the tears?"

"Think about it, Luce. I finally meet a really great guy, and he lives six hours from me. It just feels so…"

"Doomed from the start?"

"Something like that."

"I know that feeling. I've been there, but we made it work."

"You didn't have a child to think about."

"True, but please don't think any of this is insurmountable. If it's meant to be, it'll be."

"I don't know if it's meant to be, but it sure felt that way for a couple of hours today."

"So you haven't forgotten how?" Lucy asked. "That's a relief."

Emma elbowed her in the ribs, making her sister laugh.

"It was good, huh?"

Emma huffed out a laugh. "Spectacular."

"Where'd you go?"

"His new place. He's taking over Ella's lease in town."

"You sneaky devils."

"I'm really sorry, Lu. I didn't mean to totally punch out while you had Simone."

"Don't be ridiculous. That's exactly what you should do when I have her. You never get a break. You'd be crazy not to take full advantage of me while you can. Besides, Colton and I love being with her. She's never a burden to us."

"Even when her elbow is dislocated?"

"Especially then."

Emma reached out to stroke Simone's silky red hair that was so much like Lucy's. "Did she cry?"

"Um, how to answer that without adding to your guilt?"

"Poor baby. Poor you, too."

"I was a disaster. Colton was the hero. He was great with her."

"He's going to be an awesome dad someday."

"Yeah, I guess."

Emma turned to her sister. "That's not exactly a ringing endorsement."

"He will be great. I just wonder if it's ever going to happen. We never talk about it anymore."

"Like *ever*?"

Lucy shook her head. "It would come up once in a while when we were first engaged, but it's been months since we last talked about the future."

"Have you asked him what he's thinking?"

After a long pause, Lucy said, "It's weird because I feel like I can talk to him about anything—except this. Any time I try to bring it up, I freeze."

"You want the fairy tale, and you need to tell him that."

Lucy scowled. "I'm a modern kind of girl. Who needs fairy tales?"

"You do, and there's nothing wrong with wanting that, especially since your relationship with him has already been right out of a fairy tale."

"I still feel silly."

Grayson appeared in the doorway, seeming uncertain of his welcome. "How is she?"

"Out cold," Emma said.

"Could I see her?"

Touched that he would ask, she said, "Sure. Come on in."

Lucy stood to make room for him. "I'll be downstairs if you need me. I hear people are coming over for the annual holiday game night tonight."

"Ah, yes, the dog-eat-dog blood sport known as Abbott game night," Grayson said. "It's got to be seen to be believed."

"Looking forward to it," Lucy said on her way out of the room.

Grayson came over to the bed and reached out to touch Simone's hair. "She's so beautiful," he said softly. "Just like her mother." He glanced at Emma. "Are you okay?"

"I've been better."

He sat next to her, taking Lucy's spot and putting his arm around her. "I'm sorry this happened while we were off the grid."

"It's not your fault. It was an accident. I'm just thankful Lucy was with her. She's the next best thing."

"Are you going to take a step back from me because this happened?" he asked, surprising her with the blunt question.

"I should probably take a step back from you for a lot of reasons."

"Please don't do that, Emma. Whatever this is between us, it's good. It's so damned good. I want more of it." He nuzzled her neck. "I want more of you."

"It's all so ridiculously complicated."

"So what?"

She laughed softly. "Easy for you to say."

"It's not easy for me to say. I don't do complicated as a rule, but in this case… I can't imagine you and Simone leaving here later this week and not seeing you again until the next family event. I don't want to wait that long."

"You don't?"

He shook his head. "A week is going to be too long."

Though his statement made her heart flutter, she said, "Why do I feel like we're setting ourselves up for disaster? You're starting a business here. I live in the city. How do you see this playing out?"

"I have no idea, but the thought of letting you go on Friday and having this be over is completely unacceptable to me."

"It is, huh?"

"Absolutely, totally and completely unacceptable."

She smiled at his emphatic declaration.

"I know you've been off the dating circuit awhile," he said, still speaking softly as he ran his fingers through her hair, "but what happened between us earlier doesn't come along every day.

Hell, it's never come along for me. Not like that anyway. We'd be crazy not to see where it takes us."

"I feel like we'd be crazy to try to make it work under these circumstances."

"Will and Cameron made it work. Lucy and Colton are making it work."

"True, but they didn't have Simone to consider, and with Lucy here more than in New York these days, I have to think about my dad, too. I could never leave him there all alone."

"It's a lot to consider. I know it is. But all I'm asking for is a chance, Emma."

He was so sweet and so convincing and so damned sexy. She wanted to curl up to him and let him make everything that was wrong okay again, which was a rather radical thought for a woman who'd taken care of herself and her daughter on her own for such a long time.

"Let's take it a day at a time," she said. "That's all I'm capable of right now."

"I can live with that." With his finger on her chin, he turned her toward him and laid a gentle kiss on her lips. "Today was amazing."

"For me, too."

For the longest time, he held her gaze, neither of them blinking as they drank each other in.

Emma felt herself falling into something big, something so significant it had the power to flatten her if it went wrong. That scared the crap out of her. Simone relied on her for everything. She couldn't afford to be flattened by a romantic disaster.

"You want to come down for game night?"

"I don't want to leave her."

"Molly said to tell you there's a baby monitor in the room next door for when Caden is here," he said of his cousin Max's baby son. "She said to move it in here if you want to come downstairs."

"Oh, um, I don't know if I should leave her."

"Colton said she's going to sleep all night because of the pain meds they gave her. It's probably safe to come downstairs, but if you don't want to, I'll stay up here to keep you company."

"You don't have to do that."

"I want to, Emma. I want to spend every second I can with you." His hand made circles on her back that comforted and aroused her.

She leaned into him, taking the support he offered so willingly. "Please don't make me start to depend on you."

"Would that be so awful?"

"It would be if it didn't work out."

"We're taking it a day at a time, remember?"

"How could I forget?"

"Want me to get the baby monitor for you?"

"If you wouldn't mind."

He kissed her cheek and then her lips again. "I don't mind."

Watching him go, Emma was filled with longing for more of what she'd already experienced with him. In addition to the physical connection, he was easy to talk to, kind, supportive, sweet to Simone and understanding of the many challenges that stood in their way. It would be so easy to dive into this with no regard for potential consequences. And oh how she was tempted to take that dive, especially after the hours she'd spent in bed with him. A shiver traveled down her spine when she recalled the searing intimacy, the things they'd done, how he'd made her feel.

Grayson returned with the baby monitor, which he plugged into the wall behind the bedside table.

"Wow, that's cool," Emma said of the video monitor. "I had the old-school audio version when Simone was a baby."

He handed her the remote portion. "You can watch her sleep from downstairs while you have a much-needed glass of wine and some fun. What do you say?"

Emma glanced at Simone, who hadn't so much as stirred since Colton tucked her in. And then she looked up at Grayson, who was watching her with interest and desire he didn't bother to try to hide. She reached out to him.

He took her hand.

"Let's go have some fun."

CHAPTER 8

Where we love is home—home that our feet may leave, but not our hearts.
—Oliver Wendell Holmes Sr.

The annual Abbott family game night was, in fact, utter chaos and nonstop laughter, most of it due to the antics of Lucas and Landon as well as a steady flow of beer and wine.

"They really do this every year?" Emma asked Grayson as they sat off to the side watching the goings-on.

"Two days after Christmas for as long as I can remember. Aunt Molly says that with ten kids on vacation and not a lot of disposable income back in the day, they had to be creative with how they entertained the troops. Game night became a holiday-week tradition."

"What've we missed?" Charley asked as she came in with Tyler.

"Just Lucas and Landon being morons," Will said.

"Nothing new there," Charley said.

"Dad always said if you're going to do something, be the best at it," Landon said.

"You took that advice a little too literally," Hannah said from her perch on the sofa next to Nolan. She was so pregnant she could barely move, or so she said.

"I'm here to defend my Scrabble title," Ella said, arriving with Gavin.

"No one wants to play with you anymore, honey," Lincoln said.

"Bunch of chickenshits," Ella said, scowling.

"It was the ninety-point word that did you in." Linc pulled a piece of paper from the game box. "Here's the petition signed by the entire family on game night last year."

"They actually signed a petition?" Emma asked Grayson.

"Oh yeah. No one can beat her."

"I'll play with you, babe," Gavin said, patting Ella on the bottom.

"I hope we're still talking Scrabble," Colton said from the floor where he sat with Max and Caden setting up Monopoly. "And not strip poker."

"I'm happy to play whatever games your sister dreams up," Gavin said to moans, groans and flying game pieces.

"Don't mess up the games!" Linc said. "You're all a bunch of *animals*!"

"They always have been," Molly said.

Wade dabbed at his eyes. "I love when Mom and Dad get sentimental."

"I'm here to photograph the mayhem," Izzy Coleman said when she arrived, camera in hand.

"And I'm here to referee," Grayson's mother, Hannah, said as she followed her daughter into the family room, zeroing right in on Emma sitting close to Grayson on the love seat.

Emma shifted ever so subtly away from him.

He looked at her, raising a questioning brow.

Should she tell him his mother seemed to disapprove of her for him? He'd deny that. Of course he would, but Emma knew disapproval when she saw it.

"Okay," Lincoln said, "Ella is the defender of the Scrabble title, which has been banned from game night due to lack of interest from challengers."

"Bunch of babies," she said, glowering at the others.

"Hunter is the defending Monopoly champion."

"Whatever," Will said.

"He totally cheats," Lucas said.

"Since he's on his honeymoon and unable to defend his title, Hannah will act as his proxy," Lincoln continued.

Hannah flexed her muscles and pretended to crack her knuckles. "He's had me in training for this moment for months. I'm ready for you losers."

"It's not fair," Landon said. "She's got two brains to work with this year. That ought to be an automatic disqualification."

"Stuff it," Hannah said. "I could kick your ass with half a brain."

"I see game night is off to a rousing start," Elmer Stillman said when he came in, his cheeks red from the cold.

"Hannah's already swearing," Colton said to his grandfather.

"Business as usual," Elmer replied.

"I thought this was such a nice family," Cameron said.

"I know!" Lucy said. "I had no idea."

"Welcome to your first game night, ladies," Elmer said. "This is where the truth comes out."

"Lucas and Landon are the team to beat in both charades and Pictionary," Lincoln said.

"Did we agree that they aren't allowed to do any handstands this year?" Colton asked.

"After they took out the Christmas tree last year, Mom made a no-gymnastics-of-any-kind law," Lincoln said.

"Go near my tree, and I'll have you killed," Molly said.

Emma giggled uncontrollably.

"The Colemans are positively tame compared to this crew," Grayson said.

"I wouldn't go that far," Izzy said. She moved around the room taking photos, zeroing in on Max, who held his sleeping infant son in his arms. "Most photogenic father and son I've ever shot."

"You may be a little biased," Max said, smiling at his cousin.

"Nope, it's true. The two of you are going to have the ladies beating down your door."

Max nuzzled Caden's fuzzy blond hair. "We don't need ladies. We've got each other, right, buddy?"

Emma's heart broke for Max, who now had sole custody of his one-month-old son after Chloe, the baby's mother, brought him to Max during Hunter's wedding, saying she wasn't ready to be a mother. The family had rallied around Max, but it was obvious he was still reeling from the enormity of his new responsibilities. Thankfully, Caden was an easy, sweet baby who enjoyed being passed from one set of loving arms to another.

"Here we go, lunatics." Lincoln began picking names from a hat to face off against the defending champions in each game.

Emma ended up with Grayson facing off against Lucas and Landon as well as Will and Cameron in charades.

"I think this was rigged," Grayson whispered to her.

"He put us together on purpose?"

"Of course he did. He and Gramps are tireless matchmakers." He kept his voice low so he wouldn't be overheard. "When they wanted to give Hannah a nudge in Nolan's direction, they messed with her car on a day when the entire family was otherwise occupied so she'd have to call him for help."

"They did not!"

"Oh yes they did. Remember the sex toy conference Colton went to in New York?"

Emma stared at him, agog. "Seriously?"

"It gave him an excuse to see Lucy. And they hired Cameron to build the website, hoping she'd fall for one of Linc's sons. Look how that worked out." He gestured to Will and Cameron, who had their heads together to plot their strategy to defeat the cocky twins. After she fainted during Hunter's wedding, the family had found out Cameron was pregnant.

"They're diabolical."

"Gramps bought the diner and handed it over to Hunter to manage, forcing him to confront his feelings for Megan."

"Now they're on their honeymoon."

"And the matchmakers are high on their own success," Grayson said.

"I'm feeling like a deer in headlights all of a sudden," Emma said.

He barked out a laugh that had everyone looking at them with thinly veiled curiosity. "Don't make eye contact."

"Good advice."

"Oh my God, look." Grayson held up the clue they'd been given to act out in charades.

Emma laughed when she saw the words *deer in headlights*. "That's too funny." She made a face mimicking the words.

"That's perfect. You got this one, honey."

Emma's insides went haywire when he called her honey and looked at her as if he wanted to drag her out of there for more of what they'd had earlier. She wondered if or when they'd get another chance to be alone together.

Despite a noble effort put forth by Emma and Grayson as well as Will and Cameron, they were no match for the hijinks of Lucas and Landon, who ran away with another charades victory shortly before Hannah triumphed in Monopoly and Gavin quit the Scrabble game he was playing with Ella after she scored a one-hundred-point word.

"Now you see why we all quit her," Colton said.

"I get it, and I'd like to sign the petition," Gavin said.

"You sign that petition, and you'll be living like a monk for a year," Ella said, glaring at him.

Lincoln held up the petition. "What's it going to be, Gavin? Are you with us or with her?"

"Ummm, well… The monk's life doesn't really appeal to me." He grinned at Ella. "I guess I'm with her."

"Pussy," Lucas said.

Molly shrieked. "*Lucas Abbott!*"

"Sorry, Mom, but if the shoe fits…"

"It *totally* fits," Gavin said, winking at his future brother-in-law.

"I'd like to completely unsubscribe from this family," Molly said.

"Sorry, love, but that's not going to be possible," Lincoln said.

"You reap what you sow, my dear," Elmer said to his daughter.

"I did not *sow* them to use words like that in my house!"

"It's because you let them run wild, Mom," Hannah said gravely. "We got all the rules, but by the time the *babies* came along, you were worn out."

"Ahhh, I love game night," Colton said from his post, stretched out on the living room floor. "Every year it's a big fat disaster."

"Spoken like one of the younger ones who got to run wild," Will said.

"Not our fault you guys wore them out," Colton replied.

Landon used his thumb to point to Colton. "What he said."

"Maybe they'll get called into work," Hannah said.

"No such luck, sis," Landon said. "We've got the *whole* week off."

"Awesome," Charley said. "We need a petition against them for charades and Pictionary. Who's with me?"

All hands went up except for two.

"I feel discriminated against," Lucas said to his twin.

"Me, too. Screw them. Let's get drunk."

"With you, brother."

"This is when the drinking portion of the evening usually begins in earnest," Grayson told Emma. "When people start quitting in protest."

"It's amazing they all speak to each other the rest of the year."

"Isn't it?"

"Does your family do stuff like this, too?"

"Not like they do. It was different for us after my dad left."

With the others engaged in conversation and friendly arguments, Emma had the privacy to ask, "Do you have any idea where he is?"

"Nope. None of us have heard from him in years."

"So he tried to keep in touch?"

"At first we got the occasional effort, but we were all so angry with him for what he'd done to us and Mom that he stopped trying after a while."

"Did you ever find out why he left?"

"Not from him. Over the years, my mom has hinted at not being as surprised as she should've been when he bailed on the marriage. She never expected him to bail on us, though. Henry and Sarah, the youngest in our family, barely remember him living at home. They're the lucky ones."

That last part said a lot about how much his father's desertion had affected him. Not caring who might be watching—or who might disapprove—Emma reached for his hand.

He glanced at her, seeming surprised by the public display of affection.

"I'm sorry that happened to you."

Shrugging, he said, "It was a long time ago."

"Still…"

"Yeah. Still."

Over the next few hours, Emma kept a watchful eye on the baby monitor and took several trips upstairs to check on Simone, who hadn't moved. Emma ate a sandwich that Grayson encouraged her to have after reminding her she hadn't eaten since breakfast. They'd been far too busy to think about food, and the shock of returning home to find Simone injured had soured her appetite earlier.

At around eleven, Hannah stood to stretch. "Take me home, Nolan. I've had enough of this day and these people."

Before anyone could object to her comment, she let out an odd sound that was followed by a rush of fluid that formed a puddle around her feet.

"Uh-oh," she said, looking up at her husband with great big eyes.

"Ewww, *gross*," Colton said. "She's leaking!"

"Her water broke, you asshat," Landon said.

Hannah seemed frozen in place by the unexpected turn of events. Next to her, Nolan seemed equally frozen.

"It's too soon," Hannah said frantically. "I'm only thirty-two weeks. It's way too soon."

"Hannah," Molly said, her hands on Hannah's shoulders. "Breathe. Take a deep breath. Now do it again."

Hannah breathed the way her mother told her to, but she was ghostly pale and her big brown eyes were wide with fear. Her expression matched Nolan's.

Everyone talked at once.

"Will the baby be all right?"

"Is Nolan going to faint?"

"He looks like he's going to faint."

"Game night causes labor. Good to know for the future."

Molly pushed Nolan down to the sofa he'd only recently abandoned. "Put your head between your knees and breathe. Ella, get me some towels. Will, go warm up the Range Rover."

"Um," Linc said. "They have their own car… Just saying."

"Does he look to be in any condition to drive?" Molly asked her husband while gesturing to her son-in-law, who had his head between his knees.

"Maybe we could take their car?" Linc asked hopefully.

"The Range Rover," Molly said to Will. "*Now.* Charley, get their coats. Emma, you're in charge of the dogs, if that's all right."

"Of course. Whatever I can do."

"That would be a huge help. Thank you. Don't anyone who's been drinking even *think* about driving."

"Yes, mother," Lucas said.

Charley returned with the coats.

Molly got Hannah's on her and told Will to help Nolan. "Let's get them to the car. Can you walk, honey?"

Hannah clung to her mother. "I think so. It's early. It's okay if it's early, right?"

"I had you and Hunter at thirty-five weeks, and you turned out fine."

"Depends on how you define 'fine,'" Lucas said.

"I had them at thirty-four weeks," Molly said. "You can see the difference."

"Hey," Lucas and Landon said together.

"That's not nice," Landon said.

"Truth hurts," Molly said, obviously making light to keep Hannah from freaking out.

It seemed to take the entire family to get Hannah and Nolan into the Range Rover, which Lincoln drove with Molly riding shotgun. Despite the teasing and bickering, every one of her siblings left to follow them to the hospital. Thankfully, it wasn't snowing tonight, so they'd have clear roads.

"I need to be there," Elmer said.

"I'll take you, Dad," Grayson's mother said.

"Won't say no to the company. It's not every day a man becomes a great-grandfather for the second time."

"Pictures," Izzy said. "They're going to need pictures."

"Come with us, hon," Hannah said to her daughter.

"Keep us posted," Grayson said as he and Emma saw them off.

"You're not coming?" his mother asked.

"I'll help Emma with the dogs."

"Right," Hannah said with a twisted little smile. "The dogs."

Grayson shut the door and locked it.

"She hates me," Emma said.

"What? Who hates you?"

"Your mother."

"She does not." He put his arm around her and led her back to the family room. After he settled her on the sofa, he stepped around the game night carnage and threw another log on the fire before joining her. "Why do you say that?"

"It's the way she looks at me, like I'm some sort of calculating gold digger out to land a daddy for my daughter."

His smile lit up his eyes. "Are you a gold digger looking for a baby daddy?"

"No! I don't need any of those things from you or any man."

"I know that, and you know that, which is what matters."

"It matters to me if your mom doesn't like me."

Sighing, he combed his fingers through his hair. "It's not you. She has a twisted view of all things romance after what happened with my dad and then with Noah. She never liked the girl he married, and then she did exactly what my mother expected her to and hurt him badly."

"What happened between them?"

"We have no idea. One minute they were happily married, or so we thought, and the next she was gone. He's never spoken of it to any of us, but he's different than he used to be."

"How so?"

"He's extremely withdrawn and antisocial. Even though he lives right down the street from Mom, she hardly ever sees him except at holidays and perfunctory visits in which he says nothing much of anything."

"That's sad. It sounds like he's heartbroken."

"Maybe so."

"Have you tried to talk to him?"

"Many times, to no avail. When I was still in Boston, I made a pest out of myself, calling him all the time and talking about nothing for a few minutes. At least it was something."

"It probably meant a lot to him."

"Who knows? I keep hoping one of these days he might really talk to me. We used to be close when we were kids. We grew apart when I went to Boston and he got married."

She could hear the unspoken regret in his words. "Maybe now that you're back in town, you can bridge that gap."

"I suppose we'll see."

"We should clean up this mess."

"You're right. We probably should." He made no move to get up. Rather, he stared at her and ran his fingers through her hair. "I didn't expect to get time alone with you in the middle of game night madness."

"I didn't expect that either."

"I'm worried about Hannah and the baby," he said. "Thirty-two weeks is early."

"It really is, but they'll get the best possible care. Hopefully, the baby will be fine."

"I can't imagine any other outcome. Poor Hannah has already had more than her share of grief in this lifetime." As he spoke, he continued to play with Emma's hair and stare at her mouth with obvious desire to kiss her.

She should send him home. She should go upstairs and sleep next to Simone in case she needed her during the night. She should clean up the huge mess from game night. She did none of those things. Rather, she licked her lips in anticipation of his kiss and then wrapped her arms around him as he came down on top of her right there on the sofa with the fire crackling in the background.

CHAPTER 9

Love is when the other person's happiness is more important than your own.
—H. Jackson Brown Jr.

This kiss picked right up where they'd left off earlier, with all the same hungry desperation she'd come to expect and crave from him. For the longest time, they only kissed, and then his hand slipped under her sweater and up to cup her breast through her bra.

Her nipple was still sensitive from earlier, and the stimulation had her moaning against his lips.

He broke the kiss to nuzzle her neck. "I can't believe how badly I want you again, Emma."

Needy for more of the incredible way he made her feel, she tried to get closer to him.

"Let's go upstairs," he said.

"We shouldn't."

"I know, but we have so little time left together, and they'll be gone most of the night. Even if the hospital tries to kick them out, they'll want to be with Hannah."

"You're like the devil leading me astray."

"So that's a yes?"

Emma hesitated, but only for a second. "Yes. But we have to clean up first, or they'll know we jumped each other the second they left."

Groaning, he took hold of her hand and pressed it against his erection. "You're really going to squander this perfectly good boner?"

"Something tells me it'll keep for a few minutes." God, this was fun. Being with him this way, teasing and flirting and kissing... She'd never had fun like this with a man and was already addicted to the feelings of elation he stirred in her. They worked together to quickly stow the games as well as the tables Lincoln had set up in the family room.

While Emma let Ringo and George out, Grayson banked the fire and closed the glass doors to contain any stray sparks.

They met up in the family room, the dogs watching them with curiosity, as if they knew what was going on and weren't sure they approved. She wasn't sure if she approved of what was about to happen while the Abbotts dealt with a possible crisis with Hannah and the baby.

Grayson handed her the baby monitor and then followed her upstairs, where they stopped to check on Simone.

Emma bent over the bed to kiss her sleeping daughter and tugged the covers up a little higher to make sure she was tucked in. When she was done, Grayson stepped closer to run his hand over Simone's silky hair and then followed Emma out of the room.

"Leave the door open so you can hear her," he said.

"What if she hears us?" Emma asked.

"Are you planning on being loud?"

She burned with embarrassment—and desire. "Stop!"

His low chuckle followed her into the bedroom next to Simone's. His arms wrapped around her from behind, his chin landing on her shoulder. "If this is too much for you, all you have to do is say so."

"It's way too much for me." When he started to withdraw from her, she stopped him. "Not in a bad way. In an overwhelmingly good way."

"It is for me, too. I never expected anything like this when I came home for Christmas."

"I feel guilty doing this here. Like I'm taking advantage of their hospitality or something."

"Remember what I told you about my uncle and grandfather wanting to see us all happy and settled?"

She nodded.

"I think they'd approve."

"I still feel weird about it."

"I'd be perfectly content if I could hold you and kiss you and sleep with my arms wrapped around you. We don't have to do anything more than that."

"You wouldn't mind?"

"Not at all." With his hands on her shoulders, he turned her to face him. "I want you to be comfortable."

She smiled up at him. "I'm often extremely *un*comfortable around you."

"I know the feeling." He pressed his hard cock against her belly to make his point.

"I told you he'd be back."

"He's incredibly resilient, especially when you're nearby."

As he looked down at her and she stared up at him, her arms around his neck and his around her waist, Emma realized this must be what it felt like to fall in love. And then he made it even better by kissing her softly and with tenderness that had her knees going weak under her. Only his arms tight around her kept her standing as the kiss went from sweet and tender to hot and needy in the scope of ten seconds.

He lowered her onto the bed, coming down on top of her without missing a beat in the kiss. His tongue caressed hers as the press of his body against hers made Emma want so much more than she'd agreed to.

She tugged on the hem of his sweater and drew it up, smoothing her hands over his back as she went.

Grayson trembled from her touch and broke the kiss to help her remove the sweater. "Yours, too," he said, tugging on the fabric until it cleared her head. He took in the sight of her in only the formfitting tank top and bent his head to kiss the plump slopes of her breasts. "Your skin is like silk. If all I can do is kiss you, I want to kiss you everywhere." He removed her top, baring her breasts to his hungry gaze. He stroked her nipple with only the tip of his tongue, but she felt it everywhere. "Are they sore from before?"

"A little," she said breathlessly.

"Then I'll be gentle." He kept up the soft strokes of his tongue, driving her wild with one caress after another—and that was before he sucked her nipple into his mouth.

"Grayson," she gasped.

"Talk to me. Tell me how it feels."

"Incredible."

"How about over here?" he asked, switching sides.

"There, too." A sharp ache of desire between her legs had her moving restlessly beneath him as he kept up the sensual assault on her nipples, which were now rigid and tight from the attention he paid them with both his fingers and tongue. He kept it up until she was about to beg him to stop or make her come or do anything to relieve the aching need.

As if he could read her mind, he finally moved down, kissing her belly and taking little bites of her skin that sent the desire to the critical zone.

He tugged on the button to her jeans. "Yes or no?"

"*Yes*," she said, no longer caring about where they were or how desperate she sounded.

His lips curved into a smile that she felt against her sensitive skin. "You're sure?"

"*Grayson!*"

"Shhh, you'll wake your daughter."

"No, I won't." Emma tore at the button to her jeans and was wiggling out of them when he caught up and helped her get them and her panties off. She hadn't intended to get completely naked, but she couldn't be bothered with details like that when he was positioning her legs on his shoulders. "*Whaa…* What're you… Oh my *God*," she said on a long, drawn-out sigh that ended in a sound that resembled a sob.

He pushed her legs farther apart and buried his face between them, drawing her rigid clit into his mouth and making her come so hard, she saw stars and had to bite her lip to keep from screaming from the blast of heat that incinerated her. And with that, she'd had more sex in one day with him than in her entire life before him. She barely had time to catch her breath before he started over again, using his tongue and fingers to arouse her to the point of madness. Then she felt pressure against her back door and froze in shock as his finger breached her in a place where no one had ever touched her before.

"Relax," he whispered. "You'll love it."

Dear sweet baby Jesus, she'd been about to lose her mind all over again, and then he touched her there, driving his finger into her as he sucked on her clit again, making her come harder than she ever had before.

"Mmm, so hot," he whispered before withdrawing from her and pulling a blanket over her. "Don't move. I'll be right back."

Emma couldn't have moved if the house had been on fire. Her entire body twitched with aftershocks from two powerful orgasms. She heard water running in the bathroom and then he was back, dropping his jeans and underwear by the bed before crawling in and reaching for her.

"Did I shock you?"

"Little bit."

"Good shock or bad shock?"

"Umm, you couldn't tell?"

"I don't want to make assumptions."

"Everything about this with you is a good shock. The best kind of shock."

He cupped her face and turned her into his kiss. "For me, too."

Like every time they kissed, this one quickly went from a light caress to a tongue-twisting duel that had them both straining for more.

Emma flattened her hand on his chest and dragged it down to encircle his hard cock. She withdrew from the kiss so she could see his face. "Show me how you like it."

"I'll like anything you do," he said, sounding tense.

"Like this?" She tightened her grip and moved her hand up and down in a slow tease that had his eyes closing and his lips parting.

"Yeah," he said. "Like that."

"How about this?" She dragged her thumb over the head, sliding through the moisture gathered at the tip.

He gasped, and his fingers dug into her arm. "That's good, too."

Emma raised herself up to kiss his chest and the abdomen that quivered under her lips. "You're going to have to show me how," she said, feeling shy all of a sudden. "I've never done this before."

"There's no wrong way."

She bent to run her tongue around the head. "This is good?"

"Really good."

She drew him into her mouth, using her tongue to stroke him before withdrawing slowly. "How about that?"

"So good." He covered the hand she had around the base of his shaft with his and said, "Do it again."

Emma took him in again while continuing to stroke him. The combination had him raising his hips off the bed, looking to go deeper. She went as far as she could before he bumped against the back of her throat, triggering her gag reflex.

"Stop. Emma... Stop."

Concerned that she'd done something wrong, she released him.

He moved quickly to take her into his arms and press her against the mattress as he devoured her mouth in another wild kiss.

"It didn't feel good?" she asked when they came up for air.

"Too good. You didn't want me to come in your mouth the first time you ever do that."

"I thought you didn't want to make assumptions."

His eyes widened, and his mouth opened and then closed.

Emma laughed. "But thanks for the courtesy. Next time, I wouldn't mind trying that."

He took a deep, shuddering breath. "Watch what you say. You've got me right on the edge over here."

"We said we weren't going to do this, and here we are naked in bed together—again."

"I can't seem to control myself when you're in my arms." His hand roamed her back and down to cup her bottom to pull her in closer to him. The new position had his cock tight against her core, and Emma rubbed against him shamelessly while noting the twitch of a muscle in his jaw.

She pressed gentle kisses to the twitching muscle.

"I'll let you sleep," he said.

"Do you want to sleep?"

"I'd much rather be awake and kissing you and touching you, but you're going to be tired in the morning, and you have an injured girl to care for."

"Despite my earlier protests, I'm feeling a pressing need to finish what we started."

When his eyes opened, she saw both surprise and desire. "Is that so?"

She bit her lip and nodded.

"I don't have any more condoms."

She took hold of his hand and directed him to a bump under her arm. "Feel that?"

His brows knitted as he nodded.

"Long-term birth control to regulate formerly out-of-control monthly events."

"Are you saying…"

"Back to those assumptions again… I assume you're healthy."

"I am. I can prove it."

"And there's no doubt I am, seeing as how I'd been off the horse for ten years before I jumped back on with a vengeance today."

He closed his eyes again and took a deep breath. "I'm going to need a minute to get it together so it isn't over before it begins."

Emma shook with silent laughter.

"You think this is funny?" He pounced on her, pinning her arms to the bed and tickling her underarm with kisses that made her scream with laughter.

"Stop! I hate being tickled!"

"I hate being laughed at."

"I'm very sorry," she said, trying to look contrite and failing to fool him.

He grunted out a laugh. "You are not." Taking himself in hand, he began to enter her, going as slowly as he possibly could in anticipation of her being sore from earlier.

She sucked in a sharp deep breath that didn't sound like pleasure to him.

"Are you okay?"

"Hurts."

"We don't have to…"

When he would've withdrawn from her, she curled her legs around his hips. "I want to. Just go slow."

He did as she asked, entering her in small increments and then retreating before doing it again and again and again until they were moving together effortlessly and all she could feel was the pleasure.

Then he curled his arm under her leg and pressed it to her chest, opening her wider to his deep strokes, and the pleasure became nearly unbearable.

"You are," he whispered softly, his lips brushing against her ear, "so incredibly beautiful all the time. But you've never been more so than you are right now."

Sensory overload. That was the only way to describe the emotions that assailed her as he made love to her with his words and his body. Linking their fingers, his gaze locked on hers as he picked up the pace. "Emma..."

He drove into her, touching a place deep inside that set off a massive orgasm that had her trembling and quaking from the power of it.

"Jesus," he muttered in the second before he came, too. His head landed on her shoulder.

Emma curled her hand around his nape and her legs around his hips to keep him close to her. If you had asked her a week ago if a person could fall in love in three days, she would've said no way. Now...

Now she had reason to believe he had the power to change her life—and Simone's—if she let him.

CHAPTER 10

Love is the answer, and you know that for sure; love is a flower,
you've got to let it grow.
—John Lennon

Holy moly. Those two words kept running through Grayson's mind as he held Emma in the aftermath of the hottest sex of his life. And here he'd thought he'd had pretty good sex in the past, but nothing in the past could compare to what'd just happened with Emma.

Her sweet, innocent responses to everything they did only added to the amazement for him. He'd never found innocence to be particularly attractive before now, before Emma.

Grayson ran his hand up and down her arm, delighting in the goose bumps that dotted her sensitive skin when he touched her. He knew he should get up and go downstairs so he wouldn't get caught in bed with her by Max or his aunt and uncle when they returned. But he couldn't bring himself to leave the warm comfort of her body curled up to his.

It wouldn't take much to become addicted to that warm comfort as well as holding her in his arms while their bodies cooled from the kind of passion he'd never known existed until he met her. The thought of having only two more days with her filled him with the kind of panic he'd rarely experienced and reminded him all too well of how he'd felt after his father left.

He couldn't let her and Simone leave and have this be over. No way. Not after what he'd shared with Emma during this momentous day and week. They had to find a way to keep it going, even if they had enormous obstacles standing between them and any sort of happily ever after.

Did he want that? Did he want a happily ever after? He'd never really cared about such things until the possibility of such a thing included Emma and Simone. They made for an incredibly attractive package, and the idea of a ready-made family with a nine-year-old was fine with him, seeing as he'd already helped raise his younger siblings and had no burning desire to have his own kids—or at least he'd never had that burning desire before.

"What're you thinking about?" Emma asked in a sexy, sleepy-sounding voice.

"About how you rocked my world."

"*I* rocked *your* world? How about what you did to mine?"

"What did I do to yours?"

"Rocked is too small a word for it."

"Is that right?" he asked, inordinately pleased to hear he wasn't the only one who'd been thoroughly rocked.

"Mmm, that's right."

"I'm also thinking about what happens after you and Simone go home."

"What do you see happening?"

"I don't know, but I'm already certain this won't be enough. Not even close to enough."

"We're kind of in a tough spot here."

"So it would seem." He paused before he shared a thought he'd had only in passing. "Nothing says I have to open a practice here."

Her eyes flew open. "But that's your plan."

He shrugged. "Plans change, and all I've done so far is start to look for office space in Butler. I could just as easily look for a job in New York. I'm already licensed in both Vermont and New York, so I can work in either place."

"But is that what you want?"

"I'm finding that what I want is changing by the hour." He continued to caress her soft skin as they talked, which was how he felt her shiver.

"Are you cold?"

"No… I'm… overwhelmed."

"Too much too soon?"

"Of course it is," she said with a husky laugh. "It's way too much way too soon, but you won't hear me complaining. This has been… It's been amazing."

"Same here. I've never done anything quite like this."

"Like what? Jumping into bed with someone you only just met?"

"That, but the rest of it, too. I never talk about my father—with anyone—and you've gotten me to talk about him several times. I didn't even hesitate before sharing the whole ugly tale with you. That's not something I do."

"Same with the stuff I've shared with you."

"This is way more than an off-the-charts physical attraction for me, Emma."

"It is for me, too."

"So what now?"

Her deep sigh answered for her.

"Do we try to make it work and see what happens, or do we say it was a great week and leave it at that?" Grayson asked.

"What do you want?"

"You're answering my question with a question," he said, tracing the outline of her sexy mouth with his fingertip.

"If I could have anything I wanted…"

"What would you want?"

"This. You. Us. Together. Somehow…"

"Me, too."

"Soooo…"

"So we'll give it a whirl and see what happens?"

"I'm scared to get so involved with you and not have it work out. I'm already in too deep to walk away without it hurting like hell. What'll happen a few months down the road if it's not working out—"

He kissed the words right off her lips. "Let's not expect it to go bad. Let's expect it to go right."

"If it were just about me, I could do that. But it's not just about me."

"I know that, Emma. I care about Simone, too. When I heard she'd gotten hurt… I couldn't stand to think of her in that kind of pain. I want to get to know her better and spend time with both of you. That's all I know right now. I want more."

Before she could reply, a whimper came from the next room.

Grayson released Emma and helped her into the T-shirt she'd tossed over the foot of the bed.

While she went into the next room, he watched her on the monitor, soothing Simone, who hadn't woken.

He got out of bed and found his clothes on the floor.

By the time Emma returned, he was dressed and sitting on the edge of the bed, waiting for her. "Is she okay?"

"Just a little restless."

Grayson held out his hand to her, inviting her into his embrace. He wrapped his arms around her waist and rested his head against her chest. "I should go downstairs."

She held on tighter to him. "Not yet."

Powerless to resist the temptation of more time with her, Grayson helped her back into bed, pulled the covers over her and lay on top of the comforter.

"You're going to be cold out there."

"If I fall asleep, it'll look better that I'm out here than in there with you if we get caught."

"Come in here with me for a little while. I won't let you fall asleep."

"That sounds promising," he said as he got under the down quilt and snuggled up to her.

Emma laughed. "Don't even think about it. I'm surprised I can still walk after this day."

Grayson glanced at the bedside clock over her shoulder. "That was yesterday. Today's a whole new day."

"Also known as Emma's day of recovery from yesterday."

"Spoilsport."

She placed her hand on his face. "Other than Simone getting hurt, yesterday was one of the best days I've ever had."

Touched by her sweetness, he said, "It was for me, too." He gathered her in closer to him, encouraging her to use his chest as a pillow. "You need to sleep so you can tend to your girl in the morning."

"I don't want to sleep when I have to go home in just over twenty-four hours."

The thought of her leaving set off an ache deep inside him. "What time is your flight on Friday?"

"Two, out of Burlington."

"I'll take you over."

"You don't have to. Lucy can do it."

"I want to, unless you'd rather have her."

"I'd rather have you, not that I don't love my sister."

He kissed her swollen lips. "I'm glad you want me."

"I definitely want you."

"Are we still talking about rides to the airport?"

"Of course we are. What else would we be talking about?"

Grayson laughed at her saucy reply. Everything she said and did appealed to him. He'd never been able to say that about any other woman he'd spent time with. It seemed there was always something that got on his nerves, whether it be an annoying laugh or a fixation on her phone and social media accounts or insane jealousy if he had the audacity to so much as speak to another woman. His dealings with women had been exhausting more than fulfilling, especially with Heather.

She'd wanted to be married, like right now. The more she'd pushed him to make that commitment to her, the more he'd pulled back from her. The push-pull had ruined what had been a pretty good thing, and when he broke up with her, that was when he saw her true colors.

With Emma, he already knew there was no hidden agenda or other side to her that would emerge at some point in the future, disappointing him. She really was as sweet and sexy and smart and devoted to her loved ones as she appeared.

"What do you have planned for today?" he asked.

"Nothing really. It'll depend on what Simone feels like doing."

"Spend the day with me. I have an idea of something we can do that she'll love if she feels up to it."

"What's this idea?"

"A surprise for both of you."

"That sounds intriguing."

"So yes? We'll spend the rest of the time we have left together?"

"Mmm," she said, sounding sleepy. "That's a yes, Grayson."

They'd tried to stop Hannah's early labor, but the baby was determined to arrive now despite the best efforts of the doctors and Hannah to make it stop. She'd known labor would be painful, but she'd been unprepared for just how painful it was or how hard it would be on Nolan to see her in agony.

"I don't think I can do this," she said to him after another particularly awful contraction. As the hours passed and the pain intensified, Hannah began to feel panicky about having a premature baby and what might be ahead for all of them. Her panic fueled his.

"I'm going to find the doctor," he said. "You want me to send your mom in?"

Hannah nodded as her eyes filled with tears. They'd asked for some time alone, but now she really, really wanted her mom.

Nolan kissed her forehead. "I'll get her, and I'll be right back with the doctor." He left the room, and Molly came in a few minutes later.

"How're you doing, honey?"

Immediately soothed by her mother's calming presence, Hannah grasped her hand. "The pain is bad. Way worse than I expected."

"You need an epidural."

Tears she tried to fight back spilled down her cheeks. "I wanted to do it without one."

Molly took a tissue from the box on the bedside table and wiped away Hannah's tears. "There's no need to suffer when they can give you some relief. First babies can take a while to arrive. Let them make you comfortable."

"I'm afraid of the baby being so early."

"I have a feeling he or she will be just fine, sweetheart. Look how determined your little one is to be born right now."

"I'm scared. I was so ready to do this until it actually happened, and now I'm panicking, which has Nolan all freaked out."

"Focus on breathing the way you were taught in the classes. It helps."

"How in the world did you do this eight times and twice with twins?"

Molly laughed. "I have no idea."

"You were certifiably insane."

"Probably."

"Is everyone out there waiting?"

Molly wiped away more tears from Hannah's face. "What do you think? Even Max and Caden are here."

Before she could reply, another contraction started. Hannah held on tight to her mom's hand while trying to remember to breathe through the pain. When it finally passed, she was sobbing from the agony.

Nolan came in with the doctor in tow.

"I want the epidural," Hannah said. "Please."

"Let's take a look and see how you're doing," the young female doctor said with chirpiness that annoyed Hannah.

With Nolan on one side of her bed and her mom on the other, Hannah gritted her teeth for the invasive exam that seemed to take forever to complete.

"You're doing great, Hannah. You're almost there."

She moaned. "I don't know if I can do it without something to take the edge off."

"Then let's get you some relief." The doctor left the room to see to the epidural.

"I feel like a wimp," Hannah said.

"Stop," Molly said. "There's nothing wrong with taking something for the pain so you have the strength to push when the time comes."

Nolan handed her a cup of ice chips and wiped the sweat from her forehead with a cool cloth that felt heavenly against her fevered skin.

She'd waited a long time to become a mother, and she wanted to focus on the joy of her child arriving rather than agonizing pain and the debilitating fear of the baby arriving too early. It took about thirty minutes to organize the epidural other than the needle to the back, the procedure was no big deal. But the relief… The relief was almost immediate. Hannah could finally breathe again after hours in agony.

"Better?" Nolan asked when they had the room to themselves once again.

"A thousand times better."

"Thank God. I couldn't bear to see you in so much pain."

"I tried to go all natural, but—"

He leaned over the bed rail to kiss her. "You're doing an amazing job. The only thing that matters is a healthy mom and baby at the end."

"I feel bad that the baby is going to have to share his or her birthday with game night," she said, making him laugh.

"Hopefully, we'll get to midnight, and he or she will be born on the twenty-eighth."

"I think I can hold off another hour."

Taking a seat next to her bed, he cradled her hand between both of his. "I love you so much, Hannah. I hope you know how much I appreciate everything you've done to bring our baby into the world."

"You've taken such good care of both of us."

"Least I could do. I can't wait to see him."

"Or her."

"Either is fine with me."

CHAPTER 11

*We never know the love of a parent till we become parents
ourselves.*
—Henry Ward Beecher

The next half hour passed in a blur of comfort even as the monitor
recorded increasingly strong contractions. *Thank God for drugs*,
Hannah thought. Right after two in the morning, the doctor
returned to check her again and declared her ready to push. Once
again, Hannah felt the twinge of panic. What if she couldn't do
it? What if she wasn't strong enough or—

"Hannah."

While the nurses scurried around the room, making it ready
for delivery, she looked up at her husband, who watched over her
with the fierce love she'd come to expect from him.

"Focus. You got this. You're the strongest person I know.
There's nothing you can't do if you set your mind to it."

He said exactly what she needed to hear, but that was no
surprise. He knew her better than anyone, even Hunter.

Oh God. Hunter! "I can't do this without Hunter. He should
be here." She began to cry again at the thought of her twin

hundreds of miles from her while she brought her first child into the world.

"Think about what a great surprise he'll come home to," Nolan said, stroking her hair. "You want your mom?"

"Just you," she said, clinging to his hand.

"We got this, Hannah. You and me."

The nurse directed him to get on the bed behind her to support her while she pushed. Her legs were raised on contraptions attached to the bed and spread so far apart as to be comical under any other circumstances. While she was spread-eagle, people came in and out of the room, focused on the individual roles that were routine to them.

"It's funny," she said to Nolan.

"What is?"

"I've got my hoo-ha out and proud for the whole world to see, and they walk around like it's no big deal."

"It isn't to them."

"It sure is to us."

"Your hoo-ha is a huge big deal to me."

Hannah wouldn't have thought it possible to laugh. "Hopefully, it still will be after you witness what's about to happen here."

He kissed her cheek and tightened his hold on her. "It will always be a big deal to me. You, my love, are the biggest of big deals to me."

"I won't be quite so big after I get this baby out."

"Love you, Hannah. If it gets to be too much for you, hold on to me."

"That's the plan." She looked back at him. "Love you, too."

Sitting on a chair, the doctor rolled into position between Hannah's legs and eyed the monitor that tracked contractions. "You ready to rock and roll, Hannah?"

Nolan squeezed her hand.

"We're ready."

"Okay, here we go. Let's give it a big push."

Hannah pushed as hard as she could. The epidural made it so she could feel only the pressure, which was tremendous, but no pain.

"That was good," the doctor said. "Just like that again."

Nolan fed her ice chips, wiped the sweat and tears from her face and supported her through each push. Having him to lean on made all the difference.

She wanted to sleep, but the contractions were coming fast and furious, each one of them a new chance to push.

"One more big one, Hannah," the doctor said in that endlessly cheerful tone that had Hannah wishing for the wherewithal to punch her.

"Ready, sweetheart?" Nolan asked.

Replying would take focus she didn't have to spare. She took a huge breath and pushed with every ounce of reserve fortitude she could muster. She pushed until she felt the pressure let up and then sagged into Nolan's arms.

"You have a girl!"

"You did it, honey," Nolan said, sounding tearful behind her.

For once, the doctor's cheerfulness didn't annoy her. She was too full of unreasonable joy to be annoyed about anything. A girl. They had a girl!

The OB immediately handed off the baby to the neonatal specialist, who whisked her to a warmer they had set up on the other side of the room.

"Why is she so quiet? Isn't she supposed to cry?"

"She's taking it all in," the neonatal specialist said.

"It's okay that she didn't cry?"

"It's fine, but she's small. Just over four pounds, and she'll need some time in the NICU for her lungs to develop further."

"Can I see her?" Hannah asked through tears that blinded her.

"Just for a few minutes," the neonatal doctor said. "These little ones lose their body heat very quickly, so we need to get her into the warmer."

He brought her to them, attached to oxygen and wrapped in a soft yellow blanket, and carefully placed her in Hannah's arms. She'd never seen a smaller baby, and a pang of fear struck in the vicinity of her heart. "She's going to be okay?" Hannah asked the specialist.

"She should be fine in a few weeks, but we'll know more after we're able to fully evaluate her."

"Oh my God," Nolan said. "Look at her. She's so perfect."

Hannah had to agree that she'd never seen anything more perfect than the tiny baby with the big eyes and the dusting of dark hair. "Hi, baby girl." She caressed the baby's soft cheek with her fingertip.

After some additional pressure when she delivered the placenta, Hannah was filled with new energy now that she had her baby in her arms. "I can't believe she's finally here."

"What's her name?" one of the nurses asked.

Hannah looked up at Nolan, who spoke for both of them. "Her name is Caleb Abbott Roberts after Hannah's first husband and my close friend who died in Iraq. We're going to call her Callie."

"That's a beautiful, unique name for a beautiful, unique little girl," the OB said. "And a very special tribute to a fallen hero."

Hannah had never loved Nolan more than when he'd suggested they name their baby after Caleb, whether they had a boy or a girl. They'd gone round and round about what they'd do if they had a daughter. Hannah wasn't sure about naming a girl Caleb, but Nolan had insisted that calling her Callie would be perfect, and any daughter of Hannah's would be strong enough to handle a different sort of name.

"Thank you," Nolan said to the doctor. "We think so, too."

"You want me to get your parents?" one of the nurses asked Hannah when the doctor had finished tending to her.

"If you wouldn't mind."

"Of course."

Hannah couldn't take her eyes off the adorable little face and the eyes that seemed to take it all in, even though Hannah knew she couldn't actually see much of anything yet. "She looks so wise, doesn't she?"

"I was thinking the same thing. She's beautiful, like her mother."

"And her father."

"Thank you so much for her, Hannah. I'm so proud of you."

She leaned her head against his shoulder. "I'm proud of us. We make a great team."

"We sure do."

"Thank you again for her name. I really love it, and I love you for suggesting it."

"In all these months, I never had another name in mind for our child."

A knock on the door preceded Molly and Lincoln into the room, both wearing huge smiles.

"Come meet your new granddaughter," Nolan said.

"Oh, a girl," Molly said, dabbing at her eyes.

"Look at her," Linc said gruffly. "She's perfect."

"Her mom was a warrior," Nolan said. "As always."

"I would expect nothing less from my daughter," Linc said, leaning over to kiss Hannah and take a closer look at the baby. "What's her name?"

"Caleb Abbott Roberts," Hannah said. "We're going to call her Callie."

"What a perfect name." Molly dealt with a new flood of tears. "Amelia and Bob will be so very touched," she said of Caleb's parents.

"I'm so glad you agree," Hannah said.

"I love her name," Linc said. "Callie. This is my grand-daughter, Callie."

Hannah reluctantly handed over her precious package to the doctor and relaxed against Nolan, a feeling of peace coming over her now that the delivery was behind her and the baby had safely arrived. To Nolan, she said, "Will you call Amelia and Bob?" In another lifetime, they would've been there, awaiting the arrival of their grandchild. In this lifetime, they would be beloved extra grandparents to baby Callie.

"I'll take care of it," he said. "You rest and don't worry about anything."

Hannah closed her eyes, only for a minute, or so she told herself. She had a daughter to care for.

Grayson woke to the sound of voices and bright sunshine beaming into the room where he'd fallen asleep despite his plans to relocate downstairs. At least he was alone in the bed where Emma had been sleeping.

The voices, he realized, belonged to her and Simone. A glance at the monitor showed Emma in bed with her daughter, the two of them talking in low voices. He wanted to know what they were saying and how Simone was feeling, but he wasn't sure if

Emma would want him to reveal himself or the fact that he'd spent the night.

His curiosity about Simone's condition won out. He got up, made the bed and used the bathroom across the hall to clean up before he ducked his head into the room next door to check on them.

"How's the patient this morning?" he asked.

"Grayson! What're you doing here?" Simone asked.

"I came to see how you were feeling. How's your arm?"

Emma smiled at him from her perch next to her daughter, nodding her head to invite him into the room.

"It's sore, but not like it was yesterday. I'm just sad that I can't ski again today. I loved it."

Grayson sat on the foot of the bed. "I heard you were really good at it, too."

"You did? Did Colton say that?"

"Yep," Grayson said. "He told me you were great at it."

Simone beamed with pleasure at hearing that. "I want to do it again as soon as my arm is better."

"What do you ladies have planned for today?" he asked.

"Not skiing," Simone said glumly.

"Taking it easy," Emma said.

"Which is no fun," Simone replied.

"I know something fun we can do," Grayson said, deciding to go forward with his plan now that he knew Simone was feeling okay. "I'll pick you up in two hours. Dress warm."

"What is it?" Simone asked.

"You'll see," he said with a mysterious smile as he stood to leave the room. "See you soon."

"Grayson," Simone said.

Turning back, he said, "Yes?"

"Thanks for coming over to check on me. That was really nice of you."

Touched by her sweetness, he said, "Of course. No problem." He went downstairs to let the dogs out and was putting on his coat in the mudroom when Linc and Molly came in.

"How's Hannah?" Grayson asked.

"She's wonderful. We have a new granddaughter, Caleb Abbott Roberts, who will be known as Callie. She's tiny, but a fighter. The doctors say she should be fine after a few weeks in the NICU to give her lungs time to develop some more."

"I'm so glad she's okay," Grayson said, profoundly moved by Hannah and Nolan's tribute to Caleb. "And I love her name."

"We agree that it's a very special name for a special little girl," Linc said. "How's Simone?"

"She's good. She slept through the night and is more bummed that she can't ski again today than anything."

"That's a relief. It was good of you to stay with them."

Grayson raised a brow. "Really?"

"Were you expecting disapproval?" Molly asked, amused. "You're thirty-six years old, Gray. We love Emma and Simone, and we love you and Emma as a couple."

"You do?"

"We do. She's lovely."

"She certainly is. It's just... well... complicated."

Molly reached up to put her hands on his shoulders. "I'll tell you the same thing I told Will when he was in this very same situation—if she means something to you, *do* something about it. If it's meant to be, you'll find a way."

"Is it possible to know if it's meant to be in just a few days?"

Molly glanced at her husband.

"We knew the day we met that this was going to be something big and potentially life-changing," Lincoln said, smiling at his wife.

"A week ago, I would've said that's not possible for me," Grayson said. "Now…"

"Oh, Gray," Molly said, hugging him. "I'm so happy to hear you say that. I've so hoped you would find someone amazing. No one deserves it more than you do."

"Why do you say that?"

She looked up at him with exasperation and amusement. "With everything you did for your mother and siblings, you really have to ask why I'd say that?"

He shrugged off her praise. "I did what anyone would do in that situation."

"No," Linc said, "you did more than any sixteen-year-old boy should ever have to do. And your aunt is right. No one I know deserves a happy ending more than you do."

"You flatter me. Both of you."

"We speak only the truth," Molly said. "You want some coffee before you head out?"

"I'll grab some at Mom's. I've got a surprise to set up for a very sweet little girl who hurt her arm."

"What've you got up your sleeve?" Linc asked.

"You'll see." He kissed his aunt and shook his uncle's hand. "Thanks for always being right there for me. It hasn't gone unnoticed."

"We're always here for you and your siblings," Linc said. "That'll never change."

"Means the world to us," Grayson said. "I'll be back in a bit."

"We'll be the zombie grandparents asleep on the sofas," Molly said.

"We're getting *way* too old for an all-nighter," Linc added.

"You guys are just getting started."

"If you say so," Molly said, heading for the coffeepot.

CHAPTER 12

Let us love winter, for it is the spring of genius.
—Pietro Aretino

Grayson stepped out into air so cold, it seared his lungs the way it used to on the long-ago winter mornings of his youth. It got damned cold in Boston, but not as cold as up here. This was a whole other level of cold, and he wondered if the air would be too frigid for what he had in mind.

Since he couldn't disappoint Simone after promising her a surprise, he got in the car and drove to his mother's house, where she was at the table with the morning paper and a cup of coffee.

"Look at what the cat dragged in," she said.

"Morning." He bent to kiss her cheek. "Did you hear we have a new baby in the family?"

"I did. Molly called me earlier to share the happy news. Where'd you sleep last night?"

"Aunt Molly's sofa."

"You're spending a lot of time over there this week."

"Yep."

"What's going on, Gray?"

"Why're you asking me that when you already know what's going on?"

"You're getting awfully involved with a woman who lives so far from where you do."

"I don't actually live here yet."

"What's that supposed to mean?"

"It means," Grayson said, "that I'm keeping my options open."

"Since when? You left Boston intending to open a practice here, and now your options are open?"

"That's what I said."

"Grayson… How well can you possibly know her after only a couple of days?"

"Better than I've ever known any woman." As he said the words, he realized they were true. He'd shared more with her than he had with anyone he'd ever dated, and knew she'd done the same with him.

His mother stared at him. "You can't be serious."

"I hate to remind you that I'm thirty-six years old, and I certainly know the difference between something special and something not worth taking a chance on. This, with Emma and Simone, is something special."

"And you already know that for sure."

"I do."

She shook her head. "I thought you were smarter than that."

"It's not fair for you to project your disappointments onto me or anyone else, for that matter. Just because it didn't work out for you doesn't mean anyone who takes a chance on love is a fool."

"Wow. How long have you wanted to say that to me?"

"Only since you inferred that I'm a fool for knowing something special and different when I encounter it."

"It's your life. I can't and won't tell you how to live it."

"That's good to know, but I'd like to think I'd have your support in whatever I choose to do with my life."

"You always have." She got up to refill her coffee cup. "I'm sorry if you feel that I'm not being supportive. I don't want to see you hurt."

"I know that, but I refuse to live my life in fear of what *might* happen."

"Fair enough."

"Emma thinks you don't like her."

His mother turned to face him. "I don't dislike her. I barely know her."

"Give her a chance. For my sake. Please make her feel welcome in our family."

"Of course I will, if she's what you want."

"I think she might be."

"Just be careful not to risk more than you can afford to lose. I wouldn't wish that kind of heartbreak on anyone, especially you."

"I hear you. Do you have Lucas's phone number handy?"

"Yeah, it's in the book by the phone."

"Great, thanks."

"By the way, Noah called earlier, looking for you. He said he needs to talk to you about something."

"He didn't say what?"

"Not to me."

"Okay, I'll run by his house when I leave here." Grayson placed the call to his cousin Lucas, asking for his help in securing the surprise for Simone.

"You've come to the right place," Lucas said. "Meet me at the Christmas tree farm in an hour. I'll set you up."

"You're the best. Thanks."

"No problem."

Grayson went upstairs to shower and shave. In the bottom drawer of the dresser that'd been his until he left for college, he uncovered an old set of thermal underwear and put that on under his clothes.

In the downstairs closet, he found a wool blanket and the parka he kept at his mother's for skiing and other winter activities in Vermont.

"I made muffins earlier if you want to take some," his mother said when he returned to the kitchen.

"Chocolate chip?"

"Is there any other kind?"

"Not in this house. I'd love to take a few."

She packed them up for him and handed him a bag.

Grayson kissed her forehead. "Thanks, Mom."

"Have a nice time."

"I will. See you later." He went out to his SUV and stashed the blanket and muffins in the backseat and then drove down the street to Noah's house, parking behind the big truck his brother used for work.

Noah met him at the door, wearing his usual winter uniform of plaid flannel and jeans. His dark blond hair was wet from a recent shower and his face freshly shaven, but as usual since his divorce, his gray eyes were wary and an aura of bitterness surrounded him that reminded Gray of their mother. "Come in," he said to Grayson. "You want coffee?"

"I wouldn't mind one more cup."

Noah poured the coffee and put it on the kitchen table along with a container of half-and-half. "You want sugar?"

"Nah, the cream is fine. Mom said you wanted to see me?"

Noah leaned back against the counter and took a sip of his own coffee. "I saw Dad."

Shocked, Grayson said, "Where?"

"I was up in Westmore for a job. Ran into him at a lunch place there."

"He's living in freaking *Westmore*?" Could he really be that close to the family he'd abandoned?

"Apparently, he's been there all along. He said he tried to reach you through your office in Boston."

Grayson tried to wrap his brain around that info. "No, he didn't. They would've told me if anyone tried to reach me."

"He didn't leave a message."

"What'd he want?"

"To tell us he's sick. He has leukemia."

"Oh." Grayson had no idea how he was supposed to feel about that.

"And he wanted to know if we'd consider being tested for a potential bone marrow transplant."

Grayson heard the words his brother said, but his brain refused to process them. His dad needed a bone marrow transplant, and he wanted the children he'd abandoned twenty years ago to be tested.

"Gray?"

He looked at his brother. "What about his siblings?"

"None of them were a match."

"What did you say when he asked you?"

"Nothing, really. He gave me his number and told me to call him if anyone would be willing."

"I can't even believe he'd have the nerve to ask us."

"I suppose nerve doesn't factor in when facing a possibly terminal illness."

"I won't do it. I wouldn't cross the street to talk to him let alone give him my fucking bone marrow."

"Fair enough."

"What does that mean? You're going to do it?"

"Haven't decided yet. We need to tell the others. Everyone can make up their own minds."

"I'll let you spread the word. I want nothing to do with it."

"Okay."

Grayson drained his coffee cup and got up to put it in the sink. "Thanks for the coffee."

"Any time."

He couldn't get out of there fast enough and took greedy deep breaths of the cold air, wishing he could pretend the last ten minutes had never happened. He was far better off not knowing where his father was or anything else for that matter. And for Mike Coleman to expect his children to step up for him when he'd abandoned them… The very thought of it sparked the kind of red-hot rage he hadn't felt in years and would be happy to never experience again.

On the ride to the family's tree farm, Grayson tried not to think about what Noah had told him, but he couldn't seem to let it go no matter how badly he wanted to. That their father would even ask such a thing of them was unbelievable. He wished he'd told Noah *not* to inform their six siblings. Let their father go straight to hell, for all he cared.

When he arrived at the tree farm stables, Lucas already had the barn doors open for him.

Grayson took a moment to calm down and get back into the right frame of mind to orchestrate a fun outing for Emma and Simone. Under no circumstances would he ever want either of them to see the rage that only his father could generate in him. He took a deep breath and let it out before he emerged from the car.

As he approached the building, Lucas came out to greet him, gesturing to the horse-drawn sleigh they kept on hand for the holiday season at the farm. He already had the horses harnessed and everything ready to go.

"You already did all the work," Grayson said to his younger cousin.

"I can do it in my sleep," Lucas said. "What would take you an hour took minutes for me."

"I appreciate it."

"You remember how to drive this rig, city boy?"

His family loved to call him that, and Grayson knew better than to admit that it bugged him sometimes. That would only encourage them. "It's like riding a bike. Once you know, you never forget."

"Where you heading?"

"Back to your parents' house to pick up Emma and Simone and then to the trails in the back woods."

"That'll be nice today."

"I thought so, too."

"So... You and Emma, huh?"

"I was hoping you'd missed that part."

"No such luck. She's really sweet, and her daughter is, too."

"So I've noticed."

"Landon and I tried to get her to fall in love with us, but it wasn't to be, and then Colton ruined all our fun and told us we had to leave her alone."

Hearing Lucas had wanted Emma made Grayson want to punch the smirk off his cousin's face. Apparently, he didn't hide his reaction very well.

Laughing, Lucas held up his hands. "All in good fun. I swear."

"I hear you."

"You really like her, huh?"

"I really do."

"That's cool. Good for you. If she's anything like Lucy, you're a lucky man."

Eager to move on from talking about his love life, Grayson said, "Thanks again for this."

"Any time. I'll be around when you get back to help you put up the horses."

"I can do it if you've got other stuff to do."

"Nothing much going on today except visiting my new niece later. I don't mind helping."

"Appreciate it."

"You guys be nice to Grayson," Lucas said to the horses. "He's out of practice. Don't take advantage."

"I heard that," Grayson called after him.

Lucas's laughter echoed through the barn.

Grayson took a seat on the bench and snapped the reins to get the horses moving toward the path through the woods that would deliver him to Lincoln and Molly's backyard. The bells on the horses' harness were the only sound other than the glide of the blades through the fresh powder. As a kid growing up here, this had been one of his favorite things to do after a snowstorm, and he was hoping Simone and Emma would love it as much as he did.

In spite of his desire to focus on his plans with them, Grayson couldn't seem to think about anything other than the bomb Noah had dropped on him. What would his other siblings say when they heard this news? Would they agree to be tested?

Despite the cheerful jingle of the sleigh bells, Grayson couldn't shake the sense of dread-laced anxiety that came over him any time he had to deal with a past he'd much rather forget than have to confront once again.

He navigated the final turn before Linc and Molly's yard came into view and reminded himself that today was about Emma and her daughter. There'd be plenty of time after they went home for him to confront the anxiety and despair this news had resurrected in him.

This was a day for lighthearted fun and for giving Simone an experience she hopefully wouldn't soon forget. It was most definitely not the time to allow his painful past to intrude on the best week he'd ever had. He drove the sleigh into the yard, where the jingle of the bells immediately caught the attention of George and Ringo, who'd been frolicking in the snow. Grayson was amused by the way the horses totally ignored the barking dogs.

Apparently, Emma and Simone had been watching for him, because they came out of the mudroom door to greet him, both wearing huge smiles at the sight of the horse-drawn sleigh.

"Who would like to go for a ride?" he asked.

"Me," Simone shouted, raising her good arm. The other was in a sling that she wore over her coat.

"Me, too," Emma said with a warm smile for him that reminded him of the pleasure they'd found in each other's arms.

"Let's put you on this side, Simone, so nothing bumps your sore arm." After he got her settled under the blanket, he helped Emma up and then followed her, taking the middle seat. Grayson tucked the blanket in around Simone and then tended to Emma, who placed a hand on his thigh under the blanket. That was all it took to make him hard for her. Jesus… If she moved that hand even a fraction of an inch, she'd be able to tell what her touch had done to him.

Thankfully, she kept her hand where it was as he snapped the reins to get the horses moving.

"This is so awesome," Emma said. "Where'd you get the sleigh?"

"From the family Christmas tree farm. Lucas uses it to give rides during tree-harvesting season and leases it out for groups during the winter."

"You seem to know what you're doing…"

He laughed. "Driving this rig was my job every Saturday in December all through high school."

"I love how you all work for the family business in some way or another," Emma said. "Izzy was telling me how she's shooting the new catalog for the store after the first of the year."

"Did she tell you how they're expecting us to be their models?" He rolled his eyes. "Can you imagine what a calamity that will be?"

"After game night, I can picture it." She leaned in closer to him. "But you'd be a very sexy model."

"This is family day," he said, tipping his head toward Simone. "Behave."

"I am behaving." She squeezed his leg for emphasis.

He'd never been so hot for anyone, especially when he was also freezing. "What do you think of the sleigh, Simone?"

"I love it. I wish I could drive."

"You can help me." He handed her the right-side rein while keeping a tight grip on the left side and showed her how to guide the team with small corrections. "No big moves. That's the secret. You got this." He loved the way she concentrated so intently on what she was doing.

Emma squeezed his leg again, and Grayson resigned himself to being hard any time she touched him.

"Are you guys going out now?" Simone asked.

Grayson had no idea what to say to that. "Ahhh…"

"What if we are?" Emma asked her daughter. "Would that be okay?"

"Of course it would. Auntie Lu and I have been telling you for years that you need a boyfriend."

Emma laughed at her daughter's bluntness. "Yes, you have."

"Is Grayson nice to you?" Simone asked.

"He's very nice to me," Emma said with another squeeze that made him want to whimper.

"Then he should be your boyfriend."

"What about the fact that he lives here and we live in New York?" Emma asked, as if he wasn't sitting between them, listening to their conversation.

"Lucy and Colton figured that out, and so did Will and Cameron. You can, too."

"None of them had a girl named Simone to think about when they were working it out."

"That's true."

"That's all you've got? That's true?"

"For now. Give me time to think about it, will you?"

Grayson laughed at Simone's saucy reply. "Yeah, Mom. Give her some time, will you?"

Emma smiled at him, and he was so focused on her adorably red cheeks and big blue eyes that he nearly missed the huge obstruction standing before them.

He brought the team to a stop about three feet from a collision with Fred the moose.

"Oh my God," Simone whispered. "Is that him? Is that Fred?"

"That's him."

"He's *huge!*"

Fred let out a loud *moo* that had Emma moving closer to Grayson, if that was possible.

"No wonder Cameron's car was totally smooshed," Simone whispered.

"She's lucky all she had were two black eyes from the air bags," Emma said in the same whisper. "Do we need to be afraid of him attacking us?"

"Absolutely not," Grayson said. "He's a pussycat."

"Right," Emma said sarcastically. "A thousand-pound pussycat."

One of the horses whinnied, and Fred took a long, measuring look at them before ambling into the woods.

Emma released a sigh of relief. "He's way bigger than advertised."

"And totally harmless," Grayson said as they began to move forward again. "Ask anyone around here."

Emma cast a wary glance at the woods into which Fred had disappeared. "I can't believe Cameron survived running into him," she said with a shudder.

"He's totally forgiven her. They're old friends now."

"I know," Emma said. "I was there when Fred crashed her wedding."

Simone giggled. "That was so funny. He came right into the tent."

"I was sorry to miss it. I was away on work travel." Another perk to self-employment was that he'd never again have to miss an important event due to something his partners decided "couldn't be avoided." Whatever. Life was too short for that nonsense.

They completed one big loop around the trails that surrounded Butler. "Do you want to go with me to the barn to put these guys up?" Grayson asked his passengers.

"You feel up to it, Simone?"

"I'm fine. I'd love to go."

Grayson loved her spunk and how she was up for any adventure even when nursing an injury. "Then let's go home." He guided the team toward the Christmas tree farm and relaxed to enjoy the ride and the company.

"This was fun," Emma said. "Thank you so much."

"I enjoyed it, too. It's been far too long since I did this."

"You haven't forgotten how." She surprised and pleased him when she leaned her head on his shoulder, and then Simone did the same thing on the other side. For a guy who'd spent his entire adult life avoiding commitment, he ought to be feeling panicked to have the two of them leaning on him. But it wasn't panic he felt but rather a pervasive sense of contentment, a feeling so strong and so pure, he wanted to hold on to it with everything he had.

Then he remembered they were leaving tomorrow, and the contentment evaporated into a messy mix of anxiety and sadness. How would he bear to let them go?

CHAPTER 13

Love is an irresistible desire to be irresistibly desired.
—Robert Frost

Emma wished they could stay in this magical place forever. Leaning against Grayson felt so natural and comfortable. After years of flying solo, she'd fallen into coupledom with remarkable ease, especially since Simone had expressed her approval. If only they weren't due to leave right when things were getting interesting.

Though it would be hard to leave him, she had no regrets after the most amazing week of her life. Who knew that when she came for Christmas and Hunter's wedding that she'd meet someone like Grayson and have her entire life turned upside down in the course of a few unforgettable days? Things like that didn't happen to her. They happened to other people, like Cameron and Lucy. Not her.

Emma was pragmatic enough to know that one didn't make major decisions after a whirlwind holiday romance. That would be foolish, and she was anything but. While she wasn't about to write off what they had together as hopeless, she had to be realistic. She and Simone had a life in the city. She had a job that paid the bills, put food on the table and provided affordable health insurance for both of them. They also had the significant support of friends and other parents who made it possible for Simone to participate in a wide range of after-school activities and who covered for Emma when she needed an assist. Not to mention, her dad was nearby in case of emergencies and was always willing to lend a hand with Simone.

A single mother didn't walk away from a network like that, not even for someone as appealing as Grayson Coleman. Was she tempted to say to hell with it and go all-in with him? Absolutely. Would she do it? Absolutely not.

She blinked back tears that couldn't be blamed entirely on the cold. It sure had felt good to feel like a desirable woman again and to have someone to talk to about the things that weighed heavily on her heart, not to mention the laughter, the tenderness, the passion…

Emma took a deep breath of cold air, determined to keep her emotions in check, especially in front of Simone, who would tune right in to her distress. There was no hiding from a perceptive nine-year-old.

"There's Will and Cam's place," Grayson said, gesturing to the log cabin, where a plume of smoke rose from the chimney.

"Can we stop to see them?" Simone asked.

"Ahh, they might be 'busy,'" Grayson said, making Emma snort with laughter.

"Doing what?" Simone asked.

"Yes, Grayson, do tell us what they might be busy doing," Emma said, smiling at him.

"Um, ah, well, they said something about doing the laundry today."

Emma choked back a laugh.

"Oh, that's boring," Simone said. "I hate when Mommy makes me fold the laundry."

"Folding is definitely the worst part," Grayson said, giving Emma a playful glare that nearly had her laughing out loud.

A few minutes later, he drove the sleigh into the gates of the Stillman/Abbott Family Christmas Tree Farm, and after they'd traveled down a long road, he brought it to a stop in front of a big red barn.

"This is a Christmas tree farm?" Simone asked. "Like with chickens and stuff?"

"No chickens or cows. Just trees. You know the ones you see for sale in the city?"

She nodded.

"They come from places like this." He gestured to the acres of trees planted in neat rows.

"That's so cool. I never thought about where they came from."

"You want to help me put the horses away?"

"If I can," she said, scowling at the sling.

"There's a lot you can do with one hand. Wait for me to help you down."

He helped Emma down and then went around for Simone, lifting her off the sled effortlessly. Under normal circumstances, her fiercely independent daughter would've scurried down on her own and told him she didn't need the help.

"Thanks," she said.

"No problem." He talked Simone through the steps of putting up the horses and stashing the sleigh. They'd removed the bridle on the first horse when Lucas appeared on a snowmobile.

He cut the engine. "Did you guys have fun?" he asked.

"It was so fun," Simone said.

"Let me give you a hand with the horses," Lucas said as he got off the snowmobile. "Maybe you can help us brush them."

"Can I, Grayson?" she asked, looking up at him with big eyes full of excitement and wonder.

"Of course. You can be in charge of the brushing."

Emma wished she could bottle him and take him home with her. If only it were that simple. She kept a close eye on Simone to make sure she wasn't underfoot or in danger of further injury, but she needn't have worried. Grayson kept an even closer eye on her and let her do as much as she could to help.

When they'd fed and watered the horses and stashed the sleigh inside the barn, Lucas said, "I was thinking about building a snowman, Simone. You want to help me?"

"Can I, Mom?"

"If you're careful of your sore arm."

"She can do the decorating," Lucas said. "I'll do the rolling." To Simone, he said, "Run into the office over there and grab the snowman kit on the bookshelf."

She took off toward the office.

"You and Emma want to take the snowmobile for a ride?" Lucas asked Grayson.

Was Lucas trying to give them some time alone? Was he really that perceptive, or were they really that obvious?

"What do you think, Em?" Grayson asked. "Want to go for a ride?" He waggled his brows and made her laugh.

"Um, sure. That sounds fun."

Simone returned with the brightly painted box that she opened to show her mother the orange wooden carrot, the black buttons, red scarf and black felt hat contained within. "It's everything we need to make a snowman," Simone said. "How cool is that?"

"Very cool. Grayson was going to take me for a ride on the snowmobile. Is that okay with you?"

"Yep. I've got to help Lucas with the snowman."

"Take your time," Lucas said. "We'll go upstairs to make hot chocolate when we're done."

"Are you sure you don't mind?" Emma asked him.

"I'm sure. I'm on vacation this week. Nothing but time."

"Okay, then. You guys have fun." She kissed Simone's cold, rosy cheek. "We'll be back soon." To Grayson, she said, "Do we need helmets?"

"We'll go slow."

Since she trusted him implicitly, she got on behind him and wrapped her arms around his waist.

"Hold on *nice* and *tight*," he said suggestively.

Emma laughed and squeezed her thighs until they were snug against his backside.

He let out a low groan that made her giggle as he fired up the powerful machine and propelled them into a wide circular turn.

Emma waved to Simone, who was supervising Lucas as he rolled the first big ball of snow for the snowman.

"You're not holding on tight enough," Grayson said. "I wouldn't want you to fall off."

Emma smiled and rested her face and body against his back, holding on to him as tight as she could.

They took the same path they'd taken with the sleigh, around the outskirts of town. He surprised her when he pulled off the path and brought the snowmobile to a stop on a scenic overlook that faced Butler Mountain and turned off the engine.

"Why are we stopping?" she asked.

"Give me one second and I'll show you." He stood and turned to face her before sitting back down and reaching for her. "Because

I couldn't wait any longer for this." He wrapped his arms around her and kissed her with hours' worth of pent-up desperation that she returned in equal measure. The deep strokes of his tongue had her straining to get closer to him.

"God," he whispered against her lips, "what're you doing to me?"

"Same thing you're doing to me."

"How am I supposed to let you go tomorrow?"

The softly spoken question brought tears to her eyes.

"Don't cry. Please don't cry. We'll figure it out."

She shook her head. "There's nothing to figure out. You live here. I live there."

"I don't live anywhere right now. I can get a job in New York."

Emma pulled back so she could see his face. "That's not what you want."

"I want you. I want this. I want *us*."

She shook her head. "Grayson, you just made this big change to simplify your life—"

"Then I met you, and nothing is simple anymore."

"You've got a new apartment."

"That I haven't moved anything into yet. I haven't done anything that can't be undone."

Her heart raced with foolish hope. "You can't make decisions based on a few days."

"I can't?"

"No, you can't. You were excited to move home, to be closer to your family, to simplify your life."

"That was so three days ago. Everything is different now."

"Grayson, you can't—"

He kissed her again, making her forget the many reasons this could be a very bad idea and all the many more reasons it could be the best idea either of them had ever had. When they came up for air many minutes later, he said, "Give me some time to figure things out, okay?"

She tipped her head forward, resting it on his chest.

"Tell me what you're thinking."

"I'm afraid to get my hopes up."

"Don't be afraid. You can go home tomorrow knowing I want this as much as you do, and we're going to find a way. I promise."

She shook her head again. "Don't make promises."

"I never make promises I don't intend to keep. Look at me, Emma."

Drawing in a deep breath, she raised her head and met his intense gaze. "I promise you it's okay to have faith in me and in us. I promise you it's okay to feel hopeful and excited about what's to come." He brushed a soft kiss over her lips. "I promise you this is not the end, but just the beginning."

Her heart beat so fast, she felt light-headed. He made her believe anything was possible and all she had to do was have faith. She could do that if it meant more time with him, more of the way she felt when he held her and kissed her and made love to her. More. Just more.

"Do you believe me?" he asked.

"I want to."

"You can. I swear you can."

"We... We should go back. Simone..."

"Okay." But he made no move to go. Rather, he kissed her again, softly and sweetly this time, devastating her with every stroke of his tongue. "It's going to work out. Remember that I promised you, okay?"

"I'll try."

With what seemed like great reluctance, he disentangled himself from her and got back on the snowmobile to return to the tree farm, where her daughter waited for them. As he steered them back the way they'd come, Emma rested her face against his back and held on tight to him and his promises.

When they returned to the tree farm, they marveled over the huge snowman Lucas and Simone had built while they were gone. Lucas invited them up to his loft for the hot chocolate he'd promised Simone.

"What a great space," Emma said, taking in the post-and-beam ceiling, the fireplace, the knotty-pine wood floor and the other rustic touches. "I love it."

"I like it, too," Lucas said as he put a kettle on to boil. "From one barn to another. Such is my lot in life."

Emma laughed at the witty comment. "At least you're up here rather than in one of the stalls."

"There is that. My grandparents lived here for a time when they were first married, and my parents stayed here while their barn was being renovated. Lots of family history in this place."

"You all have the coolest homes up here," Emma said. "I love the rustic vibe."

"It's rustic, all right," Lucas said. "Especially when the wind chill is at thirty below zero."

Emma shivered. "I don't think I'd like that."

Grayson put his arm around her. "I'd keep you warm."

She shivered for a whole different reason, imagining how he'd do that.

They enjoyed a cup of hot chocolate with Lucas before departing in Grayson's SUV.

"How about some pizza before I take you ladies home?" he asked.

"Yes!" Simone said from the backseat.

"Pizza is her favorite food group," Emma said.

"Mine, too," Grayson said. "Especially Kingdom Pizza. It's the best."

They shared a large cheese pizza and split a salad. Over dinner, Grayson asked what Simone's favorite part of her trip to Vermont had been.

"Hmm, I really liked skiing until I hurt my arm, and the sleigh ride was pretty cool, too. I liked meeting you."

"I liked that, too."

She pushed her new iPhone across the table. "I'm putting everyone's contacts in my phone. Will you put yours?"

Emma could see that he was touched that she would ask.

"Of course, but only if you'll text me."

"I will."

"Remember that I have no cell service in Butler, so it might take me a day or two to reply, but I'll always reply." He handed his phone to her. "Add yourself to my contacts."

As Simone dedicated herself to the task, Emma and Grayson shared a smile. She mouthed the words *thank you* to him. Under the table, he grasped her hand and brought it to rest on his leg.

Darkness had descended upon Butler by the time they returned to the Abbotts'. Emma was filled with dread at the thought of saying good-bye to him and was relieved when he came inside with them. They found Molly wearing a robe over her pajamas, curled up in front of the fire with a down comforter over her lap, and Linc asleep in his chair.

"This grandparent gig is exhausting," Molly said.

"How're they doing?" Grayson asked.

"Very well. The baby is getting great reports, and Hannah actually got some sleep today."

"Can we see the baby before we go?" Simone asked her mom.

"Not this time."

"Why not?"

"Moms of new babies are very protective of them when they're first born. Usually they only allow their immediate family near the baby for the first month or two. By the time we come back to visit Lucy, baby Callie will be big enough for a visit."

"We should get her a present," Simone said.

"Definitely. Why don't you run up and get out your pajamas? I'll be up to help you in a minute."

"Okay, Mommy."

After Simone went upstairs, Molly said, "Lucy called to check on Simone. And Will and Cameron called to invite you guys to a get-together at their house tonight. Lucy said to tell you she'll be there and wants to see you before you leave."

"Simone has already had a big day," Emma said.

"She can stay here with us," Molly said. "We're early to bed tonight."

"I wouldn't want to impose," Emma said hesitantly. "You've already been such wonderful hosts."

"Oh please, honey. She's a pleasure to have around. We'd be happy to have her here with us. You two should go out while you can."

Emma glanced at Grayson, who raised his brows. "Do you want to go?"

"Only if you do."

"I'd really like to see Lucy and the others before we leave."

"Then let's go," he said.

"I need to get Simone settled first. Give me a few minutes?"

"Take your time." He took a seat in one of the easy chairs while she went upstairs to help Simone.

"How's it going up here?" she asked her daughter, who was sitting on the edge of the bed, her pajamas next to her.

"Okay."

"What's the matter?"

"I'm sad that we have to leave tomorrow. It's fun here. There's always something to do."

"I know, baby. We'll come back and visit again soon." Emma helped her remove the sling and carefully eased her sweater up and over her head, revealing her badly bruised elbow. "How's it feeling?"

"Hurts a little, but not bad."

Emma planned to have it checked by an orthopedic doctor when they got back to the city. That was one of many things on her to-do list once they returned to real life. The thought of it exhausted her as she helped Simone change into pajamas, realizing it'd been a long time since she'd had to help her daughter get dressed. Time with her was flying by so quickly. Soon, she'd be a teenager, a thought that had Emma snuggling Simone into a hug.

"Grayson and I were going to go out for a little while. Molly and Linc said you can hang out with them." The Abbotts had insisted that Simone call them by their first names, even if Emma had wanted her to call them Mr. and Mrs. Abbott. "Is that okay with you?"

"Sure. Will I see Auntie Lu before we go?"

"We'll make sure of it. Should we put the sling back on?"

"I think I'm okay without it."

"Just be careful not to overdo it."

"I will."

Emma escorted Simone back downstairs with the new doll Santa had brought her and a couple of her favorite books.

"Is that the new doll?" Grayson asked her.

"Yes, this is Ashley," she said of the doll that shared her auburn hair. "She's not American Girl, because Mommy said they're ridiculously expensive, but I think she's really pretty."

"I agree," he said. "Can I hold her?"

Emma's heart melted at the request as well as the big smile that lit up Simone's adorable face.

"Sure." She took the doll to him and set her carefully in his arms.

Watching him cradle the doll with such tender care, Emma was struck by a pang of yearning to see him holding a baby of theirs someday. *Holy hell, where did that thought come from?* Ten years into motherhood, the last thing she wanted was to start over again. But if he were the father... *Stop. Just stop.*

"She's very pretty," Grayson said. "Just like her mama." He handed her back to Simone. "Thanks for letting me hold her."

"You're welcome."

"Are you ready?" Emma asked him.

"Whenever you are."

Emma hugged and kissed Simone. "Be good for Molly and Linc, and go to bed when they tell you to."

"She'll be fine," Molly said. "Go have a good time."

"Thank you," Emma said, filled with anticipation for more time alone with Grayson.

"Night, Simone," Grayson said.

Simone crooked her finger at him.

He went to her and squatted in front of her.

"Thank you for the sleigh ride and the pizza. It was a lot of fun."

"You're very welcome." He stood and then leaned in to kiss her forehead. "Sweet dreams." To Molly and Linc, he said, "Sleep tight, guys."

"We'll sleep like zombies after this day," Linc said.

"Congrats again on the new granddaughter," Emma said. "And thanks again for having Simone."

"Our pleasure."

CHAPTER 14

Love is a friendship set to music.
—Joseph Campbell

With his hand on her back, Grayson guided Emma through the kitchen to the mudroom, where they donned their coats. He looped her scarf around her neck and drew her in close to him for a kiss. "Bonus time."

"I was thinking the same thing."

"I've never loved my aunt Molly more than I do right now."

"I was in full-on girl crush with her *before* she offered to keep Simone."

"She is pretty damned awesome." He opened the door and gestured for her to go ahead of him into the icy night.

When they were in the SUV, he said, "So we're going to Will's?"

As she did every time she got in his vehicle, she immediately turned on the seat warmer. "I thought so. Where else would we go?"

Grayson answered her saucy question with a grin. "I can't think of a single other place we might go." He reached across the center console for her hand. "How do you feel about a brief visit with Will, Cameron, Lucy and the others?"

"I feel like that might be rude."

"So?"

Emma laughed at the impatient way he said that. "They'll talk about us if we do that."

"Um, newsflash, sweetheart, they're already talking about us."

"Does that bother you?"

"Not even kinda. Let them talk." He glanced over at her. "Does it bother you?"

"No, not really. It's been a long time since I've been involved in anything worth talking about."

"The teasing is all in good fun in my family. I hope you know that."

"I do. Of course I do."

"I won't let it get out of hand. Don't worry."

"I'm not worried." What she thought but didn't say was that there wouldn't be much for them to talk about after tonight.

They pulled into Will and Cameron's driveway, which was full of trucks and SUVs. The cabin was lit up, and smoke curled from the chimney into the darkness. Above them, the night sky was full of more stars than Emma had ever seen before.

"It's so beautiful here," she said wistfully.

"Even when it's freezing?"

"Even then."

He put his arm around her shoulders as they walked to the door, escorted by Will's excited yellow Labs, Trevor and Tanner. "So yes to a brief visit?"

"Brief but not rude."

Dropping his hand from her shoulder, he gave her ass a squeeze that let her know exactly what was on his mind. "I can work with that."

Even though the air around them was frigid, heat zinged through her bloodstream at the thought of more time alone with him later.

Grayson walked right into his cousin's home, where everyone turned to greet them.

Emma felt like the proverbial moose in the headlights with all eyes on her and Grayson.

Cameron and Lucy came over to hug her.

"There you are!" Cam said. "I wondered if you'd gotten the message to come over."

Emma gave Grayson a grateful smile when he helped her out of her coat. "Molly told us."

"Where ya been all day?" Lucy asked, glancing from her to him and then back to her again.

"Grayson took us for a sleigh ride, and we hung out with Lucas for a while. Then we had pizza at Kingdom Pizza and went back to the Abbotts'. They offered to keep Simone if I wanted to go out, and here I am. That's my whole day accounted for."

"Sounds like fun."

"It was."

Lucy gave her a measuring look, letting her know there was much more she wanted to say, but she'd never do that in front of a crowd. "Come get a drink."

Emma followed Lucy and Cameron to the kitchen, suspecting she was in for a grilling about Grayson and what would happen next for them. If only she had the answer to that question.

Grayson wanted to take her by the hand and get the hell out of there. He wanted to go to his new apartment and lose himself in her for hours until the time came when he had to let her go—for now, anyway. Tomorrow was going to suck, but tonight… Tonight he would be able to hold her and kiss her and make love to her.

"What's up with you?" his cousin Wade asked.

"Nothing. Why?"

"You're tense."

"Am I?"

"Uh-huh. Something tells me it has everything to do with a gorgeous blonde who's going back to her real life tomorrow. Am I warm?"

"You're warm," he said with a sigh.

"She's really nice, and her daughter is a cutie."

"I agree."

"What're you going to do about her?"

"I don't know yet."

"Might be time to make a plan, unless you want her to get away."

The thought of that made him feel panicky and overheated. He tugged at the neck of his sweater. During the time he'd spent with Emma and Simone today, he'd done a pretty good job of forgetting about the situation with his father, but that, too, weighed heavily on him tonight. "What would you do if you were me?"

Wade laughed. "I'm the last one you should ask for romance advice."

"Why's that?"

"The only woman I've ever felt something for is married to someone else. What do I know about how to deal with things like this?"

"Who is she?" Gray asked, intrigued by the rare glimpse at Wade's private life.

"No one you know."

"I'm sorry."

"It is what it is," Wade said with bravado that sounded forced. "Have you told her how you feel about her?"

"Only that I want to see her again."

"Might be worth putting it all on the table if you're determined to make it work."

"Too soon."

"Is it?"

"For her, it probably is. She's reserved and cautious."

"Makes sense. She has a lot on the line with a daughter to think about."

Before Grayson could reply, Ella plopped down on the sofa next to him. "I was over at the apartment today and took most of my stuff. I left things like sheets, towels and pans that I don't need. If you don't want them, let me know, and I'll donate them."

"Sounds good, thanks."

"You're taking over the apartment at the Abernathy place?" Wade asked.

"That's the plan." *Or it was the plan as recently as two days ago*, Grayson thought. Now he didn't know anything for sure except he wanted more with Emma. With that in mind, he caught her eye in the kitchen and tipped his head toward the front door.

Her face turned bright red before she shook her head to say not yet.

Amused and aroused by her, he turned his attention back to his cousins, both of whom were watching him intently. "What?"

"Got some plans, cousin?" Ella asked, her eyes dancing with amusement.

"Maybe."

"Good for you," she said. "I love Emma. She's so sweet, and that daughter of hers is a trip."

"Couldn't agree more. They're both great."

"What're you going to do about it?"

"Hell if I know. I thought I had my shit all figured out, and then *wham*."

"Can I say one thing?" Wade asked, his expression more intense than Grayson had ever seen it.

"Sure."

"No matter what happens, don't have regrets," Wade said. "Regrets are tough to live with."

His cousin seemed to speak from experience.

Ella's eyes softened with compassion. "Wade…"

"That's all I want to say about it. Don't have regrets, Gray."

"I hear you. Thank you."

Colton came over to the sofa. "Gray, come help me take Will's dogs out."

"Will's dogs were just out."

"They need to go out again."

"Subtle," Ella said under her breath.

"If I don't come back, you'll look for me, won't you?" Grayson asked her.

Ella giggled. "I will. I promise."

Grayson got up, grabbed his coat off a pile on a chair near the door and followed Colton out the door, the dogs bolting out ahead of them. "Whatever you want to say to me, say it fast. It's colder than Jack Frost's balls out here."

"What's up with you and Emma?"

"I'm sure you already know."

"I want to hear it from you."

"I like her. We've had fun together this week."

"That's all? Fun?"

"What're you getting at, Colton?"

"She means everything to Lucy. It would hurt her if Emma got hurt, and if Lucy's hurt, I hurt. You follow?"

"Um, I think so…"

"Don't hurt her, Gray. She's special, and so is Simone."

"You think I don't already know that? I get it."

"What happens after they go home?"

"I don't know yet."

"Figure it out."

"No pressure," he muttered.

"Lucy is worried. If she worries, I worry. You got me?"

"I hear you. I don't want Lucy to worry or Emma to be hurt any more than you do. Give me a little credit, will you? And give me some time. We have things to work out, but it's not going to happen overnight."

"Fair enough."

"Can we go in now?"

"Yeah, sure."

"Gray."

He turned back to his cousin. "Yeah?"

"If you think it's not going to happen, let her down easy, will you?"

"Of course I will. And for what it's worth, I'm not trying to figure a way out. I'm trying to figure out how I can have more. Much more."

Before Colton could reply, Grayson went back inside where Emma was staring at the door, seemingly waiting for him to come back.

"What's Colton saying to him?" Emma asked her sister.

"I have no idea."

"No idea at all?"

"Maybe the slightest idea. I'm worried about you. He's picked up on that."

"There's nothing to worry about."

"No?"

"No. We had a really nice week, but it is what it is." The hopelessness of it all weighed on her.

"That's it? You're just giving up before you even try?"

"What would you have me do? I can't exactly split my time between here and New York the way you do. I have a child who goes to school and dance and soccer and has friends. I have a job with benefits that I need. I have a tribe in the city that makes it possible for Simone to do everything she wants to do. Dad is there, and he helps me a lot. Grayson just moved back here and is planning to set up a business. How in the world do you see this working out?"

Lucy wilted under the strength of Emma's argument. "I want it to work. I like the way you sparkle when you're with him."

"I like it, too. And I like *him*—a whole lot."

"But?"

"No buts."

"What's she saying?" Cameron asked Lucy when she joined them after playing hostess.

"That it's hopeless."

"No, it isn't," Cameron said emphatically. "You and I know better."

"In her case, it might be."

"I don't believe that," Cameron said. "If two people are meant to be together, it works out. Somehow."

"Only in the movies," Emma said with a smile for her friend.

"In real life, too," Cameron insisted. "We're surrounded by examples of that right here in this room. Me and Will, Lucy and Colton, Ella and Gavin. Not to mention Charley and Tyler and Hunter and Megan. Every one of those couples overcame tremendous odds to make it work, because it was meant to be."

Emma wished she believed in fairy tales the way Cameron did, but life had taught her to be more practical.

Grayson came in from outside and caught her gaze. Did he seem annoyed, or was that her imagination? The look he gave her left no doubt that he wanted to leave. Now.

"We're going to go," Emma said, hugging her sister and then Cameron. "I'll see you girls again soon, I hope." Life in New York had been a whole lot less fun since they moved north. "Lu, Simone was hoping to see you before we leave in the morning."

"I'll come by early," Lucy said.

"Emma," Cameron said, "I know you think I'm full of crap—"

Emma laughed. "I never said that!"

"I know you. I know what you're thinking. *Cameron has her head in the clouds.* But I really believe everything I said. If you have genuine feelings for him, and vice versa, somehow you'll figure it out."

"That'd be very nice," Emma said, hugging Cameron again.

"She's placating me, isn't she?" Cameron asked Lucy.

"I'd say you're correct."

"I heard you both. I love you both. And I'll talk to you soon." She walked over to where Grayson held her coat.

"Leaving so soon?" Will asked when he came to see them off.

"Emma and Simone have to get to Burlington in the morning," Grayson said.

Colton hugged Emma. "It was great having you and Simone with us this week."

"We loved every minute of it."

"Come see us again soon."

"I'm sure Simone will be dragging me up here for another skiing lesson before too long."

"I'm happy to give her another lesson any time she wants," Colton said.

Will shook hands with Grayson. "Drive carefully."

"Will do. Thanks for the beer."

"Any time."

Emma and Grayson ran out into the tundra, where the air was so cold, it hurt to breathe. He stayed with her until she was safely in the SUV and then ran around to his side and started the engine.

She immediately turned on the heated seat. "I'm going to miss your bun warmer."

"Is that right?" he said with a low chuckle.

She snuggled into the seat. "Mmm."

"I'm going to miss your warm buns."

Emma laughed.

"Is the bun warmer the only thing you're going to miss?" he asked.

"No. You know I'm going to miss much more than that."

He gave her a small smile that let her know she wasn't the only one wrestling with their impossible dilemma. "You want to go back to Molly's?"

"What're my options?"

"We could go to my place for a little while."

At the thought of more time alone with him, her heart beat faster and her entire body felt warm despite the frigid temperatures. She knew what she ought to do—call it a night and go home before they could make things worse. But honestly, how could it be any worse than her leaving here tomorrow and not seeing him again for a long time? "We can go to your place."

"Are you sure?"

"No," she said with a laugh. "I'm not sure of anything other than I want to spend more time with you."

He ran his finger over her cheek, and she felt his touch everywhere. "I want that, too." His hand dropped from her face to shift the SUV into reverse. As soon as they were on the road back to town, he took hold of her hand, and he didn't let go until they were parked in his driveway.

Before he shut off the engine, he leaned across the center console to kiss her. His hand sank into her hair, drawing her closer to him as the kiss went from sweet and tender to hot and bothered with one stroke of his tongue against hers.

She curled her hand around his neck and leaned in closer as their tongues engaged in a fierce duel.

He broke the kiss on a gasp. "Inside. Hurry."

CHAPTER 15

Love and compassion are necessities, not luxuries. Without them humanity cannot survive.
—Dalai Lama

His urgency sparked hers as they dashed into the house and up two flights of stairs. Outside his apartment, he fumbled with the key and swore when it didn't work on the first try.

Emma giggled at his frustration.

The door swung open, and he compelled her in ahead of him, pulling at her coat before she was even through the door. Their coats landed on the floor right inside the door. He grasped her sweater while she unbuckled his belt, both pulling and tugging until their clothes were in a pile at their feet.

His lips came down on hers in a devouring kiss that had her clinging to him and then gasping when he lowered her to the floor, coming down on top of her without missing a beat in the frantic kiss.

She took him in hand and directed him to where she wanted him so badly.

He pushed into her, taking hold of her hands and pinning them over her head. "Is this okay?"

She appreciated that he would stop in the midst of madness to ask that. "Only because it's you."

Her reply seemed to fuel his ardor, and he pounded into her in a way he never had before, wild and unrestrained.

A knock on the door had them both freezing mid-stroke.

"Ella? Is that you? Are you and that Guthrie boy hanging pictures again?"

Grayson's eyes got very big before he lost it laughing, taking Emma down with him. "That's Mrs. Abernathy, the landlord," Grayson whispered.

Another knock. "Ella?"

"Say something," Grayson said. "She'll think you're Ella."

"Everything's fine, Mrs. Abernathy," Emma said as cheerfully as she could while Grayson throbbed inside her and his chest hair abraded her sensitive nipples.

"Okay, dear. Just making sure. Good night now."

"Good night."

When they heard the older woman walk away, they began to laugh again. They laughed so hard that tears ran down their faces and they gasped for breath.

"Oh my God," Grayson said when he'd recovered somewhat. "Ella and Gavin… hanging pictures. Those dirty devils. I can't *wait* to see her again."

"If you tell her what happened, you'll be confessing that you were hanging some pictures of your own."

That got him laughing all over again, which started her up again, too.

"Have we lost the mood?" he asked when he'd recovered.

"Maybe a little, but I bet we can get it back."

He smiled down at her. "I'll take that bet." He kissed her lightly. "Shall we relocate to the much more comfortable bed?"

"Yes, please."

Grayson withdrew from her and stood, reaching out to help her up and then wrapping his arms around her. "That was the best laugh I've had in years."

"Me, too."

He held her close to him as he walked them toward the bedroom.

Emma kept her arms around his neck and followed his lead, walking backward as he navigated for both of them.

Standing by the side of the bed, he held up the covers and Emma got in ahead of him, immediately chilled by the loss of his warmth. He was right behind her, reaching for her and drawing her into his embrace, their legs intertwining and their lips meeting in another hungry kiss.

Every single thing about him appealed to her, from the way he kissed her, to his scent, to the roughness of his leg hair, to the flex of his muscles, to the tender way he held and touched her. Grasping her leg, he drew it over his hip and entered her again, the position intensely intimate with his gaze locked on hers as they faced each other. She'd never done anything remotely like this. In her distant past, sex had been fast and mostly meaningless. But this, with him… It defied description.

"Good?" he asked.

"So good." She held on to his arm while his hand lay flat on her bottom, holding her tight against him.

"Emma…" His eyes were closed, his lips parted. He was so damned sexy when he lost himself in her this way. "God, Emma… Tell me you're close."

"So close."

Rolling them so she was under him, he gave it to her hard and fast, driving deep until they came together in a moment of utter magic. There was, simply, no other word for it.

Emma clung to him in the aftermath, needing his solid weight on top of her. She'd had sex before him. Not much, but some. In the romance novels she devoured late at night when Simone was in bed, she'd read about it far more than she'd done it. She knew enough to realize the difference between sex and lovemaking. This, right here, had been all about love. Not that she could say that to him, not now anyway.

He lay with his head on her chest and his arms around her.

Emma combed her fingers through his hair, enjoying the peaceful interlude after the storm of passion that had been unlike anything she'd ever imagined for herself. *He* was far more than she'd ever imagined. And she had to leave him in less than twelve hours.

"Why did you just get all tense?"

Sighing, she said, "Because I have to go home tomorrow."

"I wish you could stay."

"So do I. I'm trying to picture going back to my normal routine after this week."

"I'm having trouble picturing my normal routine without you and Simone as part of it."

Her heart ached with the desire to be part of his normal routine—and to make him part of hers. But how would they do that? The obstacles seemed insurmountable from her point of view.

"Something happened today."

"I know. I was there."

His low chuckle made her smile. "Something *else* happened today, I should say." He withdrew from her, shifted onto his back and then reached for her, snuggling her into his embrace. "Noah heard from my dad. Apparently, he has leukemia and needs a bone marrow transplant. He's asked if we'd be willing to be tested."

"Oh. Wow. What do you think about that?"

"Truthfully? I think he can go fuck himself."

"I can certainly understand why you feel that way. What did Noah say?"

"Not much, but he never has much to say about anything."

"So you won't get tested?"

"Hell no. I couldn't care less if he lives or dies."

Emma thought about that, trying to see it from his point of view. So much had fallen to him after his father left the family, and he was rightfully bitter about that.

"What're you thinking?" he asked after a long silence.

"I don't want to presume to know you better than you know yourself..."

"It's okay to say what's on your mind. I want your opinion. That's why I told you."

"I understand completely why you feel the way you do about him. You have every good reason to despise him."

"But?"

"You're a good and decent man, Grayson. Would you be able to live with yourself if you ignore his request and he dies?"

His deep sigh answered for him.

"There's no judgment from me if you say you could live with that outcome. I'm just playing devil's advocate here."

"I hate that I feel obligated to do this, whether I want to or not, for that very reason."

"It's a simple test, right? Have the test and go on with your life, knowing you were the better man. You and he would both know it was more than he deserved from you."

"You're right," he said with a sigh, "and I guess that's what I'll do. None of his siblings were a match, so chances are none of us will be either."

"Your younger siblings will be looking to you for direction on this."

"I know. If I do it, they will, too. And if I don't..."

"You have to do it, Grayson. His life is on the line. You don't have to see him or talk to him to be tested."

"That's true." He gave her arm a squeeze. "Thanks for listening."

"Any time."

"Even when you're in New York and I'm way up here?"

"Even then."

"I'm going to miss you like crazy."

"I'll miss you, too."

"Could I come visit you and Simone?"

"I wish you would."

"I will. As soon as possible."

"I should go back to the Abbotts'."

"Not yet," he said, tightening his hold on her. "I'm not ready to let you go."

"We can't fall asleep here."

"We won't."

Because she wasn't ready to let him go yet either, Emma relaxed into his embrace, telling herself a few more minutes of utter perfection wouldn't hurt anything.

Hannah woke with a start from a sound sleep, her breasts tingling from the dream she'd had that the baby was crying.

"What's the matter?" Nolan asked, his voice thick with sleep from his post in the recliner next to her hospital bed.

"I need to check on her."

"You checked her an hour ago. She's fine. The nurses will let you know if she needs you."

"I have to see for myself."

Thankfully, he seemed to understand that there'd be no sleeping—or peace—until she was pacified. Groaning, he dragged himself out of the chair and rubbed his hands over his face before holding up the robe he'd brought her from home and wrapping her up in it.

Nolan held her hand as they walked to the NICU where they spent five full minutes washing their hands. Then he helped her into the gown and shoe covers everyone was required to wear to gain entrance.

"Back so soon?" one of the overnight nurses asked when they went in.

"I just wanted to check on her," Hannah said.

"Of course. She's feisty, that little one."

"Like her mother," Nolan said dryly, drawing laughs from both women.

Hannah gazed down at her tiny daughter, drinking in every detail for the thousandth time. She never got tired of looking at her. Callie's lips moved in her sleep, the same way her daddy's did. Hannah loved that she already saw similarities between the baby and Nolan. She stared at her, watching the rise and fall of her little chest and marveling at the miracle of her

"You ought to sleep while you can, Mom," the nurse said.

"That's what I say, too," Nolan said, yawning.

"One more minute." Though every inch of Hannah's body hurt from the delivery, her aches and pains were secondary to the overwhelming joy of finally being a mother to such a sweet little girl.

Baby Callie. Her *daughter*. She was a *mom*! Had anything ever been more exciting than that?

"You need to rest, sweetheart," Nolan said.

"I'm too excited to sleep. All I want to do is look at her."

"I love seeing you so happy."

"I'm *so* happy. I feel like my heart is going to burst or something. Are you happy, too?"

"Hannah… How can you ask me that?"

"Just making sure."

He kissed the top of her head. "I was over the moon to have you, but having her, too, is just… It's everything. She's everything. *You* are everything."

"Thank you for her and for her name. That was the single-best idea you've ever had, and it'll make a lot of people very happy."

"I don't even remember having the idea, only that we needed to name the baby for Caleb, one way or the other."

"It's perfect. And it'll be even more perfect when Hunter gets home and can meet his new niece."

"How many times did he call today?"

"Three," Hannah said with a sheepish smile.

Nolan tugged on her hand. "Come on. Let's get you back to bed."

She took a long last look at her precious daughter and then let him lead her from the NICU.

He kept his arm around her as they walked back to Hannah's room. She was due to be discharged tomorrow, but the baby would be here for a while yet.

"Come sleep next to me," she said when she was settled in bed.

"You're so sore, babe. I'd be afraid I'd hurt you somehow."

"I can't sleep right without you next to me."

"All right, then."

He snuggled up to her, his leg slipping between hers and his hard cock pressing against her backside.

"Um, what's going on back there?"

"Same thing that always goes on when you're next to me. Do we really have to wait six more weeks?"

Hannah groaned at the thought of having sex any time soon. "I hope that's *all* it takes."

"I'm teasing. I still can't believe what you did in that delivery room. You amazed me."

"I couldn't have done it without you there with me."

"I didn't do anything."

"You certainly did, too. You kept me from giving up when it got too hard."

"You were the star. I was a supporting character."

"Whatever you say. I know the truth. And by the way, I'm going to want to have another one right away." Hannah surprised herself with that pronouncement and apparently him, too, because he went totally still behind her.

"Define 'right away.'"

"As soon as we can. We're already thirty-six. We got a late start, and I don't want Callie to grow up alone. I can't imagine life without my siblings."

"You're not considering having ten kids, by any chance, are you?"

"No! Oh my God. No way. Two would be perfect."

"I can do two."

"Excellent, so you'd be willing to knock me up again ASAP?"

"If I must," he said with a long-suffering sigh that made her giggle.

"You're a good sport."

"I do what I can for the people."

"*People?* What people?"

"You and only you, of course."

"Good answer." Hannah yawned, and her eyes closed.

"Sleep, Hannah. You're going to be needed again very soon."

"Mmm, I can't wait for her to wake up and need me."

CHAPTER 16

At the touch of love everyone becomes a poet.
—Plato

Emma woke to total darkness and cozy warmth that she quickly realized was coming from Grayson sleeping next to her. They'd fallen asleep. Again! Damn it! "Grayson." She nudged him. "Gray, wake up."

"Oh crap."

"Exactly. We've got to go."

"Not yet." His arm around her kept her from getting out of bed. "Five more minutes of this. Please?"

"It's really late."

"They're sound asleep and will never know what time you came home."

Knowing he was right, Emma forced herself to relax ever so slightly. She didn't want to go any more than he wanted to let her.

"If I could have anything I wanted, I'd want to keep you and Simone here with me."

His words were like a balm on the wound opening in her heart. "Thank you for telling me that."

"Would you even consider moving? Your sister is here. I'm here… I know it's crazy and too soon, but would you think about it? Simone loves it here."

"I know she does. I do, too." Emma sighed. "Our whole life is there, though."

"Lives can be moved."

"It's hard for me to explain how important my network is to me and to making it possible for Simone to do the things all the other kids do. Not to mention, my job, health insurance, my dad…"

"I know it all seems insurmountable right now, and under normal circumstances, I never would've brought it up so soon. But these aren't normal circumstances. We've found something here that I've never had with anyone else."

"I haven't either," she said softly.

"The thought of letting the two of you leave later today makes me feel sick."

"It makes me feel sick to think about leaving."

"I haven't done anything here that can't be undone, so I'm not opposed to moving to New York."

"You just left another city to move home. Your whole family is here."

"If I got to be with you, I'd move, Emma. I'm not just saying that."

Her eyes burned with tears. He made her want things she'd never thought she'd have, not in a million years. "Could we… maybe… take a little more time before we make any big decisions?"

"We can do whatever you want. I'm not going anywhere except to New York to see you next weekend."

"Next weekend?"

"If I make it that long."

Just that quickly, her sorrow turned to joy at knowing she would see him again—soon.

"I'll get a hotel. Don't worry. We'll keep it all on the up-and-up for Simone."

"Don't get a hotel. Stay with us. We'll make sure you're back on the sofa by the morning."

"Are you sure?"

"Yes!" She laughed. "I'm very, very sure."

"Are we being ridiculous for diving all-in to this so soon?"

"Probably."

"All I know is I'm way past the point in my life where I have any desire to play games."

"I never got to have that stage. I had to grow up awfully fast."

"I want to give you everything you've never had."

"Grayson…"

"Too much?"

"You're making my heart beat fast."

He laid his hand over her rapidly beating heart. "I've never made anyone's heart beat fast."

"Now you have." She covered his hand with hers. "We should go."

"I know," he said, but he made no move to let her go. Rather, he moved them so he was above her, gazing down at her with so much emotion that Emma couldn't process it all. Then he kissed her, making her forget about the late hour, her impending departure, the question he'd asked her and everything other than the pleasure she found in his arms.

He made slow, sweet, sexy love to her, as if they had all the time in the world rather than only a few hours before they would go their separate ways. For now, anyway.

She wished she could bottle the way he made her feel when he touched her. He loved her with unrestrained passion that he didn't try to hide or mask as anything other than exactly what it was. The raw emotion she saw in his expression touched her deeply and had her clinging to him when she came harder than she ever had before. He was right there with her, holding her tight against him as he lost himself in her. It was, without a doubt, one of the most beautiful moments she'd ever experienced.

His lips brushing her cheek made her aware of tears that she hadn't known were there. "Don't cry, sweet Emma. We're going to figure this out. Now that I've found you, I'm not letting you go."

With her arms around him, she held on tight to his assurances. "I have to get back to the Abbotts'."

"I know."

She felt his reluctance as he withdrew from her and helped her up. They took a hot shower together and got dressed in silence, the weight of the intense intimacy they'd shared hanging over them as they ventured into the predawn darkness. By then, it was after four o'clock, and Emma felt ridiculously guilty for staying out so late.

"I'm sure you're worried about offending my aunt and uncle, but after having raised ten children, there's literally nothing that surprises them anymore."

"I'd never want to take advantage of their hospitality."

"You haven't. Don't worry. They're super cool. They'd never think a thing of it. Besides, my uncle and grandfather have made it their mission in life to see us all married off. If that were to happen with us, they'd find a way to take full credit."

His use of the word *married* in relation to them did crazy things to her insides, which were already a jumbled mess of emotion after the night she'd spent with him.

"I'll pick up you and Simone around nine, okay?"

"Will that give us enough time to make a two o'clock flight in Burlington?"

"More than enough."

"You don't have to walk me in," Emma said after they pulled into the driveway at the barn. "Go get some sleep."

He raised his hand to her face and leaned across the console to kiss her. "I wish you could've stayed all night."

"Me, too."

"I'll see you soon." He kissed her one more time, lingering, letting her know he didn't want to let her go.

Emma pulled back, smiled at him and opened the door to an icy blast. She jogged the short distance to the mudroom door and ducked inside, feeling like the naughty teenager she'd once been, sneaking into her parents' home long after curfew. Thankfully, the dogs were upstairs with Linc and Molly and didn't hear her come in.

She stepped into the kitchen and came to an abrupt stop at the sight of Max, seated at the kitchen table, giving baby Caden a bottle, a gentle lullaby playing on Max's cell phone. "Oh, um… Hi, Max."

"Hey."

Emma's face burned with mortification. "I… um…"

"No worries," he said with a chuckle. "I won't tell Mom and Dad."

"This is so embarrassing."

"I trust you had a nice time with Grayson."

"Ahhh, yeah." Could a person actually expire from humiliation? "We had a nice time."

"He's a good guy. One of the best guys I know. He was very helpful to me after Caden was born."

"That's, um, good to know."

"Could I ask you something that's none of my business?"

"Sure," Emma said, wondering what was on his mind.

"When you first had Simone and knew you'd be raising her on your own, were you scared?"

Emma's heart went out to him as she took a seat at the table. "Terrified."

"I don't know if I can do it."

"Yes, you can. You absolutely can. You have this amazing family all around you. They'd do anything for you and Caden. You can do this, Max. Will it be easy? No. It'll be the hardest thing you ever do, but it'll also be the most rewarding. I didn't plan to have Simone when I did, but with hindsight, I wouldn't change a thing. She's the best thing to ever happen to me, and he will be for you, too. I know it."

"He is pretty great," Max said, gazing down at his son sleeping in his arms.

"You can't believe this now, but it'll go by so fast. He'll be almost ten before you know what happened. And another thing—he won't always be as needy as he is now. Before long, he'll be able to do a lot of things for himself, and you'll feel like you can breathe again."

"That's very helpful. Thank you."

"Any time. I'll give you my number. You call me any time you need to talk."

"That's really nice of you."

"I remember being right where you are, and I know how you feel. You're not alone in this. Caden is so lucky to have a dad who cares so much about getting it right."

"That's all I want—is to get it right and to make sure he has the best possible life."

"If those are your goals, you're already a wonderful dad."

"You really think so?"

His insecurity was so very endearing. "I know so." She picked up his cell phone from the table and added her number to his contacts. "You call me any time you need a single-parent friend. Okay?"

"I will. Thank you so much, Emma."

"Happy to help, and thanks for not ratting me out to Mom and Dad," she said with a wink.

"If you only knew the secrets I've kept in this house. You think it's easy being the youngest of ten?"

"You wear it well. I'm going to bed." She nodded to Caden. "Looks like you're good to go for a while, too. Sleep when he does."

"That's what everyone says."

"Night, Max."

"Night."

Emma crept up the stairs and peeked into Simone's room to check on her before going to her own room and closing the door, breathing a sigh of relief not to have encountered Molly or Lincoln.

As she got ready for bed, she thought about her conversation with Max as well as the night she'd spent with Grayson, the things he'd said, how he wished she and Simone could move to Vermont. It was funny how that never would've crossed her mind until she came for Christmas, met Colton's incredible cousin and had her orderly little world turned upside down.

She tiptoed across the hall to use the bathroom and brush her teeth, finally breathing easier when she was tucked into the comfortable bed in Hannah's old room. Sleep proved elusive, however, as she allowed herself to entertain the tempting fantasy that Grayson had suggested. They could move to Vermont. She could find another job here. The Abbotts and Colemans knew everyone. Surely they could help her find something. They would have Lucy back in their daily lives, along with Colton and his big family.

And they would have Grayson… The very thought of spending every day with him, having him act as a father to Simone, sleeping next to him every night and making sweet, sexy love with him whenever she wanted… Even after knowing him less than a week, she already knew she'd do anything to make that fantasy a reality.

But when she thought about her dad, alone in the city while both his daughters were six hours away, her fantasy crashed back to earth. She couldn't leave him. She *wouldn't* leave him. It would break his heart not to be able to see Simone any time he wanted and vice versa. Emma couldn't do that to either of them.

Her heart ached as the fantasy slipped out of reach. Not only did she have her dad to consider, but her job and the benefits it provided that gave her peace of mind, the support network that had taken years to cultivate… The life that had been lonely at times but mostly satisfying didn't look quite so satisfying post-Grayson Coleman.

She couldn't let that happen. She couldn't allow a few days with a sexy, wonderful man to color her perception of the life she'd worked so hard to build for herself and Simone.

Emma tossed and turned and tried to find a position that was anywhere near as comfortable as she'd been sleeping in Grayson's arms. At some point, she must've dozed off, because she woke to sunlight streaming through the window and realized she'd forgotten to draw the blinds during her early morning sneak-in. Tears pooled in her eyes that couldn't be blamed entirely on the ruthless glare of the sun.

Today they had to leave this magical place where they'd had such a wonderful Christmas break. Tomorrow, she had to go to work. The dentists she worked for held Saturday hours that were always booked solid. Simone had her friend's birthday party. They had to pick up a gift for the party, and she needed to hit the grocery store, too.

Reality had a nasty way of intruding on a lovely fantasy, reminding her that no matter how wonderful the visit to Vermont had been, it was time to go home.

CHAPTER 17

'Tis better to have loved and lost than never to have loved at all.
—Alfred Lord Tennyson

After returning to the apartment, Grayson didn't sleep for shit. His brain was a muddled mess of dilemmas, including Emma and Simone's pending departure, embarking on a long-distance relationship with Emma—at least for now—and the request his father had made of Grayson and his siblings.

And here he'd thought his biggest challenge this week was going to be securing office space for his new practice in Butler. Now he had no idea if he was going to practice in Vermont or make use of the New York license he'd gotten years ago so he could be with the woman who'd captured his heart in a few short days.

Grayson had no idea what to do. Nothing like this had ever happened to him before, and the next step wasn't at all clear to him, not like it had been only a few days ago.

At seven o'clock, he gave up on trying to sleep and took a shower, hoping to clear the cobwebs from his racing mind. He got dressed and headed out to the diner for some badly needed coffee. As he stepped into the brightly lit diner, he wasn't surprised to see his grandfather sitting at one of the tables reading the *Burlington Free Press*.

Elmer Stillman's face lit up with pleasure at the sight of his grandson.

"Mind if I join you?" Grayson asked.

"You know better than to ask me that. Sit your ass down." He signaled to Butch, who was running the diner in Megan's absence. "Can we get some coffee for my grandson, Butch?"

"Coming right up."

"Why is he so nice to you and cranky with everyone else?"

"I'm a silent partner," Elmer said, as if that was the most obvious thing in the world.

"Silent?" Grayson asked, brow raised in amazement.

"Megan and Hunter are in charge. I just do what I'm told." Grayson laughed. "That'll be the day."

"Enough about me. What brings you out so early looking like something the cat dragged in? What's wrong?"

For a second, Grayson thought about saying nothing was wrong, but his grandfather was far too perceptive to be lied to. "Emma and Simone are leaving today."

"Ahhh. I wondered if that was it. You've taken a shine to that girl."

"You could say that," Grayson said with a grunt of laughter. More like he was obsessed with her, but his grandfather didn't need to know that.

"It's about time," Elmer said with satisfaction.

Butch plunked a heavy mug full of coffee onto the table in front of Grayson. "You guys eating?"

"I'll have a full stack of pancakes with sausage," Elmer said.

"Make it a double," Grayson said.

"Coming right up."

"You're doing a good job running the place, Butch," Elmer said.

"Megan can get her ass back here any time now."

"Couple more days," Elmer said.

"Damned honeymoon."

They laughed at Butch's scowl as he stormed off.

"We need to find him a wife," Elmer said. "Then he'll be all for the damned honeymoon."

"Seriously."

"Enough about him. Tell me about you. What're you going to do about the lovely Emma and the absolutely adorable Simone?"

"They are rather lovely and adorable," Grayson said, smiling as he thought of them. "I'm going to New York next weekend to see them, and we'll go from there."

"If you feel something special for this woman, son, and I can already tell that you do, don't let her get away. You'll regret it for the rest of your life."

His grandfather's blunt statement struck Grayson square in the chest, leaving his heart aching. "I feel… almost desperate to hold on to her. I've never felt that before."

A big smile stretched across Elmer's face. "You're falling in love with her. If you haven't already fallen."

"That can't happen in four days."

Elmer laughed. "You don't think so? I'm here to tell you that I took one look at your grandmother, who was dating my cousin at the time, and saw my entire future laid out before me with her by my side. One look, Gray. That was all it took."

Grayson felt light-headed and despondent at realizing his grandfather was right. He was falling hard for her—and her daughter. But what did he do about it? "She has a life in the city that works for her and Simone, a support network, a job with insurance that she needs... Her dad is there."

"Okay..."

"What does that mean? Okay to what?"

"So she isn't willing to uproot a life that makes her feel safe and secure. The way I see it, you have two options—one, go there and be part of her safe, secure life in the city. Or offer her the same safety and security here, and see if it appeals to her."

"Why does it sound so simple coming from you when it's anything but to me?"

"Because it *is* simple, Grayson. You've found a woman and a little girl you could make a life with."

"It's too soon for talking about making a life together."

"Is it? You're thirty-six years old. If not now, when?"

"Is it normal to feel like you're having a heart attack when you realize you might be in love with someone you met a week ago?"

Elmer roared with laughter. "I assure you it's entirely normal. This is a *good* thing, the best thing that'll ever happen to you. No matter what, don't let her get away."

"The thought of her leaving today makes me sick."

"Make sure you tell her that. Don't let her leave without knowing you're serious about her—and her daughter. Including Simone will matter to her."

"Of course she's included. I think I fell for her the first time I ever talked to her and she told me I was silly for asking if she likes scotch." He smiled at the memory of her sassy comebacks.

"This makes me so very, very happy," Elmer said. "The only thing I've ever wanted for you kids is what I had with your grandmother. I'm kind of bummed that Linc and I might not get to nudge you in the right direction the way we have some of your cousins. You always were one to get things done on your own, although I suppose you didn't have much choice in that."

"Speaking of my father…"

Elmer's amiable expression hardened. "What about him?"

"Noah heard from him. It seems he has leukemia and needs a bone marrow transplant. None of his siblings were a match, so…"

"You gotta be freaking kidding me. He's got some kind of nerve thinking he can ask such a thing of the children he abandoned."

"It may be nervy, but he's asking just the same."

"You're under no obligation. None of you are."

"I know."

"You're going to do it anyway, aren't you?"

Grayson shrugged. "I can get tested and donate without ever having to see him. Why would I want to have to live with knowing I could've saved someone's life and didn't do it? Doesn't matter whose life it is."

"Doesn't it? Doesn't it matter tremendously?" After a pause, Elmer said, "You're a far better man than he is. You always have been."

"Thanks." Grayson smiled at him. "With you and Uncle Linc around, we never felt the void."

"Sure you did, but we filled in where we could."

"You were—and are—the most important man in my life. Don't discount your contributions, Gramps. They meant—and continue to mean—everything to us."

"Awww, for crap's sake. You're gonna make me cry."

"Don't do that."

Butch delivered their pancakes, and they passed the jug of maple syrup that came from the family's sugaring facility back and forth, liberally coating the pancakes and sausage.

"So good," Grayson said around a mouthful.

"There's no place like home."

"I would've totally agreed with you until a few days ago. Now, I'm not sure where home is."

"It's wherever she is. Figure it out, Grayson."

"I promised you guys I'd still handle the company account."

"You did that from Boston. You could also do it from New York."

"It'd be easier here, especially with the changes Uncle Linc is making in January with the catalog set to go into production, the website due to go live, the distribution center opening…"

"You can handle the legal end of it from anywhere. And by the way, why're you waiting for next weekend? What's stopping you from going home with her today?"

Grayson was struck dumb by the question. "Ahh, well… I don't know. Exactly."

Elmer cracked up laughing. "You suck at this."

"Thanks a lot," Grayson said dryly, amused as always by his irrepressible grandfather.

"I'll tell you what… If I could have even one more day with my Sarah… Hell, I'd be thrilled with one more *hour*… Nothing would stop me from doing whatever it took to have that. Not one damned thing."

"It's too soon. She'll think I've lost my mind."

"No, son, she'll be quite certain you've lost your heart. If she's as excited to have found you as you are to have found her, trust me, she won't be anything other than thrilled if you tell her you want to go back to New York with her and Simone."

"Is it too much too soon for Simone?"

"She's not your average nine-year-old, is she?"

"No, she's so far above average, she's right off the charts."

"If you show her and her mother nothing but love and respect, you won't have any problem whatsoever with Simone."

"I... I think... I have to go. I have to... I..."

Once again, Elmer laughed as he reached for the check Butch had left on the table. Elmer insisted on paying to eat at Megan's even though he owned the place. "I got this. You go get your girls."

Grayson stood and did something he hadn't done in years. He kissed his grandfather's lined cheek. "I love you. I love you so damned much."

Elmer's eyes filled. "Back atcha, boy," he said gruffly. "Right back atcha."

Fortified by the conversation with his grandfather, Grayson left the diner and jogged to his SUV, which he'd parked behind the family's store across the street. He had a plan to make and not a lot of time to do it.

His first stop was his mother's house, where he took a few minutes to shovel drifted snow off the back stairs before sprinkling salt on the icy patches and scraping the ice off the windows of her car. Then he went into the mudroom, kicked off his boots and stepped into the kitchen, where she was having coffee with the morning paper. "Morning."

"Morning." Her disapproval of his night out came through in the way she said that single word and made him feel like a teenager again. "Heard you shoveling out there. Thank you."

"No problem." Though he'd already consumed his daily dose of caffeine, he poured a cup of coffee and topped off hers. "I wanted to let you know I'm going to New York for a few days."

"With her?"

He didn't like that she referred to Emma as "her," but he chose not to say so. "Yes, with Emma."

"This is kind of sudden."

"Certainly is," he said with a chuckle.

"I'm surprised you would go chasing after a woman you just met. That's not like you."

"I know, but I'm still going."

"What about the new business you're starting here?"

"I'll be working from New York on some things for Uncle Linc and the store, and I have several other clients from the firm that have asked me to stay involved. I won't starve." He took a seat at the table, dreading the other thing he needed to tell her. "Noah heard from Dad."

His mother stared at him, unblinking. "And?"

"He's sick."

"With what?"

"Leukemia."

She still didn't blink. "What does he want?"

"Bone marrow."

Grayson watched as she connected the dots, finally blinking when her expression went from blank to furious in the span of second. "No. *Absolutely not*. He will *not* ask that of you or the others. I won't allow it."

"Mom, you have every right to feel the way you do. We all do. But I, for one, don't want his death on my conscience. If I can do this for him, then I will. It won't cost me anything other than some time."

"It's outrageous that he would even ask such a thing of you all. What about his siblings?"

"None of them are a match."

"I can't believe his audacity."

"He's desperate." Grayson shrugged. "I can't imagine it was easy for him to reach out to Noah."

"Easy for him," she said spitefully. "Who cares about him?"

"None of us do."

"Then why would you do something so huge for him? I don't understand you lately. I thought I knew you as well as I know anyone, but since you came home, you're like someone totally different."

"Because I met a woman who interests me and don't want my father's potential death weighing on me?"

"It wouldn't be your fault."

"It would be if there was something I could do to save him. I want nothing to do with him. That hasn't changed."

"It's not fair of him to ask this of any of you, but you in particular."

"It's a cheek swab. It's nothing. I'll do it and be done with it."

"Do the others know?"

"Noah was going to reach out to them."

"Why didn't he tell me?"

"I suspect he didn't want to upset you. We all know Dad is a hot button for you."

"You ought to stay single, Grayson. You're much better off."

"I know you believe that, and I get why you do, but I really like Emma a lot. I want to spend more time with her. I'm not making a lifetime commitment here, so you don't need to be worried."

"Of course I do. I never wanted to see any of my children go through what I did, and Noah already had it happen to him."

"We can't hide out in fear of heartbreak. I don't want to live like that, and it's not fair to ask us to."

"Not fair," she said with a huff. "Don't talk to me about what's 'fair,' Grayson."

Knowing he was fighting a losing battle, he got up, put his mug in the dishwasher and went upstairs to pack. He brought enough clothes to stay a week. After that, he'd either have to do some laundry or come home.

When he was packed, he logged on to his computer to book a ticket on the two o'clock flight to LaGuardia and took a quick scan of his email. He read a message from Noah about where they needed to go if they chose to be tested and wrote down the address of the clinic that was on the way to Burlington. A short time later, he went downstairs, carrying his suitcase and the backpack containing his laptop and ongoing-case files. "I'll call you," he said to his mother as he wrapped his scarf around his neck.

She nodded.

Grayson hated to leave with unusual tension between him and his mother, but he also refused to be talked out of going with Emma and Simone. He had nothing keeping in him in Butler at the moment and every good reason in the world to go to New York.

CHAPTER 18

Love is a hole in the heart.
—Ben Hecht

Emma moved through the motions of packing for herself and Simone, who'd woken grumpy and unusually out of sorts. Her elbow hurt, and that made everything difficult for both of them as Emma helped her through a shower, getting dressed and packing her belongings.

Molly came to the door to the room Simone had stayed in. "I could use some help bagging up the cookies I made yesterday, if anyone is interested."

"I'll help," Simone said, immediately cheered by the sight of someone other than her mother, especially if that someone was Molly, whom she adored. "If I can do it with one arm."

"Your one arm gives me one more than I'd have without you."

"Thanks, Molly," Emma said with a grateful smile. "We'll be out of your hair very soon."

She put an arm around Simone. "You're not in our hair. We're going to miss you girls."

"Can we come back sometime soon?" Simone asked.

As Emma said, "Simone!" Molly said, "Sure, any time."

"I'm trying to make her civilized," Emma said.

"She's very civilized," Molly said with a warm smile for Simone.

"Yeah, and she ought to know," Simone said. "She has ten kids."

"Many of whom are highly *un*civilized most of the time. I know civilized when I see it."

Emma and Simone laughed at that.

"Let's go bag up some treats for the plane," Molly said.

"Thank you," Emma said silently to Molly, who nodded. She'd probably overheard Simone being cranky and had come to the rescue.

Feeling like she was wading through hip-deep mud, Emma moved through the motions of getting dressed and finishing packing. She had zipped up Simone's suitcase and was working on her own when Lucy appeared at the door.

"Help has arrived," her sister said.

"You're about twenty minutes too late."

"I wish you guys didn't have to go," Lucy said, pouting as she stretched out on the bed Emma had stripped of sheets and recovered with the down comforter.

"So do I. Believe me."

"It's like that, is it?"

Emma sat on the bed next to her sister and rested her head on Lucy's shoulder. "Did it hurt this bad when you met Colton and had to leave him?"

"It hurt so bad any time we had to be apart. Still does. Have you talked about trying to keep it going?"

"He said he wished we could move here, and that he'll be coming to visit next Friday."

"That's so awesome, Em. He's totally into you."

"And vice versa. I feel like I've lost my mind or something, talking this way about a guy I hadn't said more than hello to a week ago."

"When it's right, it's right."

"Like you and Colton. Did you talk to him?"

"Not yet."

Surprised by Lucy's unprecedented reticence where Colton was concerned, Emma raised her head and looked her sister in the eye. "What's that about?" Lucy further surprised her when her eyes went shiny with tears. "Lucy! What's wrong?"

Lucy spun her engagement ring around on her finger. "I don't know what the hell is wrong with me. Why can't I bring this up with him? Why don't we ever, *ever* talk about actually getting married or anything beyond what's for dinner or when we're going to the city or... Logistics. We talk about logistics."

"Why is it that you don't feel you can talk to him about this?"

Lucy sighed. "We both agreed to our current arrangement. I worry that he'd think I was changing the rules on him, and he'd be right."

"You have to tell him this, Lucy! He'd want to know that you're unhappy."

"I'm not unhappy. He makes me so happy."

"You're ready for the next step. There's nothing wrong with letting him know that."

"What if he's not ready?"

"If you're wondering if he still wants you, the answer is yes. *Emphatically* yes. The guy never takes his eyes off you if you're in the room. The second you walk through the door, he's looking at you and only you."

"I've never noticed that."

"Well, I have, as recently as last night at Will and Cam's. He loves you, Luce. If something's bothering you, he'd want to know."

Lucy wiped away her tears. "It makes me feel stupid and weak to be crying over a guy."

Emma laughed. "You are anything but stupid or weak. You're in love with a great guy, and you want a life with him. There's nothing wrong with that."

"I have a life with him—a great life."

"Okay, so you want the next step. *Tell* him that. You know as well as I do that sometimes guys have to be led to where they want to go."

"What if he says he never wants to get married, that what we have now is working just fine for him?"

"He's not going to say that. If I know Colton at all, and I've come to know him pretty well, he'll hear that you're unhappy about something, and he'll want to fix it. Because he loves you that much."

Lucy sighed deeply.

"You'll talk to him?"

"Yeah, I guess."

"And you'll tell me what happens the minute you talk to him?"

"Yes," Lucy said, laughing. "I'll tell you."

"Have you said anything to Cam about this?"

Lucy shook her head. "I didn't want to put her in a weird spot with Will. If she told him, he might feel compelled to say something to Colton, and that'd be way too high school for me."

"You don't need anyone to do your dirty work for you with Colton. Has it occurred to you that he might be waiting for you to bring up the wedding? Maybe he's wondering the same thing you are—why doesn't Lucy seem to want to plan a wedding? Don't all women live to plan their wedding?"

"Hmm," Lucy said, "you may be right about that."

"Just put it out there, Luce. You love him. He loves you. It'll be fine."

"Thanks for listening."

"That's what sisters are for."

"Let's talk about you and that sexy Grayson Coleman."

"Mmm, he is some kind of sexy. My body feels like I've just taken up kickboxing after not working out in ten years."

Lucy snorted with laughter. "I love that kind of working out."

"Turns out I do, too. Who knew?"

"I'm so damned happy for you, Em. You've waited so long to find someone special."

"And when I finally do, he lives six hours from me."

"Try not to focus on the obstacles. I know it's hard not to. Believe me, I get how hard it is. Just focus on *him*. He's what matters."

"I'll try." Emma glanced at the bedside clock and saw it was five minutes until nine. "I need to get our stuff downstairs. Grayson will be here any minute."

Lucy hugged her. "Come back again soon. Promise?"

"I promise."

Feeling as if he'd run a marathon since he left the diner, Grayson arrived at the Abbotts' barn a few minutes before nine. He couldn't remember the last time he'd been more excited about anything than he was about surprising Emma with his plan. What if she didn't go for it?

"Don't be stupid," he muttered as he let himself into the mudroom. "She'll go for it." Though he was fairly confident that she would be excited, he wouldn't relax until he was sure.

In the kitchen, Max held Caden as he ate breakfast, Linc read the morning paper, and Molly was doing something with Simone, who smiled brightly at the sight of him.

"Want a cookie, Grayson?" she asked.

"I never say no to a cookie or a pretty girl."

Her smile did crazy things to his insides. She handed him a napkin containing two chocolate-chip cookies.

"Gray," Linc said. "A word in the study?"

"Sure." Eating one of the cookies, Grayson followed his uncle to the study he used as a home office. "What's up?"

"Mary called from the office. We've received a letter from a law firm in Burlington that's been retained by a former employee at the Christmas tree farm. Ed Sheehan was let go after he told Gavin, in a bar, that we wasted our time in Iraq and the two of them got into a fight over it."

Shocked, Grayson stared at his uncle. "Someone who worked for our family *actually said that* to Gavin of all people?"

"He did, and when Lucas found out about it, he fired him on the spot."

"Which is exactly what he should've done."

"Sheehan disagrees. He's retained an attorney, and he's looking for damages. Can you get the letter from Mary and see what you can do?"

"Absolutely. I'll start by talking to everyone involved, if you agree."

"Please do."

"Don't worry. I'll deal with it."

"Thank you."

"I should tell you I'm going to be working from New York this week and for the foreseeable future."

After a long pause, Linc said, "Is that right? I didn't realize you and Emma were to the point of making plans."

"We're not," Grayson said with a laugh. "Not even close. I haven't told her yet I'm going with them today."

"What brought this on?" Linc asked.

"A conversation with Gramps. He told me if I feel something special for her, which I definitely do, don't let her get away." Grayson shrugged. "So I'm not letting her get away. Had a go-round with my mother about it, but that's a whole other story."

"She doesn't want you to leave. You just got home."

"I understand that, but I need to do this. I have no idea what it is I'm even doing. I just know I have to go with her."

"For what it's worth, I agree with you and your grandfather."

"It's worth a lot, as you certainly know by now."

"I was supposed to spend a semester in England that I was so excited about, but I never made it there. You know why?"

Grayson shook his head.

"I met your aunt Molly the summer before when we were down South building houses for the needy. One week with her, and England didn't look quite so good to me anymore."

Grayson smiled at his uncle. "Thanks for telling me that. It makes me feel less certifiably insane for chasing after a woman I just met."

"You're not insane. In fact, I think you'd be insane *not* to chase after her. She's a sweetheart and so is her daughter."

"I've noticed."

"You've given a lot of yourself to your family and worked like a dog for that firm in Boston. If anyone has earned the right to focus on himself for a while, it's you, Gray. Go do what you want and don't worry about what anyone else thinks. You only get one life. You should live it the way you see fit, as long as you're not hurting others with what you're doing."

Moved by his uncle's heartfelt encouragement, Grayson said, "I'm only hurting my mother."

"She'll get over it. She's gotten over worse."

"I guess. So listen to this…" He told him about his father's illness and what he'd asked of his children.

"You gotta be kidding me."

"Wish I was."

"He's got some nerve."

"My mother said the same thing."

"She must be furious."

"That's one word for it."

"I'll tell Molly to call and check on her."

"I'd appreciate that. She wasn't too happy with me when I left."

"Because you're going to do it, right?" Linc asked. "You're going to be tested?"

"Like I told her, I don't want his death to be my fault in any way. I don't want to have to wonder for the rest of my life if I could've saved him, you know?"

"I do. I get it. I don't like it any more than you do, but I get it."

Grayson checked his watch and saw it was inching closer to nine. "We've got to get going to make the flight."

Lincoln extended his hand. "Have fun in New York."

"I will. Thanks." Grayson's throat closed around a lump of emotion. "For everything. You'll never know…"

Linc dropped his hand and hugged him. "I do know, and being there for you and your siblings has always been my pleasure."

On the verge of losing his composure, Gray nodded and ducked out of the study before he could embarrass himself. Emma was coming down the stairs with her suitcase and stopped short when she saw him there. His heart lurched at the sight of her, and he knew—he absolutely, positively *knew* in that one second of charged glances—he was doing the right thing going with her.

He went up the stairs to relieve her of the suitcase.

She smiled at him, and he noticed the sadness in her eyes.

"Are you okay?" he asked softly.

"No. I'm terrible."

He loved that she didn't tell him what she thought he wanted to hear, but rather laid out the truth. "I have a little surprise for you that I hope will make you feel less terrible."

"What kind of surprise?" she asked warily, as if life had conditioned her to fear surprises rather than relish them. He'd have to work on changing her expectations when it came to surprises.

"The kind I hope you'll be happy about."

"Are you going to tell me?"

"Mom! I need you! I can't get my sweater on."

Emma handed him the suitcase and turned to go back up the stairs, but the look she gave him over her shoulder told him she was dying to know what he'd been about to say.

Grayson smiled at her and then took the suitcase downstairs to wait, impatiently, for them to come down.

They appeared a few minutes later, Simone wearing a cardigan with her sling on over it.

"You don't need your coat for the car," Grayson said. "You'll be too hot on the ride."

"Keep it handy in case we stop anywhere, though," Emma added.

Lucy, Lincoln, Max and Molly, who was holding Caden, came to the mudroom to see them off with hugs and bags of cookies for the ride.

"Come back any time," Molly said when she hugged Emma and then Simone. "Our barn is your barn."

"We had the best time ever," Simone said.

"So did we," Linc said, tweaking the little girl's nose and making her giggle.

Simone gave Caden noisy kisses while Molly held him low enough for her to reach, and when Max kissed Emma's cheek and said, "Thanks for everything,"

Grayson knew a moment of pure jealousy at realizing she had formed a friendship with his younger cousin. Ridiculous. He wasn't a jealous sort of guy. Or he never had been before.

"I've got to get to work," Max said. "You're all set with him, Mom?"

"We'll be perfectly fine. Go on ahead."

Max went out as Elmer came in, bringing freezing air and drifting snow. "Glad I caught you," he said to Emma. "Wanted to say good-bye—for now—to you and Simone."

"That's so sweet of you, Mr. Stillman," Emma said.

"Call me Elmer. Please."

"Can I call you Elmer, too?" Simone asked.

"Of course you can." He bent to carefully hug her. "You take care of the crooked elbow, you hear?"

"I will. I can't wait to get to ski again. Can we come for February vacation, Mom?"

Emma laughed and rolled her eyes. "Let's get home from Christmas vacation before we start planning February. Thank you again, everyone. We'll never forget this week."

Lucy hugged them both at the same time. "I'll see you very soon. FaceTime me tonight, Simone."

"I will, Auntie Lu. You'll get sick of me FaceTiming you."

"Not possible." She hugged Simone again. "Safe travels."

"I'll text you when we get home," Emma said to her sister.

Grayson took their suitcase to the back of his car and stowed it next to his, smiling at the possibility of keeping his secret until they got to Burlington. Yes, in fact that was a brilliant idea. It would be so much better to tell her there, right when she thought they had to say good-bye.

CHAPTER 19

There is always some madness in love. But there is also always
some reason in madness.
—Friedrich Nietzsche

Grayson held the passenger doors for both "ladies" and waited
for them to get settled before closing the doors and going around
to the driver's side. When he got in the car, he said, "I have to
make a quick stop in town and then one more stop on the way to
Burlington, but I'll have you there in plenty of time. Don't worry."

"What were you going to tell me before?"

"It'll keep until we get there," he said, winking at her.

"Seriously?"

"Uh-huh."

"That's just mean."

Grayson smiled. He couldn't wait to tell her the surprise—and
he hoped she was as happy about it as he was. They pulled into the
parking lot behind the store. "Why don't you take Simone into
the store and let her pick out something from me for Christmas?"

Simone let out a happy squeal and had her seat belt off and
door open far faster than she should've been able to with one
working arm.

"That's not necessary, Grayson."

"Mom! Come on!"

"I didn't give her a present for Christmas. Simone, you can pick out whatever you want."

"No way! You can't give her carte blanche!"

"I just did."

"What is carte blanche?"

"It means," Grayson said before Emma could, "you can pick out whatever you want."

"Within reason," Emma added. "You have to be able to carry it on the plane."

"Well, that rules out a pony or a go-kart," Grayson said.

Simone giggled, and he lost his heart to that joyful sound.

He held out his hand to her. "Come on. I'll show you where the good stuff is, and you can pick something out while I run up to the office, okay?"

"Okay," she said, taking his hand. "Thank you, Grayson."

"You're very welcome."

He left them browsing the extensive toy department and dashed up the back stairs to the offices, eager to get back to them as soon as possible. It was ridiculous, really, how gone over the two of them he was. "Hi, Mary," he said to the family's longtime administrative assistant.

"Hey, Grayson. How's it going?"

"Very good. Uncle Linc told me you had the letter from Sheehan's lawyer."

"Right here." She handed him the packet. "Hope you can make that go away."

"That's the plan."

"I hear you're moving home. Your mom must be thrilled."

"She is. It's nice to be home, but I'm actually heading to New York for a week or so."

"That sounds fun. I'm hoping to get down there myself in the next few weeks."

"Have you been before?"

"Yes, I have," she said, blushing.

"To visit anyone we know?"

"A friend."

"A friend, huh? Does this friend happen to be related to my cousin Will's wife, Cameron?" Rumor had it that Mary was seeing Cameron's dad, Patrick Murphy, the billionaire businessman.

"Possibly," Mary said, blushing madly.

Grayson laughed. "All these New Yorkers invading our tranquil little town."

"I know! It's so wrong."

"Actually, it's feeling kind of right to me."

"I might've heard you've been hanging out with Emma."

"I forget how the information pipeline works in this town."

"It's more about how it works in your family."

Grayson laughed at that, knowing it was true. "I've gotta run to Burlington." He handed her a business card. "If you hear any more from Sheehan's attorney, let me know."

"I will, thank you. Have fun in New York, and Happy New Year."

"That's the plan, and same to you." Grayson waved and headed down the stairs, rejoining Emma and Simone at a huge display of doll clothes. "What's the verdict, Simone?"

She held up a dark blue gown on a tiny hanger. "I think this dress would look nice on Ashley. Do you?"

Grayson gave the dress a careful examination. "I agree. That color would complement her eyes."

Emma coughed, and when Grayson glanced at her, he saw that she was covering a laugh.

"Don't you agree, Emma?" he asked.

"Absolutely." She rubbed her hand over her lips, clearly trying not to lose it laughing.

"I would say she needs at least two more outfits to complete her wardrobe. What about this one?" He held up a suit with five different pieces as well as two pairs of shoes.

"I like that," Simone said, eyeing it carefully. "Are you sure? One is fine."

Could she be any sweeter? "I'm sure. Get that one and another one. Anything you want."

She took a careful survey of all the options before landing on a set of red plaid flannel pajamas with a matching red robe and fuzzy slippers. "How about this one?"

"A girl definitely needs PJs," Grayson said, taking note of the others she considered for future gifts. "Let's hit the register and then hit the road." He steered her toward the front of the store, with a side trip to the penny candy aisle to fill a small bag, before they checked out.

"Thank you so much," Simone said, holding her big green bag by the handles as they made their way to the car.

"You're very welcome. I can't wait to see how she looks in her new outfits."

He held the door for Simone and waited until she was settled before closing it.

"Thank you," Emma said softly. "She loved that."

"I did, too."

"It complements her eyes. Really?"

"It did!"

Her gaze dropped to his lips and then returned to his eyes. "You're too much."

"Nah, I'm just enough." He winked and waggled his brows. "We've got to go."

"I know, but I don't want to."

"It's going to be okay, Emma. Remember, I promised."

She nodded and got into the car, but when he got in, he noticed she had tears sliding down her cheeks. That was when he knew he couldn't keep his surprise from her any longer.

"Hey."

She looked over at him.

He raised his hand to her face and brushed away her tears. "I was thinking I might come with you guys, if you don't mind." To his great horror, Emma began to cry harder. "Emma, honey." He glanced at Simone, who also seemed on the verge of tears. This surprise was not going as he'd planned.

And then Emma released her seat belt and reached for him.

Grayson pulled her in as close as he could get her with the center console between them. "Shhh. I don't have to go if you don't want me to."

Emma shook her head. "I want you to," she said softly. "I can't believe you're actually coming with us."

"Only if it's okay with you guys." He looked to Simone, who nodded enthusiastically.

"It's more than okay." Right there, in front of her child, Emma kissed him square on the lips.

"Ewww," Simone said, covering her eyes.

"That's a relief," Grayson said. "For a second there, I thought I'd read this all wrong."

"You didn't. I can't believe this. I was so sad this morning to have to leave you here."

He felt breathless and off-kilter when he stared at her lovely face. "You know this is totally crazy, right?"

"Totally." She reached for his hand and held on tight. "The best kind of crazy."

Grayson looked into the backseat, where Simone was still hiding behind her hand. "It's safe to come out now."

She spread her fingers.

"Are you okay with me coming with you guys?"

"Will you stay with us?" she asked.

"If that's all right with you."

"Sure. That'll be fun. I can show you my room, and you can meet my friends."

"I'd love to meet your friends."

Emma squeezed his hand again.

He started the car and tried to focus on driving on the way out of town, but he stole frequent glances at Emma. More than once, he caught her looking at him, as if she still couldn't believe this was happening. He knew how she felt. He couldn't believe it either, but if this was crazy, he never wanted to be sane again.

He was coming home with them! Emma could barely contain the excitement that came from knowing they had more time together. She didn't have to leave him and go back to her "normal" life and be forced to pretend that nothing had changed when *everything* had.

The relief was so profound it left her feeling dizzy and off kilter. She held on to his hand and repeatedly looked over at him, trying to confirm he was real, that *this* was real. Emma had never experienced this kind of joyful excitement, except in relation to her daughter. But that was a different kind of excitement. This, with him, was something all new, something private and deeply personal.

The man who'd fathered Simone had been the only real "boyfriend" she'd ever had, and it was a stretch to call him a boyfriend or what they'd had a real relationship. Grayson was the first man she'd ever been seriously involved with, and she couldn't wait to show him their home, introduce him to their friends and spend more time with him.

Under normal circumstances, she'd never have introduced a new man to her daughter so soon. However, Simone had been a part of "them" from the beginning, acting as a matchmaker by encouraging Grayson to ask her to dance at Hunter's wedding. Simone liked him. He liked her. Was it too soon for the three of them to be acting like a little family? Absolutely, but she couldn't seem to find the wherewithal to take a step back from something that felt so damned good.

She glanced over at him again, and he caught her looking.

"What?" he asked.

Emma turned to check on Simone, who was listening to the music Lucy had put on the phone for her, earbuds in place, her gaze focused on the scenery. "Just doing a reality check."

"What do you mean?"

"Making sure you're real and you're really coming with us."

"I'm really coming, and this is as real as it gets, at least for me."

"For me, too," Emma said softly. "It's kind of scary."

"What is?"

"How fast it all happened." She ventured another look at him, and her gaze connected with his until he returned his attention to the road. There was no denying the powerful connection that zinged between them, and when he looked at her that way...

Her heart raced, and the surge of emotion was almost too much to process.

"I've decided that something that feels this good can't be treated lightly. I want to run with it, and I hope you'll run with me."

She raised her free hand to her chest. "My heart is racing."

"Mine, too, sweetheart."

"We're crazy. This is crazy. I don't do things like this."

"Neither do I," he said, smiling as he glanced over at her. "At least I never have before."

"What did your mom say about you coming to New York?"

"She was…"

"Less than thrilled?"

"That's one way of putting it, but please know that her issues have nothing at all to do with you. She doesn't even know you. If she did, she wouldn't have the first objection."

"I'm sorry if her concerns are taking something away from your happiness. I hate that for you, especially after all you've done for her over the years."

"It's sweet of you to say that, but I'm used to it. She's an unhappy person. Has been since my dad left."

"Does she know that he's resurfaced?"

"I told her this morning, which didn't help anything. She's furious."

"With good reason."

"Speaking of that," Grayson said as he signaled to exit the highway. "I have to make a quick stop to be tested. Should only take a minute."

Emma gave his hand a squeeze, wishing there was more she could do to support him in this situation with his father.

"Be right back," he said when he'd parked in front of a walk-in clinic, leaving the car running so they'd have heat.

Emma watched him go in the main doors and could see him speaking to a receptionist inside.

"Mom," Simone said from the backseat.

Emma turned to her.

"Is Grayson really coming back to New York with us?"

Emma nodded. "Are you sure that's okay with you?"

"Where is he going to sleep?"

"On the sofa."

"It's not very big, and he's kinda tall."

Emma didn't mention that Grayson would spend most of the nights in her bed. "He'll be fine." She was so damned thankful that they didn't have to say good-bye today. She wasn't anywhere near ready to leave him.

"I'm glad he's coming. It'll be fun."

"Yes, it will."

Ten minutes after he entered the clinic, Grayson emerged with a woman who Emma recognized as his sister Isabella. She followed him to the car. He got in and put down the driver's side window.

"I hear you're stealing my brother away for an extended vacation," Isabella said with a friendly smile.

"This is all his idea," Emma said, returning her smile. The woman they called Izzy was stunning, with curly auburn hair and striking green eyes.

"Have a good time."

"We will," Gray said. "Gotta run. We've got a plane to catch. Happy New Year."

"Same to you. Safe travels. Bye, Simone."

"Bye," Simone said from the backseat. When they were back on the highway, Simone said, "She's your sister, right?"

"That's right," Grayson said. "I also have Vanessa, Ally and Sarah and three brothers, Noah, Jackson and Henry."

"You're so lucky to have all those brothers and sisters. I wish I had one."

Emma sucked in a sharp deep breath. Simone had never said that before.

"Maybe someday you will," Grayson said to Simone, looking up to catch her gaze in the rearview mirror.

"Maybe."

Emma turned to say something to Simone, but she'd put her earbuds back in and was once again watching the world go by out the window. Emma turned back to face the front.

"I take it she hasn't said that before?"

"Never," Emma said softly. "I had no idea she felt that way."

He reached for her hand. "It's probably all the time with the Abbotts that made her see what it's like to have a lot of siblings around."

"Maybe."

"Hey," he said, meeting her gaze. "Don't let it bum you out. From what I can see, she lacks for none of the important things, thanks to her amazing mom, who makes sure she has the best of everything."

"I've tried."

"And you've succeeded. She's the nicest, sweetest little girl. You have so much to be proud of where she's concerned."

"Thank you. That means a lot to me. I got really lucky that she was a sweetheart from day one. She makes it easy. For now, anyway. I'm dreading the looming teenage years."

"She'll be fine. She doesn't have it in her to be a monster."

"Time will tell."

"What were you like as a teenager?"

"I was as rebellious as I could be given that my mom was sick for most of my teenage years. I got away with murder because they weren't really paying attention. That's how I ended up with a dirtbag boyfriend who treated me badly."

"I'm trying to picture you rebellious."

"I was quite feisty back then," she said, smiling at him. "Now I'm a very upstanding, responsible mother who leads a life of routine and predictability and is focused entirely on my child. Until recently, that is."

"What happened recently?" he asked with a teasing grin.

"I met this guy, you see, and he's got me doing all sorts of things I've never done before, and now he's running away with me and my daughter."

"You're sure it's okay if I come with you?"

"Yes, Grayson," she said with a soft laugh, "it's very okay."

"If it's too much for Simone, I can stay elsewhere. That's not a problem."

"She's glad you're coming."

"She is? How do you know?"

"She told me so when you were in the clinic."

"Oh," he said. "That's good. That's really good."

"I can't remember the last time I felt as happy as I do right now."

"I can't either." Grayson grasped her hand a little tighter and looked over at her with a fierce expression on his face that had her counting the hours until bedtime.

CHAPTER 20

If you find someone you love in your life, then hang on to that love.
—Princess Diana

After seeing off Emma and Simone, Lucy went to the office at the store to spend a few hours working with Cameron. With the store's long-awaited website due to go live on January first, they were running final tests, making sure any potential bugs had been addressed and generally being their usual anal-retentive selves when it came to launching a new site.

"This is the best work we've ever done," Lucy said when they took a break after two hours of intense concentration. If you'd told her in high school that anything would ever hold her attention for that long, she'd have said you were crazy. But she loved her work and found it easy to get lost in the details, despite battling attention deficit disorder. Cameron was the same way, and they'd bonded over their ADD as well as their love of technology.

"I don't know how I'll ever top this project," Cameron said. "Everything else will seem boring in comparison."

"This was a true labor of love for you, and that comes through in every page on this site. You'll have plenty to keep you busy managing it and adding to it when the catalog comes to fruition. Not to mention the sex toys," Lucy added with a dirty laugh.

Cameron rolled her eyes. "I can't wait to build those pages."

"What's the timeline for that product line?"

"Linc is aiming for March to roll it out, which means the staff training will happen in February. That ought to be interesting. All those grandmothers who work on the floor are going to get quite an education."

"Oh to be a fly on the wall." Lucy checked the time. "I'd better get back to the mountain to deal with the rest of our clients."

"How are things with the business? I've been so absorbed in this site that I haven't even asked. Worst ex-partner ever."

"Amazingly, we're making it work. Diana has been a godsend. She's fantastic at bringing in the new business and running the office while I'm here, and I'm doing a lot more of the hands-on development than I've done in years."

"Is that a good thing?"

"I love it. That's the reason we got into this business, and having the time to be creative and to just *breathe* is such a relief."

"I know what you mean. Sometimes I wonder how much longer I would've been able to keep up that pace in the city if I hadn't met Will and ended up here."

"And look at you now—married and thoroughly knocked up."

Cameron's smile stretched across her pretty face. "I was dying to tell you, but we'd agreed to wait a bit. I'm superstitious that way."

"Can't say I blame you, but passing out in front of the whole family messed with your plans."

"That was so embarrassing."

"The only thing that matters is that you're all right."

"I'm fine, but I'm staying away from sweaters and fireplaces for the next few months. The heat was what took me down."

Lucy stood and put on her coat. "Congratulations on the site launch, the marriage, the baby, all of it. Seeing you happy makes me happy."

"Never could've done it without your support of me moving. You made it easy for me."

"What're we going to do about Emma, who's gone stupid over Grayson this week?"

"I don't know. I was saying to Will last night that theirs is a much more complicated situation with Simone in the mix. Emma can't just up and move here, and he just left one city to move home for a simpler life. I don't envy them that dilemma."

"I suppose if it's meant to be, they'll figure it out the same way we did."

"I guess. Wouldn't it be something to have her and Simone here?"

"It would be fantastic, but can you picture what Troy would have to say about it?" Cameron asked of their close friend in New York.

Lucy grimaced. "Yeah, and it won't be pretty."

"I feel bad for him. I know how I'd feel if all you guys had moved and left me alone in the city."

"Very true. I'll check in tomorrow to see if you need anything for the launch."

"Thanks again for all the help."

"Always a pleasure to have the chance to work with you."

"Same here."

Lucy left the office and got into the four-wheel-drive SUV she'd bought to get around in Vermont and headed back up to the mountain where she lived with Colton. As she drove through town to the one-lane covered bridge and then past Hell's Peak Road, where the Abbotts lived in their big red barn, she thought about everything that'd happened in the months since she met Colton. She'd come to Vermont with Cameron to present the first cut of the website and had taken one look at the burly mountain man, and her entire life had changed for the better.

She, who'd never needed a man to make her feel whole, now needed him as much as she needed air and water and food to survive. He was everything to her, and the life they'd put together between Vermont and New York worked far better than she'd ever expected it to. For the next few months, Vermont would be home during the upcoming sugaring season that she couldn't wait to experience firsthand after hearing so much about it. This year, the season promised to be more intense than ever before due to the additional acreage the family had procured on the mountain, adding more than ten thousand new sap-producing trees to the twenty-five thousand they already had.

In April, they'd head to the city, where she'd meet with clients and he'd work on his side business of selling syrup to a wide array of gourmet shops in the city.

When she first met Colton and was faced with the enormous challenge of how to meld her city life with his mountain life, she never would've imagined the arrangement they'd ended up with. It was perfect for them, and things that had once seemed preposterous, such as the lack of indoor plumbing at his home on the mountain, now were routine. The cabin on the mountain was home to her as much as it was to him.

He'd brought color and adventure and laughter—*so much laughter*—to her staid and boring existence. A day without Colton would be like a day without chocolate, and that rarely happened. Emma was right. It was time for her to put her cards on the table with him and tell him what she wanted. She had nothing to fear from telling him the truth.

One thing in her life she was absolutely sure of was his love for her. He demonstrated that love in a thousand big and small ways every day, from the way he looked at her, to the way he cared for her, to the passionate way he made love to her every chance he got. She needed to have faith in him—and in what they'd built together—by being honest with him.

She drove up the winding road that led to home, noticing it had been sanded since she left and realizing Colton had probably done that with her in mind. In the driveway, she parked next to Max's Subaru. He'd started back to work today, part time for now, until he got Caden on a more reliable schedule. As Lucy approached the front porch of the cabin, Max emerged from the retail building.

"Hey," she called to him. "Have you seen Colton?"

"He's up on the hill. I'm heading up myself. Want me to deliver a message?"

"Just tell him I'm back. I'll see him later."

"Will do."

Lucy went into the retail building where they'd set up an office space for her and went straight to the woodstove to add more logs. Sarah and Elmer were asleep on their dog beds. She gave each of them a scratch behind the ears before she sat down to get some work done.

An hour later, she heard Colton's distinctive footsteps on the wooden stairs. In addition to Max, Colton had several other helpers who worked with him on the mountain, but after nearly a year with him, she could distinguish his footsteps from everyone else's.

And no one came crashing into a room the way Colton Abbott did.

Sarah and Elmer were jolted from a sound sleep and got up to greet him. Amused, Lucy spun around in her chair. "Hi, honey, you're home."

"Hey, babe. How'd the send-off go? You told them I had to work, right?"

"It went fine, and I did. They said they'll see you soon."

He unzipped the heavy coveralls he wore to work outside in the winter and removed the first of two insulated hats. "You okay?"

"Why wouldn't I be?"

"I know it's hard for you to see them go home."

"I'll see them when I go down for Simone's birthday."

"That's true. So what's going to happen with Emma and Grayson now?"

"I don't know, but she was pretty sad to be leaving him. They really hit it off."

Now down to jeans and a flannel shirt with another layer of thermal beneath it, Colton came over to press his cold lips against her neck. "We know how that can happen, don't we?"

Lucy jolted from the chill. "We certainly do." *There*, she thought. *He's given you an opening. Take it.* "Colton…"

"Hmm?" He wrapped his arms around her shoulders and leaned into her, surrounding her with the now-familiar scents of fresh air and wood smoke.

"Can we talk?"

"Any time you want."

"About something we never talk about but probably should?"

He looked down at her, hands resting on the arms of her chair. "What's on your mind, Luce?"

She looked up at the face she loved so much and swallowed hard. "Our wedding."

"What about it?"

"I'm just wondering if we're going to have one."

"Of course we are. We're engaged, aren't we?"

"Yes, we're engaged, but *when* are we getting *married*?"

"Whenever you want to. I'm ready when you are."

She stared at him, wondering if men truly were from Mars. "We have to plan a wedding."

"Or we can just get married. I don't need the big production if you don't."

"It doesn't have to be a big production, but I'm thinking something slightly better than town hall."

"Whatever you want, whenever you want. Let me know, and I'll be there."

"That's not how this works, Colton. We have to plan our wedding *together*."

"We do? Really?"

She tugged on a lock of his hair. "Really."

Without seeming to exert an ounce of effort, he lifted her out of the chair and brought her back down on his lap. Lucy let out an inelegant squeak at being hauled around like a sack of potatoes. "Quit doing that!"

"What?"

"Picking me up and moving me around like I'm a sofa pillow or something."

He snorted with laughter. "You're much more important to me than a sofa pillow, as you well know. How about you tell me about this wedding you envision and how we might make it happen?"

"If I could have anything I wanted..."

"You *can* have anything you want."

"What about a tent in your parents' yard in the spring after your season is over? Nothing too crazy. Just our families and closest friends?"

"That sounds good to me. You're sure you want to do it here and not in the city?"

"I'm sure. At some point over the last year, Butler has become home to me."

"*You* have become home to me. I'm at home wherever you are, and I absolutely hate the idea that you've been stressing out about whether or not we were actually going to get married."

"I haven't been doing that. Not really..."

He raised a brow. "No?"

"Well, kinda. We never talk about it, so I didn't know—"

He kissed her. "What didn't you know?"

"If you still wanted to."

"Lucy," he said on a long sigh. "How could you wonder that for even one second when you have to know that my whole world revolves around you?"

"I let my old insecurities take over, I guess."

"Don't do that. You don't have one single reason to be insecure in this relationship." Suddenly, he was standing up and heading for the door with her in his arms.

"Colton! What're you doing?"

"You'll see."

"You aren't going to dump me in a snowdrift, are you?"

"Would I do that to you?"

"Ummm..."

He laughed, knowing she was right to be concerned about the unexpected with him. Rather than drop her in a drift, he walked her across the wide expanse of yard between the store and their cabin, kicking open the door and then kicking it shut behind them. "Slide the lock," he said gruffly.

"What're you up to, mountain man?" Lucy asked as she pushed the lock they rarely used into place.

"Apparently, I need to show my woman that she has nothing to be insecure about."

"Colton, you don't have to—"

Again, he kissed the words right off her lips as he deposited her on the bed and came down on top of her.

Lucy curled her arms around his neck and her legs around his hips, wanting him as close as she could get him. When they'd first gotten together, she'd been under the mistaken assumption that the intensity of their relationship would wane over time. But the opposite had been true. The more time she spent with him, the more she craved him—his smile, his laughter, his earthiness, his scent and the wild, untamed way he loved her.

"Yes, I have to, Luce. I have to show you right now. I can't have you doubting me or our relationship."

"I don't doubt you or us."

"Then why didn't you just tell me you wanted to talk about the wedding?"

"I don't know, but whatever the reason, it was more about me than you."

"If something involving us is on your mind, it involves me, and I always want to know. I can't bear the thought of you worrying about whether I actually want to get married."

"You've hardly said a word about a wedding since we got engaged."

"Not because I don't want to marry you." He shook his head in obvious disbelief. "You're the one thing in this entire world I can't live without, Lucy. My only explanation for not mentioning our wedding is that I'm so damned happy with what we already have. I got comfortable and complacent, and I'm sorry if that hurt you."

"I feel like a jerk now."

His smile lit up his eyes. "You're not a jerk. Don't say mean things about my fiancée. She's everything to me." He kissed her once and then again, never taking his eyes off her face. "What do you think about the first weekend in May? We've never boiled past the thirtieth of April, so that ought to be safe."

"How about the second weekend in May so you have time to recover before the honeymoon?"

His eyebrows lifted. "Are you planning to wear me out on this so-called honeymoon?"

"You know it."

"Then I suppose it would be a good idea to give me a week to recover my stamina after the boil."

"And you can be away for a week or two after the wedding?"

"Uh-huh." He nuzzled her neck. "I'll leave Max in charge. It'll be fine." Rolling her earlobe between his teeth, he bit down and sent a charge of desire rippling through her body. "Where do you want to go on this honeymoon of ours?"

"Anywhere. I don't care. As long as it's just us for days and days and days on end."

"Don't forget the nights."

"Mmm, that, too."

"So second week of May," he said. "It's a date?"

"Yes, Colton, it's a date."

"Good, now let's get naked to celebrate."

Lucy laughed at his boyish glee as he said those words and started tugging at her clothes, which were removed with the impressive efficiency she'd become accustomed to. Usually he was all about driving her out of her mind before they got to the main event, but today he skipped all the preliminaries and entered her in one deep stroke that had her gasping from the impact.

"Ah *God*, Lucy…" Raising himself up on his elbows, he gazed down at her, brushing the hair back from her face. "Don't ever be afraid to talk to me about whatever is on your mind. Promise?"

"I promise. I'm sorry. I didn't mean to doubt you or us. I should've known everything would be okay."

"You have nothing at all to worry about where I'm concerned, Luce. You've owned me from the first day I met you and every day since. I love you so much. You have no idea."

"I think I do, and I love you just as much."

"We got this, Luce." He gathered her in even closer to him. "Don't ever doubt that."

With her hands on his face, she kissed him. "I won't."

CHAPTER 21

Love cures people—both the ones who give it and the ones who receive it.
—Karl A. Menninger

Grayson switched seats with another passenger so he could sit next to them on the plane. Emma sat in the middle, between him and Simone, who'd wanted the window seat. Since they'd driven to Vermont with Emma's dad, this was Simone's first-ever ride on a plane. She was all but vibrating with excitement and had asked a million questions about what to expect.

"Is this really happening?" Emma whispered to him as the plane taxied out for takeoff.

"It's really happening."

"I was so sad when I woke up this morning."

"And now?"

"Soooo not sad."

"Good. I don't want you to be sad about anything."

Emma leaned her head on his shoulder, and Grayson realized right in that moment that he felt more at home with her and Simone sitting together on an airplane than he had with anyone else since he left his mother's home to go to college. The powerful feeling of rightness that came from spending time with them was impossible to deny. He could only hope that feeling would continue when they returned to Emma's real life in the city. Would there be a place for him in that life? That remained to be seen.

Grayson enjoyed watching Simone's excitement as the plane roared down the runway and lifted into the sky, rocking and rolling a bit due to the gusty wind.

"Is it supposed to do that?" Simone asked, her brows knitted in concern.

"It's the wind," Grayson said. "Once we get up above the clouds, it'll be fine."

"How long will it take to get to New York?"

"About an hour and a half. It's a quick flight."

"I don't know if I like it," Simone said as the plane encountered more turbulence in the clouds.

"I don't think I like it either," Emma said.

Grayson extended hands to each of them. "Hold on to me until we get above the clouds where it will be a nice smooth sunny day." At least he hoped so. Both of them took him up on his offer, which had him leaning in close to Emma so he could reach Simone. After making sure Simone was captivated by the view outside the window, Grayson nuzzled Emma's neck and whispered in her ear, "Relax. It's all good. Just a few bumps on the climb out."

"I hate to fly. I haven't done it in years."

"I do it all the time, or at least I used to. I've done so many long-haul flights to Europe and Asia on behalf of clients. I won't miss that. There'll probably only be nice short flights from Vermont to New York in my future now."

She smiled at him and seemed to relax ever so slightly as the plane reached altitude and leveled off in smoother air.

Grayson ordered Bloody Marys for him and Emma and a Sprite for Simone.

"Mom never lets me get soda," she said after he'd gotten her what she said she wanted.

"Are you trying to get me in trouble?" he asked.

"Special occasion," Emma said. "Don't make a habit out of it. Either of you."

"Yes, ma'am," Grayson said with a pretend glower at Simone that made her giggle. God, she was so cute and so fun to be with. He wanted to spoil her rotten but knew Emma would never allow it. He'd have to choose his moments carefully. It was curious, at least to him, that he, who'd had heavy responsibility for his siblings at such a young age, was looking forward to spending more time with Simone. If you'd asked him a couple of weeks ago if he could picture himself involved with a single mom—and her daughter—he would've said no way.

Now, everything was different, and he was fine with that.

Simone had a million questions about how the plane stayed in the sky and why some clouds were big and puffy and others were wispy. He and Emma did what they could to answer her questions, but explaining aerodynamics and meteorology to a nine-year-old was complicated business.

All too soon, the plane began descending, which sparked more questions from Simone, who watched the flaps rise and fall on the wing with endless fascination. As the plane descended, Grayson explained what would happen when they landed to prepare Simone for the bump of the wheels touching down and the roar that would follow as the pilots slowed the plane.

She bounced with excitement as the city came into view in the distance. "This was the best trip ever, Mom. Can we do it again soon?"

"We'll see," Emma said.

"She always says that. 'We'll see.'"

"My mom used to say that, too," Grayson said. "It's a mom thing."

"I can hear you two," Emma said.

Grayson smiled at her and took hold of her hand again, needing that small connection to her after hours of trying to behave around her daughter.

The plane touched down with a thud and then the roar.

Simone's eyes went wide as the reverse thrusters roared. "*Whoa*," she said. "That was so cool."

"She has a need for speed," Emma said. "The crazier the cab driver, the happier she is."

"Thus her affection for skiing."

"And sledding," Simone added. "I liked that, too."

"We've created a winter monster," Grayson said.

"I *love* Vermont," Simone said, looking out the window at the activity on the tarmac. "It's so fun compared to here."

Emma's smile faded at that, only slightly, but Grayson noticed just the same. He noticed everything about her.

"New places are always more fun than home," he said, "but there's no place like home."

"I guess," Simone said.

They disembarked and walked through the airport on the way to baggage claim, Simone keeping up a steady stream of chatter about the trip, her plans for the weekend, the book report she needed to finish before school resumed next week and what they were having for dinner.

"We need to make an appointment to have that elbow looked at," Emma said.

"Aw, Mom, it's fine! I don't need a doctor."

"Yes, you do. We want to make sure it's healing properly so you don't have trouble with it later."

"Your mom is right," Grayson said. "You don't want an elbow that doesn't work the way it should."

Simone scowled, but she didn't argue the point.

Thank you, Emma mouthed silently.

He winked at her and went with Simone to get the bags off the belt. Within minutes, they were in the backseat of a cab on the way to Emma's apartment on the Lower East Side. Simone sat between them and pointed out landmarks to Grayson, who didn't tell her he'd been to New York many times. This time, he wanted to see the city through her eyes.

When the cab pulled up to Emma's building, Grayson ran his card through the credit card machine before Emma could do it.

"You don't have to pay for us," she said when the cab had departed.

"It's no biggie."

"Yes, it is."

"Let's have that argument later."

"Fine, but we *will* have it."

"I look forward to that," he said, patting her on the ass as he sent her up the stairs ahead of him.

She tossed him a saucy look over her shoulder that set his blood to boiling. How many hours until bedtime, he wondered. They lived on the second floor of a walk-up. Emma disengaged three locks to get them inside an apartment that was small but cozy. Right away, Grayson noticed that the place was all about the child who lived here. Her framed artwork adorned the walls, her dollhouse took up an entire corner of the living room, and her umbrella hung from a hook on the coat tree right inside the door.

"Make yourself at home," Emma said with a shy smile that made him want to kiss her so badly, he burned from the need.

"Grayson, come see my room!" Simone said as she took off down a short hallway.

"Yes, ma'am," he said, hanging his coat on the tree and following her into a bedroom with pink walls, a princess comforter, dolls, stuffed animals and other toys. "Wow, that's a whole lot of pink."

"I know! It's my favorite color."

"I can see that. Who are these ladies?" he asked, sitting on the bed next to several lifelike dolls.

"Those are the American Girls that Auntie Lu got me last Christmas. She says they're more expensive than college, but I think she's exaggerating."

"Possibly, but those are some rather amazing dolls."

"I know! See this one? She looks like me, doesn't she?"

"She certainly does. What's her name?"

"Valerie. She even has green eyes like mine."

"I see that. Will the clothes you bought at the store earlier fit her?"

"I think so. Let me go get them, and we can see." She bolted from the room, leaving Grayson sitting on a princess comforter with a doll named Valerie in his arms. His brothers and cousins would have had a field day with this if they'd seen him now.

"You're a trouper," Emma said from the doorway where she leaned against the doorframe, watching him.

"We're going to see if the new stuff we bought this morning fits Valerie."

"Don't let me interrupt."

"Yeah, Mom, we're really busy," Simone said when she returned with the bag from the store. "Can I take this stupid sling off? I can't dress Valerie with one hand."

"I can help," Grayson said. "I've dressed a few little girls in my time."

"I thought you didn't have kids."

"I don't. I have baby sisters."

"You can take it off for a little while," Emma said in response to Simone's question, "but don't overdo it."

She removed the sling and tossed it across the room. "I won't."

"And don't drive poor Grayson crazy. He just got here."

"He doesn't mind. Do you, Grayson?" She looked up at him with big green eyes full of trust and affection.

The most curious feeling struck him in that moment, something he could neither define nor explain. "I don't mind," he said gruffly.

Emma went through the motions of unpacking their suitcase while listening to the steady flow of chatter coming from Simone's bedroom. The last time she'd looked in there, Grayson had been stretched out on the floor while Simone dragged out everything she owned to show him.

He had the patience of a saint and was earning a permanent place in her daughter's loving heart whether he wanted to be there or not. The thought of Simone being hurt if their relationship didn't work out made her ache over something that hadn't even happened yet.

One of her New Year's resolutions was to try to live more in the moment and to not fear the future. Over the last ten years as a single mom, she'd learned that the future tends to take care of itself no matter how you try to affect the outcome. Her relationship with Grayson would work out or it wouldn't. Either way, she and Simone would be fine—or so she told herself.

Emma was folding laundry she hadn't gotten to before their trip when Grayson emerged from Simone's room after an hour. "You're so good with her," Emma said, smiling at him as he sat next to her on the sofa.

"She's fun to be with."

"I think so, too."

He took hold of her hand and brought it to his mouth, running his lips over her knuckles and setting off a wildfire inside her. How did he do that so easily? "Her mom is fun to be with, too."

Unnerved by her overwhelming desire for him, she said, "What do you feel like doing tonight?"

"What would you guys normally do?"

"Probably get takeout and watch *Frozen* for the two thousandth time."

"That sounds good to me."

"You don't want to go out?"

"I don't want you to feel like you have to entertain me. I'm totally happy to hang here with you guys and do nothing. Besides, don't you have to work tomorrow?"

"I do," she said, frowning. The first day back from vacation was always so depressing, especially after a vacation as great as this one had been.

"What's the plan for Simone tomorrow?"

"Her sitter is taking her to get a gift for her friend and delivering her to the birthday party. I'll pick her up there after work."

"Could I maybe do that?"

Emma stared at him, still trying to decide if he was for real or if she'd dreamed him.

"What? Too much too soon?"

"No," she said. "I just can't believe you're really here and offering to help with Simone and playing dolls with her for an hour and—"

He leaned across the pile of laundry to kiss her. "I'm here, and there's nowhere else in this world I'd rather be."

"You've got my heart doing backflips in my chest."

"That sounds uncomfortable."

"It's actually far more comfortable than you'd think."

Smiling, he kissed her again, seeming to pull back reluctantly. "Can I help fold?" He hooked a finger around a pair of her panties from the basket of clean clothes and lifted them for a closer look.

Emma grabbed them. "No, you may not help."

Grayson laughed. "You're no fun."

"Be a typical man and watch football or something, will you?" She handed him the remote.

"Don't mind if I do."

While she finished folding, he clicked through the channels until he found a college football bowl to watch.

Emma caught him taking surreptitious glances at her instead of watching the game. "Do you really want to help out with Simone tomorrow?"

"I really do, or I wouldn't have offered."

"Okay, then. I'll text the sitter."

"Anything I can do to help while I'm here, just let me know."

"You'll tell me if it gets to be too much for you?"

"It won't."

"Grayson…"

"*Emma*… It's fine. I like being with her."

She folded Simone's favorite fuzzy pink sweater and added it to her pile, which was twice the size of Emma's. "Could I ask you something?"

"Anything you want."

"Do you want kids of your own someday?"

"Depends."

"On?"

"Who their mother would be, for one thing. How far into the future we're talking, for another. I'm thirty-six. I don't want to be a senior citizen sending them off to college."

"That's a good point. You are getting kind of old."

"Hey!"

Emma dissolved into laughter. "Sorry, that was a softball."

"I had no idea you were so mean."

"I feel your pain. I'm going to be thirty in March."

"You feel my pain," he said with a scoff. "You're a baby compared to me. I'm probably way too old for a young girl like you."

"You're not too old. I was only kidding."

"I know, babe. What about you? Do you want more kids?"

"I used to when Simone was younger. For years, I half expected to meet a single dad and blend our families so she wouldn't have to grow up alone."

"No single dads in the play group?"

"None I wanted to date."

"Thank goodness for that," he said with a meaningful look. "I'd have hated to find out you had someone else."

"Me, too," she said softly.

"So more kids? Yes or no?"

"I don't know. I've already been a mom for ten years. If I have another one, I'll be bringing up kids for thirty years. That's a lot of years of parenthood."

"You wouldn't be doing it alone the next time."

There went her heart doing backflips again as his meaning registered with her. "True."

"Before I met you and Simone, I would've answered the kid question very differently."

"How would you have answered it?"

"I would've said my life was fine the way it was, and I didn't think kids were in the cards for me."

Emma licked lips suddenly gone dry. "And now?"

"The cards have dealt me a whole new hand to play, and anything is possible."

The way he looked at her, as if he could see everything with her, was unnerving to say the least. "Things like this…"

He picked up the piles of laundry and transferred them to the coffee table so he could move closer to her, putting his arm around her. "What, sweetheart?"

"This sort of thing doesn't happen to me."

With his finger on her chin, he compelled her to look at him. "It does now. You've turned my whole life upside down this week, Emma. I had a plan. And now… Now, I just want you—and Simone."

Emma leaned in to kiss him.

"I'm afraid we're going to get caught doing that," he said, glancing toward Simone's room.

"I don't think she'd mind. She likes you as much as I do."

"Maybe you should talk to her to make sure she doesn't mind before she catches us."

"I will."

"Mom! What's for dinner?" Simone came bounding into the room, stopping short at the sight of Grayson sitting close to her mom on the sofa.

"Come here, hon." Emma held out a hand to Simone and encouraged her to sit between them. When she was settled, Emma said, "I wanted to ask if you mind if Grayson is my boyfriend."

He grimaced playfully at the word *boyfriend*.

"You might see us holding hands and maybe kissing each other," Emma continued, her face heating with embarrassment. "Would that be okay with you?"

"Kissing is kind of gross."

"Well, no, not really," Emma said, noticing his attempt to withhold laughter. "It's actually very nice when you like the person you're kissing."

"What about germs?" Simone asked. "You're always telling me not to share drinks with my friends, but when you kiss someone, you get their germs."

Grayson shook with silent laughter.

He and Simone watched Emma expectantly as she tried to formulate a response.

"I, um, if you and the person you're kissing are both healthy, you don't need to worry about germs. Now go take a shower and make sure you actually wash your hair."

"Because I don't want to have germs."

"Exactly. Do you need help with your arm?"

"No, I can do it." She took off toward the bathroom, and Emma collapsed into the couch.

"That... was *awesome*," Grayson said, laughing out loud now.

Emma sighed dramatically. "She kills me."

"I love her. She's the best."

Glancing at him, she said, "I guess we're official now."

"I guess so." He gathered her into his embrace. "How about you share some of your germs with me?"

"I'd love to share my germs with you."

"If we're going to get all germy, we may as well really go for it," he said, running his tongue over her bottom lip.

"I couldn't agree more. Infect me."

He laughed as he kissed her with all the desire they'd been forced to contain during the long day of travel. Laughter turned to moans as they feasted on each other with the kind of ravenous hunger Emma had come to expect when they were together this way.

"God, you make me crazy," he whispered gruffly.

"Same." She ran her fingers through his hair and gazed up at him, drinking in every detail of his handsome face. She'd never get tired of looking at him, especially when he stared at her with such dazzled affection.

"How many hours until Simone's bedtime?" he asked.

"Three."

"I don't know if I'll make it."

"Me either."

He drew in a deep breath and appeared to be summoning patience as well as control.

"So dinner. Takeout is okay?"

"Whatever you want is fine with me."

"This has been the best day ever. Thank you for coming home with us."

"Thank you for having me."

Emma brought him in close enough to whisper in his ear, "I can't wait to have you."

CHAPTER 22

A loving heart is the truest wisdom.
—Charles Dickens

He was crazy about her, and then she said that and took him right over the edge into utter insanity. He'd never felt this way about any woman ever. He'd never wanted to spend every waking second with anyone before her, and he was counting the minutes until he could be alone with her.

They ate Italian from their favorite local restaurant and watched *Frozen*, listening to Simone sing every word of every song at the top of her lungs.

While Emma tucked Simone in after the movie, Grayson found himself humming "Let It Go" while he washed the popcorn bowl and tidied up the living room.

As Emma walked back into the room, the buzzer to the door sounded. "Wonder who that is at this hour." She went to the intercom.

"Hey, it's me," a male voice said. "I saw your lights on."

"Come on up." She buzzed him in. "My friend Troy," she said for Grayson's benefit. She opened the door and welcomed her handsome visitor with a big hug.

He returned her hug, lifting her right off her feet. "So glad you're back! It's been so boring around here this week."

Grayson watched the scene unfold with an uneasy feeling unfurling inside him. Who was this guy who was so familiar with her?

Troy put her down and came to a halt when he saw Grayson sitting on one of the barstools at the counter that divided her kitchen and living room. "Oh, sorry. I didn't know you had company."

"Come meet Grayson," Emma said. "Grayson Coleman, this is Troy Kennedy."

Grayson shook Troy's hand. "Nice to meet you." He took in the other man's dark hair and intense brown eyes, which quickly moved from him to Emma.

"You, too."

"Gray is Colton's cousin," Emma added, her cheeks flushing with color.

Troy looked at her and then at him before returning his incredulous gaze to her. "Not you, too! Emma! Are you *serious*?"

His heated words had Grayson standing to put a possessive arm around her.

"I can't even believe this," Troy said, hands in his hair as he spun around to head for the door.

"Troy! Wait. Let me explain!"

"What's there to explain? First Cameron, then Lucy and now you. I wish I knew what the hell was so special about these guys in Vermont." He pulled open the door.

Emma went after him, grabbing his arm. "Don't leave. Let's talk about it."

"What's there to talk about, Emma? Are you going to assure me that you're not going to move away, too? Remember how

Lucy was going to 'divide her time' between here and Vermont? We both know how that's worked out." He pulled his arm free of her grasp. "I gotta go before I say something that can't be unsaid—or unheard."

"Will you call me tomorrow?"

"Yeah, whatever." He went through the door and bounded down the stairs.

She closed the door, turned the locks and leaned her forehead against it. "Sorry about that."

"You don't need to apologize."

"I feel like I need to explain his reaction."

"Only if you want to."

"The four of us were like a little family, always together, until Cam left and then Lucy. He's afraid I'm going to go, too, and he'll be alone here."

"Did you... Were you guys ever..."

"No, we didn't date. Not really. We were each other's plus one a few times at weddings and other events, but there was never anything between us besides close friendship."

"He's a good-looking guy."

"Is he? I haven't noticed."

"Sure you haven't," he said with a chuckle.

"You don't have any need to be jealous of him or any other guy."

"That's good to know." He slid his arms around her waist and drew her in tight against him, hoping she could feel what her nearness did to him. "Is it bedtime yet?"

"We need to give her another half hour or so to make sure she's asleep."

Grayson walked backward to the sofa, bringing her with him. Emma surprised him when she snuggled into his lap.

He wrapped his arms around her, content to hold her close—for now, anyway. "This was fun tonight."

"This is my life."

"It's a nice life."

"I like it, but it's better with you here."

Her words touched him deeply. "I don't know if I can stand to wait another half hour to touch you the way I've been dying to all day." Because he was holding her so close, he felt the tremble that traveled through her.

"You can do it."

"I feel like I'm having the best dream of my entire life since I met you."

"I'm having the same dream," she said softly.

Grayson ran his fingers through her hair. "Are you upset about what Troy said?"

"Sort of. He's a very good friend, and he's had a hard time with everyone falling in love with guys in Vermont and leaving the city. I've felt the same way since Cam and Lucy left. It's been a huge adjustment."

"I'm sorry if I've made trouble for you with your friend."

"It's not your fault."

"Are you sure he's not interested in you as more than a friend?"

"Very sure. Cam and Lucy tried for years to make us into a couple, but I never thought of him that way. There's no spark between us. We're just friends."

"That spark makes all the difference, doesn't it?"

She smiled at him. "It certainly does."

"Has it been half an hour yet?"

"More like ten minutes."

"No way. That was totally thirty minutes."

"How about I check to see if Sleeping Beauty is actually asleep yet?"

"That's the best idea you've had all day."

She leaned in to kiss him, lingering long enough to get his hopes—among other things—up. "Hold that thought."

"Been holding that thought since you left my bed early this morning."

Grayson watched her walk away, noticing the way her jeans hugged her sweet ass and how her blonde hair reached her mid-back. He loved looking at her, watching her move and the loving but firm way she mothered her daughter. He loved talking to her, laughing with her, kissing her and making love with her. He loved everything about her.

"Holy shit," he whispered to himself as the earth-shattering realization registered all of a sudden. His grandfather was right. He was in love with her—completely and totally and absolutely in love. He wanted a million more days with her and Simone just like today, here or in Vermont, or in both places if that was what they wanted. His mind raced with scenarios and possibilities and plans, even as he told himself it was far too soon for any of these thoughts. The last thing he wanted to do when things were going so well was to freak her out by asking for too much too soon. *Patience* was the word of the day.

Emma returned to the living room a few minutes later. "Sleeping Beauty is out like a light. She's even snoring a little."

Grayson launched off the sofa and had her in his arms two seconds later, lifting her right off the floor to carry her toward the apartment's other bedroom.

"Tell me how you really feel," she said with a teasing grin.

"You're not ready to hear that."

"Says who?"

"Me." He put her down next to the bed and went to shut and lock the door. "What if she wakes up?"

"I'll hear her. My ears are calibrated to her, even through a closed door."

Grayson whipped the sweater up and over his head, tossing it aside on his way back to her. He put his hands on her hips and took a long, greedy look at her gorgeous face.

"What do you think I'm not ready to hear?" she asked.

"My true feelings about you—and Simone."

"I want to know."

He shook his head. "It's too soon."

"Grayson…"

Bending his head, he placed a series of kisses on her neck that had her leaning into him. He loved when she did that.

"Please tell me."

"You already know."

"No, I don't."

"Yes, you do, and if I say the words, it'll change things. It'll put pressure on you that you don't need right now, and I don't want to do that to you."

"You really feel that way about me? And Simone?"

"I really do."

Sighing, she closed her eyes and tightened her hold on him. "I do, too, and I keep asking myself how that's even possible."

"It happened that first night for me, when I talked to you about things I never talk to anyone about."

"That's when it happened for me, too." She pulled back to look up at him. "Are you happy about it?"

"So happy. What about you?"

"Very happy. I'd given up on anything like this ever happening to me."

He rested his forehead on hers, caught up in an emotional firestorm the likes of which he'd never experienced before. And then he kissed her with all the love he felt for her, even if he hadn't said the words. He wanted her to know how he felt.

They undressed each other slowly, reverently, both seeming to understand that the stakes had been raised in the last few minutes. Everything was suddenly more important, more fraught, more intense. Grayson pulled back the floral comforter for her and then followed her into bed, immediately reaching for her. Being in her arms felt like coming home, and he needed her the way he'd never allowed himself to need anyone.

He'd intended to go slow, to give her sweetness and tenderness, but the desire that had been on slow burn all day flared to life when she slid her leg between his and put her arms around him. Their lips came together in a burst of passion that had him clinging to her as he kissed her and cupped her breast.

She arched into him, letting him know she wanted the same thing he did—right now.

Grayson couldn't wait. He needed to be inside her immediately. "Emma," he said as he broke the kiss. "I want you so badly."

"I want you, too. Hurry."

Her urgent tone made him crazier for her than he already was. He took himself in hand and slid into her, gasping at the incredible feel of her tight, wet heat surrounding him. "God, that feels so good. *You* feel so good."

"Don't go slow, Grayson. Please don't go slow."

Her words were like gas on a simmering fire, igniting the kind of passion he wouldn't have thought himself capable of before her, before this. Never had he felt so transported during sex. But this wasn't just sex. It was far more than that, and having her soft body wrapped around his was becoming as necessary to him as oxygen. This was the kind of thing that came along once in a lifetime. This was the kind of thing people changed their lives to accommodate.

"Emma," he whispered, her name like an oath on his lips.

She clung to him, her fingers digging into the muscles on his back, her legs wrapped around his hips and her breasts pressed tight against his chest.

As he drove into her, surrounded by her, engrossed in her, it still wasn't enough. He wanted everything she had to give. He wanted to give her everything he had and then some. He wanted to hold her and kiss her and protect her and provide for her and Simone and maybe even have children of his own with her. And he'd known her a week.

"Talk to me, sweetheart," he whispered, his lips hovering just above hers. "Tell me how it feels."

"Amazing. Like nothing I've ever felt before."

"Same here." He withdrew from her, making her whimper from the sudden change of plan, and took her nipple into his mouth, sucking and teasing until it stood up tight and firm. Then he did the same to the other one before moving down to kiss her quivering belly.

"Gray…"

"Hmm?"

"What're you… Oh… Oh *God*…"

He slid his fingers into her and caressed her clit with his tongue.

She squirmed under him, trying to get closer and to move things along. "I… I can't…"

The nearly frantic tone of her voice spurred him on. He sucked her clit into his mouth and ran his tongue back and forth until he felt her inner muscles clamp down on his fingers.

All the air seemed to leave her body in one big exhale as she came, silently but forcefully.

Grayson moved quickly to trade his fingers for his cock and drove into her, triggering a second wave that was stronger than the first and took him with her in an explosive release that made him see stars and left him gasping for air in the aftermath. *Christ have mercy.*

He collapsed on top of her, and she welcomed him with her arms and legs wrapped tight around him, as if she couldn't bear to let him go, which was totally fine with him.

"Wow," she whispered after a long period of silence. Her heart beat so hard, he could feel it against his chest and against his lips, which covered the pulse point in her neck.

"Wow isn't a big enough word for that."

"I never knew it could be this way. It's like it gets better every time."

"It does get better every time."

"Don't let me forget to set my alarm. I can't believe I have to work tomorrow. The party is over."

"No, baby," he said, kissing her. "The party is just getting started."

CHAPTER 23

He who loves, flies, runs, and rejoices; he is free and nothing holds him back.
—Henri Matisse

Lincoln found his father-in-law right where he expected him to be on a Saturday morning—at the Green Mountain Diner with the *Burlington Free Press* spread out on the table and a cup of coffee in hand. He slid into the booth across from Elmer and smiled at his daughter-in-law Megan when she approached with a pot of coffee and another mug.

"Welcome home," he said. "How was the trip?"

"Amazing," she said, blushing ever so slightly. "We had a great time. Back to reality today."

"It's good to have you home safely."

"Thanks."

"Where's Hunter this morning?"

"At the hospital with Hannah. He went there first thing." She poured his coffee. "Have you heard anything about how the baby is doing today?"

"Same," Lincoln said. "Holding her own, but she's going to be in the NICU until she gains some weight and her lungs get stronger."

"But they think she's going to make it, right?"

"The prognosis is good. Yes."

"Thank God. We've been so worried. Hunter was climbing the walls wanting to get home. I suggested we cut the trip short, but he didn't want to do that. It was hard for him to be away from Hannah when she was going through this."

"I'm sure it was. The two of them are thicker than thieves."

"Do you want breakfast?"

"Maybe in a little while."

"I'll be back to check on you guys."

"That's one happy gal," Elmer said when Megan had moved on to the next table.

"It's nice to see. She sure does make Hunter happy." Lincoln took a sip of his coffee and then dove into the reason he'd sought out Elmer this morning. "I got a call from Mary earlier."

"Mary from the office?"

"The one and only."

"Everything okay?"

"Everything seems great with her, but she gave me her notice."

"What? She's worked for us for decades. Where's she going?"

"Apparently, she's relocating."

"To where?"

"She didn't say, but I suspect it has something to do with Patrick Murphy. They danced together for hours at Will and Cameron's wedding, and she drove him home afterward, even though he could've come with us. She's never mentioned him again, not to me anyway, but he asked to use the house in Burlington a couple of months ago, and she's taken a few more days off than usual. He was here for the wedding and Christmas, but he didn't stay with Will and Cam."

"Is that right? Well, good for her—and for Patrick. He'd be a lucky man to have her in his life."

"I agree, but I'm sad to lose her in the office. She's the glue that holds us all together."

"True. I'd sure like to know how that romance transpired."

"You and me both. She hasn't said a word about it to any of us, and we don't know for sure that it has anything to do with Patrick. I'm only speculating."

"But you're going to find out?"

"Of course I am," Linc said, sounding offended that he'd even ask. "Anyway, after Mary called, I had an idea I wanted to run by you."

"What's that?"

"Emma Mulvaney."

"What about her?"

"Did you know she's the office manager for dentists in the city?"

"I didn't know that."

"Well, she certainly has the skills we need. I'm thinking about offering her the job."

Elmer stared at him, unblinking. "You're serious?"

"Dead serious. Grayson doesn't want to relocate to New York. He wants to be here, but now that he's met Emma, he wants to be where she is. I thought this might simplify things for them."

"Have you talked to him about this idea of yours?"

"Nope."

"Are you planning to?"

"Nope. I'm planning to talk to *her* about it. All I can do is offer the job. The rest is up to her."

"That's kind of a big bomb you'd be dropping on her."

"I prefer to see it as a nice opportunity, and there's no obligation for her to take the job."

"Hmm," Elmer said, rubbing at the white whiskers on his chin.

"You don't seem too excited about this brilliant idea of mine."

"I'm actually thinking about Ray being all alone in New York if Emma moves here. I mean, Lucy gets down to the city, but she's spending more time than ever here."

"Maybe he'll come, too."

"You're getting awfully full of your own self with this grand plan," Elmer said.

"Right… Like you're not full of your own self and fat with your own matchmaking success."

"Who you calling fat?"

Lincoln snorted with laughter. "Admit it. This is a *good* idea. You're just mad you didn't have it first."

"It's not a *bad* idea—and how could I have had it first when I didn't know Mary was leaving?"

"If this works, it counts in my column."

"That's fine. I'm still way ahead, and thinking about my next plan of attack."

"Who've you got your eye on?"

"I'll be keeping that to myself for the time being. I'll let you know when the time is right."

"Is that how it's going to be now?"

Megan returned to refill their coffee cups. "Are you two fighting?"

"Nah, we're bickering," Elmer said. "Big difference."

Lincoln laughed right along with Megan. "I'm going to skip breakfast today, sweetheart. I've got an important call to make."

He sent a meaningful look Elmer's way before he got up to leave the diner. On the way out, he gave his new daughter-in-law a kiss on the cheek. "Good to have you home."

"Good to be back."

Hunter stared down at his new baby niece, who had an array of wires and monitors attached to her tiny body. He could see her heart beating frantically in her chest and the outline of blue veins in paper-thin skin. But her face, dear God, her face was so lovely and angelic, with her mother's fine features. "She's absolutely stunning, Han," he said to his sister, who stood at his side gazing down at her daughter. The doctor had told Hannah that immediate family could visit one or two at a time, but everyone had to wear protective clothing.

"Isn't she?"

"Never seen a prettier baby in my entire life. I'm sorry I wasn't here when everything happened."

"Don't be sorry. You called, and it helped to hear your voice. You were where you needed to be, with your new wife."

"It must've been scary to have her arrive so early."

"It was terrifying. We're just thankful that she's going to be okay. It'll take some time, but we've got all the time in the world to give her."

"I absolutely love her name. What an amazing tribute to Caleb. He'd be so proud of you."

"You really think so?"

Hunter slid his arm around his twin's shoulders. "I know so. You've been so strong and courageous through everything, and now you have a new family with Nolan. No one would be happier for you than Caleb."

"I hope so. Sometimes I wish I hadn't been such a holdout on having kids with him. I said I was waiting for him to finish growing up. I didn't know he'd never get the chance."

"He wasn't ready to be a dad yet. He was still sowing his wild oats. You were right to wait."

"Still, it would be nice to have something of him left behind in a child or two."

"Yeah, it would, but imagine what a handful his kids would've been."

Hannah laughed at that. "I used to have nightmares about procreating with him."

"He would've been a great dad."

"Yeah, he would've." She nudged him with her elbow. "So how was Bermuda?"

"Terrible," he said with a dirty grin. "We hated everything about it."

"Sure you did," she said with a laugh. "I can see married life is agreeing with you."

"Best thing I ever did. I can't believe I get to keep her forever."

She leaned her head on his shoulder. "Happy for you."

He put his arm around her. "Happy for you, too."

Nolan came into the NICU, his hair damp from a shower, his eyes red from exhaustion, and a joyful smile on his face. "Hey," he said to Hunter. "Welcome back."

"Thanks. You guys like to keep things interesting when I'm out of town."

"Not on purpose, that's for sure." Nolan bent for a closer look at his daughter. "How's she doing?"

"The doctor was here a little while ago," Hannah told him, "and said she's doing great."

"Thank goodness."

No kidding, Hunter thought. When he got the call from his mother that the baby had arrived eight weeks early, he'd nearly had a heart attack from the fear of something happening to the child Hannah had wanted so desperately. He'd been frantic with worry about what would become of her if the baby didn't make it. Thank God little Callie was as strong as her mother.

"You'll be her godfather, right?" Hannah asked him.

"Of course I will. I'd be honored."

She glanced at Nolan. "We'd like to ask Megan to be her godmother. Do you think she'd be okay with that?"

"She'd be thrilled, Han. Thank you. That's so sweet of you guys."

"We picked the best people for the job."

"She was so mad that she had to go to work while I got to come see baby Callie."

"Bring her by tonight after work."

"I will."

A nurse came in to let then know that Amelia and Bob Guthrie were asking for them.

Hunter kissed Hannah's forehead. "I'll go so they can come in, but I'll be back later."

"Thanks for coming, and I'm so glad you're home safe."

"Good to be home, and I'm so happy to meet my niece. Great job, Mom and Dad."

"It was *all* Mom," Nolan said.

"Not all," Hannah said with a saucy smile for her husband.

"And with that, I'm outta here." Hunter hugged Amelia and Bob as he left, pulling off the special gown and shoe covers he'd been required to wear inside the NICU and heading for the exit, excited for Hannah to ask Megan to be the baby's godmother. He knew how much that would mean to his wife.

Hannah hugged Bob and Amelia and stepped aside so they could take a closer look at baby Callie.

"Oh, Hannah, she's simply *gorgeous*," Amelia said, sniffling as she gazed down upon the baby.

"She sure is," Bob agreed. "And we love the name Callie."

Once again, Hannah looked to her husband, smiling with anticipation. She'd asked her mom to tell the Guthries only the baby's nickname, so she could tell them the rest herself.

"Her actual name is Caleb Abbott Roberts," Hannah said. "Callie is her nickname."

"Oh," Amelia said, seeming momentarily stunned. "Hannah... Oh my goodness."

"It was Nolan's idea."

His arm came around her shoulders, always right there to support her no matter what.

"What a beautiful tribute that is," Bob said gruffly, blinking back tears. "You honor us by honoring him. Both of you."

"We hope you know," Nolan said haltingly, "that even as we move forward together and start our family, we never forget him. Not for a minute."

"We know that," Amelia said. "We've always known that."

"Callie is going to be so lucky to have you as her grandparents," Hannah said.

"We couldn't be more delighted to have her as our granddaughter," Bob said. "And you, Hannah, as our daughter."

She hugged them both and accepted a tissue from Nolan to wipe tears from her face. Unlike the grief-stricken tears of the past, these were tears of joy for the second chance she'd been given with her new husband and daughter.

Emma's alarm going off at six in the morning was an unwelcome shock to her system. She had absolutely no desire to leave the warmth of Grayson's arms to go to work, but she'd already had a week off. Besides, the office was open only until two, and the day would fly by because Saturdays were always extra busy.

She tried to slide free of Gray's heavy arm, but he tightened his grip on her. "You've got to let me go."

"Don't wanna."

"Just for a few hours."

"All right. If I have to."

Emma sat up and turned to look at him. "You're absolutely sure you don't mind having Simone today?"

"I'm a thousand percent sure. She knows where we need to be, right?"

Emma nodded. "And she can get you around on the subway, too."

"Why am I not surprised?" He took her hand and gave it a squeeze. "Don't worry about anything. I'll take good care of her."

"I'm not worried. Just don't spoil her rotten and undo ten years of my hard work in one day, you got me?"

"I'll do my best to resist the temptation to spoil her rotten."

Emma leaned in and kissed him. "Thank you."

While she was in the shower, he relocated to the sofa so Simone would find him there rather than in her mother's bed when she woke up. Wearing the scrubs that were her work uniform, Emma emerged from her bedroom to the smell of coffee percolating. *So this is what it would be like*, she thought, *to have a partner in life and parenthood.* They say you don't miss what you've never had, and she'd made it all work somehow. But having him here made everything so much better, especially when he got up at six o'clock on a Saturday morning to make her coffee.

"This earns you huge, *huge* points," she said as she accepted a travel mug from him.

He put his hands on her hips and took a good long look at her. "I'm digging the scrubs, babe. Sexiest office manager I've ever met."

"Right," she said, laughing.

"I mean it." He gathered her in close to him and held on tight for a long moment. "How do I go about redeeming these points I've earned with the coffee?"

"I'll tell you later."

"I'll look forward to that all day."

She looked up at him, studying his handsome face and wondering once again if it was possible for a life to change so completely in the span of one monumental week.

"What're you thinking right now?"

"Still thinking I should pinch myself to make sure this is real."

"I'd be happy to pinch you any time. Everything about this is real, especially the way I feel about you."

"And how is that?"

"That's a longer conversation than we have time for now."

She whimpered. "So not fair to send me off to work with these questions."

"I'll make it up to you later."

"I'll hold you to it." She kissed him. "I really have to go."

"Okay."

Emma stepped reluctantly out of his embrace and grabbed the lunch she'd made the night before from the fridge. Back to her same old boring routine, but with a twist. When she got home, Grayson Coleman would be waiting for her, and there was absolutely nothing boring or routine about him.

CHAPTER 24

There is no remedy for love but to love more.
—Henry David Thoreau

Grayson never did go back to sleep and was watching the news when Simone emerged from her room at around eight o'clock. She wore flannel pajamas that had little pink flowers on them. With her hair a mass of red spun silk around her head and her cheeks flushed from sleep, she was even more adorable than usual. Then he noticed she was holding her sore elbow at an awkward angle.

"Morning."

"Morning."

"How's the elbow this morning?"

"I think I slept wrong on it or something. It's stuck."

He grimaced. "Ouch. How about some breakfast so you can take a pain pill?"

"That sounds good."

"What do you like to eat?"

"Cereal or whatever."

"How about pancakes? You like them?"

"I love them."

"You're in luck. I'm a master pancake maker."

They went into the kitchen, and she told him where to find everything he needed to make the pancakes.

"I'm glad your new uncle keeps you guys in the good stuff from Vermont," Grayson said when he broke open a new jug of Colton's syrup that he found in the pantry.

"He sends us a jug a month," Simone said. "We love it."

"There's nothing like the real thing." While he kept watch over the griddle, he said, "Tell me about this birthday party today. What's the plan?"

She told him about the party planned for her friend Talia at a pizza place that also had indoor games.

"Your mom left some money for a gift. Where should we go?"

Simone's green eyes sparkled when she said, "Can we go to American Girl?"

"Wherever you want." He couldn't miss the somewhat guilty look that crossed her expressive face. "What?"

"Mommy would say there's no need to go all the way uptown when we have stores right around here where we could get something."

"Hmm. Well, would your mom be mad if we went there?"

"No, but she'd tell me I took advantage of you."

Grayson laughed, because how could he not? "If I know you're taking advantage and I don't mind, would that be okay?"

She thought about that for a long moment. "I suppose she couldn't be mad at me for that."

"Then that's what we'll do."

"Really?"

"Sure, why not?" He served up the pancakes, with butter and syrup. "You need help cutting?"

"I can do it, but thanks."

Grayson leaned against the counter while a second batch of pancakes cooked. "Let me ask you something else."

"Sure."

"The night we met, you told me that your mom loves to dance but never gets to."

"'Cuz of me," she said matter-of-factly.

"She would say that she'd much rather be with you."

Simone shrugged. "I guess."

"So where does she like to dance?"

"I'm not sure, but I could ask Auntie Lu."

"That would be great. And if I wanted to take her out tonight, do you think your grandpa would be willing to stay with you?"

"I bet he would. He likes when I sleep over. He says it's more fun when I'm there."

"I have no doubt about that."

"You do know it's New Year's Eve, right? And that's kind of a big night in New York."

"So what you're basically saying is I won't be able to take her anywhere tonight because I didn't plan it out months in advance."

"Possibly."

"Hmmm."

"Do you need to go somewhere to dance with her?"

"Not necessarily."

"You could get her favorite dinner from the Thai place down the block and dance right here."

"That's true. I suppose we could, but I wanted to do something special for her."

"My mom doesn't like to go out when it's crazy in the city. She says the crowds make her ragey."

"That's some really good info. Thanks for letting me know."

"You want me to ask Pop if I can sleep over?"

Endlessly amused by her, he said, "Are you really only nine, or are you actually nineteen?"

"Mom says I'm an old soul."

Grayson nearly choked on a mouthful of coffee. "I can definitely see why. And yes, if you think your Pop wouldn't mind."

"He won't." She finished her pancakes, took the pain pill he gave her and loaded her plate into the dishwasher before running off to get dressed while he finished his own breakfast and cleaned up the kitchen.

He poked his head into her room where she was sitting among her doll collection. "I'm going to grab a shower and then we can go, okay?"

"Yep."

Before he showered, he called up the American Girl store on his phone to see what he was getting himself into. Clicking around on the site, he noticed the café, made a reservation for lunch and hoped she would like the surprise. One of the things he enjoyed the most about both Emma and Simone was they were easy to please—and fun to surprise.

When they were ready to go, Grayson helped her put on the sling over her coat. "How's it feel?"

"Better than it did when I woke up. Mom says I have to go to the ortho... ortho..."

"Orthopedic doctor?"

"Yeah, that, on Tuesday." She looked up at him. "Will it hurt?"

"Nah. They'll look at the X-rays and see how it's healing. Your mom is being thorough to make sure there's no permanent damage. Everyone needs two working elbows."

"I just want to know when I can ski again. That was so fun."

Outside the apartment, Grayson hailed a cab.

"Cabs are too expensive," Simone said. "We can take the subway."

"I don't get to spend much time here, and I want to see the sights. How about we make an exception this one time?"

"Okay."

He held the door for her, and she went in ahead of him. She kept up a steady stream of chatter as they made their way uptown, pointing out various landmarks along the way, including the New York City Public Library, which was one of her favorite places to visit.

The American Girl store was mobbed with little girls bursting with excitement. His biggest fear was losing track of Simone in the crowd, so he kept his hand on her shoulder as she led him through a sea of pink frills and lifelike dolls and every conceivable accessory.

She spent a full hour contemplating the dizzying array of gift possibilities for her friend, who had received a new doll for Christmas. "Sorry," she said. "I'm taking way too long. Mom would be losing it by now."

"I don't mind. We've got until two to get you to the party."

She looked up at him, seemingly prepared to say something that she apparently thought better of.

He nudged her. "What?"

"You're just really nice."

Touched by the compliment, he said, "You're pretty nice yourself."

"You like my mom."

"I like her a lot."

Simone bit her lip.

"Whatever you want to say to me is fine, Simone. I hope we can be friends."

"We already are."

"I'm glad you think so."

"It's just my mom… She's really special, and she does a lot for me. I just… I wouldn't want…"

Around them, chaos ruled with delighted young girls and harried parents, but everything else faded away except her. He bent to bring his face down to her level. "I'm going to try my very hardest not to do anything to ever hurt her, if that's what you're worried about."

"That's good," she said, sounding relieved. "I want her to be happy."

"So do I." After the incredible week they'd spent together, that had become his top priority.

"Are you going to move here?"

Leave it to a perceptive nine-year-old to cut right to the chase. "I don't know yet. Your mom and I are still figuring it out."

She thought about that for a minute. "She smiles a lot when you're around."

"Does she?"

Simone nodded.

"I'm glad to hear that, and I'll do everything I can to make sure she has lots of good reasons to smile."

"Okay." Seeming pacified, for now anyway, Simone went back to shopping and finally made a decision on a dress for her friend's new doll.

"I can't believe they have a doll hospital here," he said, noticing a sign. "What goes on there?"

"Repairs. Kids are hard on toys."

"Wow. This is serious business."

She giggled, and he fell a little deeper in love with her.

"I was thinking… I need something to remember my first time here. Maybe you could pick out something for me."

"*You* want something from *here*?" The disdain dripping from her tone gave him a good preview of what her teenage years might be like.

"What's wrong with that?" he asked, faking offense.

She giggled again and shook her head at his foolishness.

"What if you pick out something for me and hang on to it until I need it? Something you might want for one of your dolls. I'll let you borrow it."

Looking up at him with a baffled expression on her face, she said, "If you want."

"I do. I never want to forget my first trip to the American Girl store."

"You're crazy, but okay."

That was how Grayson became the proud owner of a ruby-red ball gown and matching slippers that would look "perfect" on one of the dolls Auntie Lu gave her for Christmas last year. He was rather proud of the way he'd convinced her to get something for herself while also dodging Emma's rules on spoiling her.

After they waited in a line twenty deep to pay, Grayson directed her toward the café.

"Where're we going?"

"Lunch." He rubbed his belly dramatically. "I'm starving after all that shopping."

Her eyes bugged when she saw where he was leading her. "*Here?* We can't eat *here*! It's ridiculously expensive!"

"Special treat to celebrate my first time. You wouldn't want to deny me, would you?"

"Mom is going to flip out."

"Let's send her a selfie."

"You're going to get in big trouble for this," Simone said with wisdom beyond her years.

"That's okay. For you, I'm willing to risk it."

CHAPTER 25

There can be no deep disappointment where there is not deep love.
—Martin Luther King Jr.

Emma was on a fifteen-minute lunch break when her phone dinged with a text from Simone that contained a photo of her and Grayson eating at the American Girl café, both wearing big smiles.

Is he spoiling you? Emma asked her daughter in a text.

Maybe a little. But don't worry. I know it's a special treat.

Tell him we will talk about this later.

She replied with laughing emojis—Simone was wild about the emojis. *I told him he'd be in big trouble for this!*

You were right about that. Have fun and don't be late for the party.

We won't. Grayson likes cabs. This comment was accompanied by a wink.

Emma stared at the picture of the two of them for a long time, hoping she was doing the right thing allowing her daughter to get attached to a man who may or may not be part of their lives going forward. An ache settled in her chest at the thought of him not being part of their lives. It hadn't taken long for her to become attached to him and addicted to the way he made her feel when he touched her, or even looked at her, for that matter.

She took a minute to text Troy. *Are you speaking to me?*

The text showed up as delivered and then read.

After a minute, he wrote back. *Just barely.*

You have to speak to me. You're one of my best friends.

All my best friends are leaving me.

But we still love you, and I'm not going anywhere. Not now, anyway.

Seems I've heard that before… After another long pause, he added, *Don't mind me. I'm being cranky. If you're happy, I'm happy.*

You mean it?

Of course I do. But clearly I need to drink some of that water in Vermont.

Grayson has sisters… Beautiful sisters.

Hahaha. Shut up.

Emma was relieved to have avoided a possible rift with someone who was such a good friend. She was about to go back to work when her phone rang, displaying an 802 number she didn't recognize, but she took the call since that was the Vermont area code.

"Emma, this is Linc Abbott. I hope I'm getting you at a good time."

Surprised to hear from him, she said, "Hi there. This is a good time. What did we forget?"

He laughed. "Nothing that we've found yet, but if we do, we'll let you know. I'm sure you're wondering why I'm calling and how I got your number."

"I assume you got it from Lucy."

"You assume correctly, and I'm calling because I had an idea I wanted to run by you."

"Okay…"

"I found out this morning that our longtime admin, Mary, is going to be leaving us in a couple of weeks."

"Oh. Wow. That's too bad. I know how much you all love her."

"We really do, but she's making some exciting plans for herself, so we're happy for her."

Emma's mind raced as she tried to figure out what the heck any of this had to do with her.

"I wondered—and you can call me crazy if you want. You wouldn't be the first to do that. But for some reason, when Mary told me her news, I immediately thought of you for the job."

Emma felt weightless, like a trapdoor had opened beneath her, hurling her into the deep unknown, like Alice in Wonderland.

"Emma? Have I shocked you speechless?"

"You've certainly shocked me. Why me?"

"Well, Lucy is here most of the time these days, and I know how close you two are, and I thought that maybe, in light of other recent developments, you might like to be here. Not to mention, your daughter took to the place like a duck to water."

Emma couldn't deny that Simone absolutely loved Vermont. "I… um… I have no idea what to say."

"I know this is totally out of the blue, and you should take all the time you need to think about it. It would be a big deal to uproot yourself and your little girl, and I don't want you to feel any obligation. I had the idea, and I figured it couldn't hurt to run it by you."

"I'm incredibly flattered that you thought of me." And shocked and stunned and elated and depressed, because she already knew she couldn't consider the opportunity, not as long as her dad would be left behind if she and Simone moved north.

"Take some time. Give it some thought. Nothing needs to be decided right away. I'd like to have someone in the position by the end of January, if possible, so we've got time. Things are really humming here. The website goes live tomorrow. We're about to start work on our first catalog. We're building a distribution center and doubling our output at the sugaring facility. I'm also really excited about our new line of intimate accessories that'll be launched in the spring. It's an exciting time, and I'd love for you to be part of it." He named a salary that exceeded her current salary by ten thousand dollars and mentioned full medical coverage for herself and her daughter that had her wavering. She paid four hundred dollars a month for the same coverage she'd get for free in Vermont.

"I don't know what to say."

"Say you'll think about it and get back to me next week."

"I will." The salary and benefits had gotten her attention, not to mention the more affordable cost of living in Vermont. Anywhere would be more affordable than New York City. "I'll definitely think about it."

"You have a happy New Year, Emma. We hope to see you back here again soon."

"Same to you, and thank you so much for thinking of me for this. I'm really overwhelmed by the offer."

"My pleasure. I'll talk to you soon."

Emma ended the call and sat in stunned amazement until one of the hygienists came to find her.

"We need you," she said bluntly.

Emma got up to go back to work, still reeling from the call with Linc. For ten years, she'd existed inside her tidy little bubble, taking care of her daughter, running the dentists' office, spending time with family and friends. Every day was more or less the same, and nothing all that exciting ever happened, which had been fine with her.

The downside was that she had no idea, *no idea whatsoever*, how to deal with life outside the bubble that had kept her and Simone safe and secure. Linc's offer, while shocking and unexpected, had left her feeling momentarily euphoric about the possibility of a new professional challenge, the opportunity to live near Lucy again and a solution to the looming problem of what would become of her relationship with Grayson.

But thinking of her dad, all alone in the city while his daughters and granddaughter lived six hours away, brought her right back to reality. Her dad was a New Yorker through and through. He would never want to leave his beloved city, and leaving him wasn't an option. She should've told Linc as much while he was still on the phone.

So while the possibility of a big change was tempting, it wasn't going to happen. Feeling unusually dejected, Emma went back to work, forcing herself to concentrate on her existing job while trying not to think about the one Linc had offered her.

After delivering Simone to the birthday party with a gift bag in hand that they bought at Duane Reade, Grayson went back to Emma's to deal with the flurry of text messages from his siblings about the situation with their father.

The consensus was divided down the middle with the four oldest—himself, Noah, Izzy and Vanessa—generally apathetic about wanting to help their father, while the younger four—Alison, Jackson, Henry and Sarah—were feeling much more generous. Of course, the younger ones had been less affected by their father's abrupt exit from the family than their older siblings. While it had been traumatic for all of them, Henry and Sarah, in particular, were too young to remember how incredibly frightening it had been to briefly wonder how they would survive without their father's income to support the family.

Following Linc's advice, their mom had immediately hired a lawyer who made sure that Mike Coleman continued to provide financial support for his children, but he only sent exactly what he was required to and not one dime more. Grayson, Noah, Izzy and Vanessa had been forced to get nearly full-time jobs while they were still in high school to help keep the ship afloat.

He might be an asshole, Jackson said by text. *But he's still a human being. If we can help him, why wouldn't we?*

I can't even believe he'd ask us to help him, Vanessa said.

It's just DNA, Henry said. *And besides, none of his siblings matched, so maybe we won't either and all this will be for nothing.*

Mom is enraged that he asked, Noah said. It was rare for him to contribute to the group discussions, mostly because he didn't own a cell phone and had to catch up when he got to his computer. *I got an earful today. Had to remind her that I'm not the one who thought it would be a good idea to ask us to get tested.*

Who got tested and who didn't? Sarah asked.

Everyone but Ally and Vanessa said they'd been tested. Both said they were still thinking about it.

Anyone heard anything? Jackson asked.

They said we'd only hear if we're a match, Grayson said.

In other news, Izzy said, *I heard from Uncle Linc today that he's definitely going to ask all of us—Abbotts and Colemans—to model for the catalog. That ought to be a fun shoot.*

A flurry of laughter emojis followed her text.

Grayson laughed, imagining the chaos of the eighteen of them modeling for the catalog.

I want the cover, Sarah said.

Always the diva, Henry replied.

Grayson smiled at Henry's predictable retort. He and Sarah had been pushing each other's buttons from the time they were little kids.

With the conversation among his siblings waning—for now—Grayson turned his attention to the packet he'd picked up at the store, outlining Ed Sheehan's complaint. He was suing for unlawful termination, emotional distress and other damages.

Sheehan, a seasonal employee at the tree farm for five years, had been fired by Lucas Abbott after word got back to the family that Sheehan had told Gavin Guthrie that the US had wasted its time in Iraq. The comment had led to a fight in a bar between Gavin and Ed, both of whom had been arrested.

Gray made a note to get a copy of the police report from the incident.

Expressing one's opinion, the attorney had written, wasn't grounds for termination under the First Amendment right to free speech. He went on to make a case for damages based on the harm done to Sheehan's reputation and his inability to secure new employment since the reason for his termination had gotten around town.

As he read, Gray made a long list of questions he wanted to ask Gavin and Lucas about the incident, which had come to a head at a company gathering in November where Lucas had fired Ed.

Grayson totally agreed with the decision to fire Ed and didn't think he or his attorney had a leg to stand on with this case. Thanks to language Grayson had drafted himself, all their employees were classified as "at-will," meaning they could be terminated at any time for any reason. That anyone could say such a thing to a man who'd lost his only sibling in Iraq was mind-boggling. Ed was lucky that all Gavin had done was punch him, and Lucas had done the right thing firing him.

Ed was embarrassed and lashing out, but he didn't have a case.

Grayson picked up his cell phone to call his uncle to let him know that.

"How's it going?" Linc asked when he answered the home line at the barn.

"Good. I've been looking over Sheehan's complaint, and it's nothing to worry about. He doesn't have a case."

"I sort of suspected as much, but it's always good to get confirmation."

"I'll do the legwork and respond to his attorney, but I'm fairly confident I can make it go away."

"Whatever you need to do. Did you get a chance to look at the info about the proposed site of the distribution facility and the contract with the company that will walk us through developing the catalog?"

"Not yet, but that's next."

"I'm interested in your thoughts on both. With the website going live tomorrow, I want to keep things moving forward."

"I'll be back to you early next week on both items."

"What're you up to this weekend? The boys and I might be getting together to play some cards, if you're interested."

"I'd love to, but I took your advice, and I'm in New York."

"Well, that's an interesting development."

"You could say that."

"I had a little chat with your friend Emma earlier today."

"About what?" Gray asked, trying to imagine what Linc would need to talk to Emma about.

"How about I let her tell you?"

"Are you playing games, Uncle?"

"Me? Play games? I have no idea what you mean."

"Sure you don't," Gray said with a laugh.

"I hear your aunt calling me. Got to run. Happy New Year to you, son."

"Same to you and Aunt Molly. I'll talk to you next week."

"I'll look forward to it."

Equal parts amused and exasperated, Grayson ended the call with his uncle. He was dying to know what had transpired between him and Emma but would have to wait for her to get home and tell him. He checked his watch. Simone's party was due to end in about thirty minutes, and then they'd be home. He couldn't wait to see them both. Before they arrived, he had some plans to make for this evening.

CHAPTER 26

Where there is love there is life.
—Mahatma Ghandi

Emma caught the last hour of Talia's party and got to catch up with parents who had become close friends since the girls started school. The kids were out of their minds with excitement and an overabundance of sugar. She signaled to Simone that it was time to go and waited while she hugged each of her friends, as if she wasn't going to see them at school in a couple of days.

Simone had fallen into a nice group of kids with parents Emma liked and respected. They helped each other out and had created a village of sorts that revolved around the kids and their activities. The thought of leaving that support network made her feel queasy, even if they'd be going somewhere with built-in support. With Lucy and Cameron nearby, as well as the rest of the Abbotts—and Grayson—they'd never be alone or lonely, but Simone would have to leave friends she'd known, in some cases, since preschool.

Walking home with her daughter, these were the thoughts that spiraled relentlessly through Emma's mind even as the futility of it all served as a reminder that there was no point even thinking about it. If only there was a way to stop her brain from imagining the possibilities for both of them.

She enjoyed the job she had now, working for husband-and-wife dentists who'd been very good to her over the years, accommodating her whenever Simone was sick or if she needed to leave early for conferences or activities at school. The people she worked with were more like family than coworkers after eight years, but the job itself wasn't particularly challenging or interesting. It hadn't been in a long time. It was, at the end of the day, just a job. What Linc had offered interested her for many reasons, not the least of which would be a whole new professional challenge.

That plus more money, better benefits, proximity to Lucy and Colton for most of the year and Cameron all the time, no more Saturdays to frantically cover for Simone while she went to work, a more affordable cost of living and… Grayson. He'd be there, and they'd be free to continue what they'd started, without the challenge of distance hanging over them.

"What's wrong, Mom?" Simone asked.

That was when Emma realized she'd sighed rather loudly. "Nothing, baby. Just tired from my first day back to work."

"Was it busy?"

"Really busy. So you had fun with Grayson?"

"So much fun. He let me shop for a whole hour at American Girl, and then we went to the café. He's kind of silly, though."

"Why do you say that?"

"He actually bought a dress that he wants me to hang on to for him until he needs it. Silly, right?"

Sweet, she thought. *So very sweet.* "He found a way around my orders not to spoil you."

"What do you mean?"

"The dress is for *you*, sweetheart, but he knew I wouldn't be happy if he bought you something else when he'd already gotten you presents from the store in Vermont."

"Ohhh, wow. I didn't get that at all. I couldn't figure out what he'd want with a doll dress." She laughed. "That's pretty funny."

"It's very nice of him, and you need to say thank you."

"I did. I thanked him for taking me to the store and to lunch and to Talia's party and for making me pancakes for breakfast."

"You guys had a big day."

"It was fun. It was kind of like…"

Emma looked down at her. "Like what?"

"Having a dad."

Those three little words were a punch to Emma's gut. Simone never asked about her father or why other kids had one and she didn't. Emma suspected her daughter knew that was a sore subject for her.

"He asked me about taking you out for New Year's Eve, but I told him you'd rather stay home. I hope that's okay."

"You know me too well."

"Pop is coming to get me at five, and we're going to the movies. I'm going to sleep over at his house so he's not all alone for midnight."

"When did this happen?"

"Before." Simone skipped up the stairs to their building. She hadn't a care inside the beautiful bubble in which she lived, and Emma was determined to keep it that way. By the time Emma caught up to her daughter, she was giving Grayson a full debrief on the party, how much Talia had liked the gift she'd picked out, how hard it had been to play the games at the party with one arm in a sling, her plans with her grandfather for the evening and how she needed to go pack because Pop would be there any minute to get her.

She took off for her room, leaving Emma alone with Grayson.

As she removed her coat and hung it in the closet, he came across the room to greet her. He wore a faded Red Sox T-shirt with equally faded jeans and bare feet. She loved that he already looked like he belonged in the place she and Simone called home. Maybe he did. Maybe he could come here, and they could make it work in New York.

That possibility gave her a glint of hope that was quickly extinguished when she recalled what he'd told her the night they met about wanting to simplify his life. He'd left one city to move home to Butler. The last thing he probably wanted at this point in his life or career was to start all over again in another city.

"Welcome home, dear," he said, kissing her. "Did you have a nice day?"

"I had a hectic day. How about you?"

"I had a rather delightful day with your daughter, who showed me the ropes at American Girl. Not for the faint of heart, that place. Did you know we could have her birthday party there? I picked up a flyer. How fun would that be? She'd love it."

"Yes, she would. What's this I hear about you buying a dress that you want her to hang on to until you need it?" She raised a brow in the universal "mom" look.

"Um, well, you see…"

Emma laughed. "You have no defense, Counselor, so don't even try it."

"She couldn't go there and not get a little something for herself. It wouldn't have been right."

"Yes, she could, and yes, it would."

"Do I have to return my dress, Mom?" he asked with a teasing grin.

Biting back a smile at his adorable contrition, she said, "Not this time, but don't let it happen again."

"Yes, ma'am."

"Thank you so much for running her around today."

"Trust me when I tell you it was entirely my pleasure. She's... Well, I don't have to tell you how fantastic she is."

"I'm glad you think so," Emma said, truly touched by his kindness to her child. "I hear we have plans for tonight."

"You heard correctly." He wrapped his arms around her and held her close to him, speaking close to her ear. "I was told by a reliable source that Emma doesn't like the city when it's chaotic, and a night at home would be far preferable to going out."

Emma shivered from the desire that came from being close to him and breathing in his distinctive scent. "You have good sources."

When Simone came out of her room, banging and crashing as she dragged her suitcase behind her, Grayson released Emma and took a step back. She appreciated that he didn't overdo the public displays of affection when Simone was around.

"Did you remember your toothbrush?" Emma asked.

"Nope." She dropped the suitcase in the hallway with a thud and ran for the bathroom.

"Use it before you pack it," Emma called after her.

"How much stuff does she need for one night?" Grayson asked, eyeing the stuffed suitcase.

"About a third of what she packed. Lucy says Simone is prepared to be a bag lady as an adult. She loves to pack bags. When we clean her room, it's all about the unpacking."

"That's cute. She's always ready to go."

His words had more significance than he realized in light of today's events.

"What?" he asked.

"Nothing." She shook it off to focus on her daughter and then her dad when he arrived to pick her up, stopping short at the sight of Grayson standing in Emma's living room. In the span of a second, Emma witnessed a blatant flash of despair that he quickly tried to mask.

"Nice to see you here, Grayson," Ray said, shaking his hand.

"Nice to be here."

"Are you guys going out?"

"I hear that Emma prefers to stay in on New Year's Eve," Gray said.

"That she does. She's a homebody, my Emma."

There was no mistaking the hidden message in Ray's gruffly spoken words.

"Are you ready, pumpkin?" he said to Simone.

"Ready."

"Kiss your mom."

Simone hugged and kissed Emma.

"Happy New Year, baby," Emma said, holding her squiggling body for a second longer than Simone preferred these days.

"I'm gonna be ten this year! That's double digits!"

"I'm so not ready to have a ten-year-old," Emma said. She could tell that Simone took Grayson by surprise when she hugged him, too. In typical Simone style, she did it so quickly that he barely had time to react before it was over and she was reaching for the handle of her overstuffed suitcase. She handed Ashley to Ray, who took the doll from her like the professional grandfather he was.

Emma went up on tiptoes to kiss his cheek. "Thanks for having her, Dad."

"Happy to have her anytime. You know that."

She saw them off, standing in the hallway as they went down the stairs before returning to the apartment and closing the door, leaning back against it for a moment. "I still feel weird, like something is missing, every time she leaves me, even when it's with someone who loves her as much as I do."

"She's your soul mate," Grayson said as he joined her at the door.

"She really is." She studied his handsome face. "Does that bother you? That I already have a soul mate?"

He shook his head. "The way I see it, someone with a heart and soul as big as yours probably has room for more than one."

She reached for him, and he drew her into a kiss that made her thankful for more than twelve hours to spend alone with him. "This is all very devious, the way you conspired with my daughter to have me all to yourself."

"Is it? I hoped you wouldn't mind. I reminded Simone of how she told me the night we met that you like to dance and asked where I could take you." He lifted her into his arms. "And that led to dinner and dancing at home and her spending the night with Ray. That part was her idea."

"I don't mind at all. If she's helping you to surprise me, that means she likes you and approves of us being together."

"I want her to approve, and not just because I want you, but I want her in my life, too. She's so fun to be with, cute and smart and funny and polite. We had the best time today."

As she listened to him talk about Simone, Emma's eyes filled with tears that she couldn't contain no matter how hard she tried.

"Hey," he said. "What's this? What's wrong?"

She shook her head and nuzzled his neck, wishing there was some way she could have everything she wanted for once in her life. Just once. Was that too much to ask?

"Emma, sweetheart. Talk to me. Tell me what upset you."

Her cell phone rang, and she withdrew from him to answer it, even if she'd rather ignore it and focus on him. If Simone was anywhere other than with her, she'd never ignore a call. She saw Lucy's name on the caller ID and took the call. "Hey, what's up?" she asked, forcing a cheerful tone.

"I have news!"

Emma wiped the tears from her cheeks, acutely aware of Grayson watching her intently. "Are you going to tell me?"

"We're getting married the second Saturday in May."

"Oh, Luce." Emma sat on the sofa. "That's great. I'm so happy for you guys."

"You'll be my maid of honor, right?"

"Of course I will."

"I'm only going to have you and Cam and Simone. We're going to do it in Molly and Linc's yard under a tent."

"Sounds perfect," Emma said with a sigh, thrilled for her sister and Colton, a man Emma loved and respected. "Have you told Dad?"

"He's my next call."

"He's got Simone, so you can tell them both at the same time."

"Are you home alone for New Year's Eve?"

Emma glanced at Grayson. "Umm, not exactly."

Lucy shrieked. "Emma! *Is he there?*"

Emma held the phone away from her ear. "Maybe…" She glanced at Grayson, who was smiling because Lucy was so loud, he could hear her, too.

"Oh my God! When did this happen?"

"Yesterday."

"He went *home* with you guys?"

"Maybe."

"Emma! Stop being a one-word sally, and tell me what's going on."

"You already know. He came home with us, and we're hanging out for a while."

"What's the plan?"

Emma glanced at Grayson again. "We don't have one."

Lucy's voice was much quieter when she said, "Are you okay, Em?"

"I'm trying to be."

"Remember my mantra. If it's meant to be, you'll find a way."

Emma desperately wanted to believe that was true, but all she could see were the many obstacles standing between them and finding a way. "I know. I'm really happy for you and Colton, Luce."

"Thanks. I'm happy for us, too. Hey, did Linc call you?"

"Yes, he did."

"What was that about?"

"Just something Simone forgot at the house. They're mailing it to us." If she told Lucy about the job offer, she'd get her hopes up about Emma and Simone moving to Vermont, when that couldn't happen. And then Lucy would feel bad that she'd gotten to move when Emma couldn't. What was the point of even talking about it? "What're you guys doing tonight?"

"Going to Hunter and Megan's for a New Year's Eve party. What about you?"

"Staying in and watching the ball drop on TV. Talk to you tomorrow?"

"Sounds good. Love you."

"Love you, too." Emma ended the call and put the phone on the coffee table.

"Big news from Vermont?"

"In case you or the people next door couldn't hear her, they've set a wedding date. Second weekend in May, and I'm the maid of honor."

"Good for them. They're a great couple."

"Yes, they are, and this is what she wants. I love seeing her get what she wants."

Grayson sat next to her and put his arm around her.

Emma curled up to him.

"Are you going to tell me what had you upset before Lucy called?"

Emma wanted to tell him. She wanted to unload on him and rail about the many ways that life simply wasn't fair sometimes. But again, what would be the point? There wasn't anything he could do to fix the situation, and hearing that his uncle had offered her a job in Vermont would only get his hopes up for no good reason.

"I'd much rather enjoy this evening with you than dwell on things that upset me, if that's all right with you."

He studied her in that intent way of his, seeing her more clearly than anyone ever had before. "That's all right with me. For now. But if something makes you sad, I want to know what it is."

Emma took his outstretched hand and let him draw her onto his lap.

He wrapped his arms around her. "I can't bear to see you sad."

She closed her eyes against the rush of emotion. Wouldn't it be nice to have him, to have *this*, every day for the rest of her life? Wouldn't it be nice if he could be an actual father to Simone rather than "like a father" for a day? Wouldn't it be so very, very nice to have it all?

She couldn't have it all, but she had right now, and that was going to have to be good enough.

CHAPTER 27

I am in you and you in me, mutual in divine love.
—William Blake

From the second she came home with Simone, Grayson had sensed a change in Emma. Something was wrong. They'd shared their deepest secrets, so why wouldn't she tell him what was bothering her? Had she changed her mind about him during the day they spent apart? Was she wishing she hadn't allowed him to invade their home and their life in the city?

He wanted to relax and enjoy this evening he had planned for them, but how could he do that when she was obviously upset about something? Though he told himself to leave it alone the way she'd asked him to, he couldn't do it.

"Em," he said, running his fingers through her long hair, "I can't stand that something's upset you and I don't know what it is."

"I… It's nothing to do with you. Not really."

"Not really? Come on. Talk to me the way you have from that first night. Tell me what's on your mind."

She took a deep breath and looked up at him with those blue eyes that gave away her every emotion. "Lincoln offered me a job in Vermont."

Grayson felt like he'd been sucker punched. "He did? When?"

"Today. He called and told me their admin, Mary, is leaving the company and asked if I might be interested in her job."

"That cagey bastard," Grayson said, smiling.

"Did you know about this?"

"Nope, but I'm not surprised. With him and my Gramps on a quest to get us all coupled up, they've apparently set their sights on us." He looked down at her. "What'd you tell him?"

"That I'd think about it, but really… There's just no way I could do it."

"How come?"

"Many reasons, but mostly because I couldn't leave my dad here alone. He'd be heartbroken if Simone and I moved away from him. And Simone is doing really well in school and has a great group of friends. Their parents are a huge source of support to me. I just… I can't…"

He laid a finger over her lips. "I understand, sweetheart. It's too much to even contemplate."

"I want it," she whispered, her eyes filling. "I want the job and I want you and I want Vermont and… I want it all."

"Aww, baby." He kissed away her tears. "Maybe you should talk to your dad and see what he says before you make any decisions."

"I can't. He'd tell me to go and that he'd be fine, but I'd never be able to do it knowing he'd be here by himself. We're all he has, and with Lucy in Vermont more than she's here these days… I just can't."

It meant so much to him that she wanted to, and it made him determined to find a way to make this work for everyone. That was what he'd done for his entire professional life—figure out the details and get people what they wanted. He needed to approach this situation as if it were the most important case he'd ever worked on.

"I need to tell you something," he said, deciding to lay his cards on the table even if it was far too soon for such things.

"What?" she asked, her brows knitting with concern.

He rubbed the furrow between her brows with his index finger. "I love you, Emma. I love Simone. I want both of you in my life to stay, and I'm very determined to make that happen one way or the other. So I don't want you to worry. We're going to figure this out."

"You…"

"Love you. I think I fell in love with you that first night at Linc and Molly's when you trusted me enough to tell me something you've never told anyone else. And every minute I've spent with you since then has only made me want more—of you and Simone." He cupped her face and compelled her to look at him. "I'm not going anywhere as long as you want me here. I'll figure out my work situation, whether it's here or there or whatever. I worked my ass off for years in Boston, and I socked away a lot of money that I didn't have time to spend. If you want me the way I want you, you've got me. I'm right here."

"I still can't believe this is happening."

"Believe it. This has been the best week of my entire life, hands down, and all I want is more. If that's what you want, too—"

She kissed him. "Yes, it's what I want. *You're* what I want. I love you, too. How could I not love you after this incredible week we've spent together and how amazing you are with Simone?"

Hearing she loved him was the greatest gift he'd ever been given. "Promise me you won't worry about how it's going to work. Everything's going to be fine."

"I'll try not to worry."

Grayson could tell he took her by surprise when he stood with her in his arms and headed for her room. He'd waited forever to find a woman who looked at him the way she did, as if he'd single-handedly hung the moon just for her. He laid her on the bed and came down on top of her.

She welcomed him into her embrace by wrapping her arms and legs around him. "Grayson…"

"What, sweetheart?"

"Tell me again. Tell me this is real, and I'm not dreaming."

"You're not dreaming. It's so real, and I love you." He kissed her with all the love and desire and passion he felt for her, wanting to reassure her that she truly had nothing to worry about where he was concerned. Was it too soon for words of love and commitment? Probably, but with so much at stake for both of them, he didn't see the need to hold back. What had Linc and Molly said about knowing the first day they met that they were going to change each other's life? The same was true for him and Emma.

That first night, when he'd found himself spilling his guts about his father and she'd told him about the violent act that had resulted in her precious daughter, he'd known she was the one for him. With hindsight, that was patently clear to him. He withdrew slowly from the kiss and rose to his knees to help her out of the scrubs she'd worn to work.

"There was supposed to be dancing," he said.

"Doesn't this count as dancing?"

"I suppose it does."

As he undressed her, she watched him with expressive eyes gone soft with emotion. When she was bare, he whipped his sweater over his head and tossed it aside and then reached for the button to his jeans.

"Let me," she said, sitting up to do the honors. She pushed the button through the hole and unzipped him slowly, working around the huge bulge, and then pushed his pants and underwear down until they were around his thighs.

His cock was so hard, it ached, but he held off, waiting to see what she would do.

She wrapped her hand around the base and drew the tip into her mouth, making him see stars as he tried to find some control.

"Lie back," he said gruffly.

Without releasing him, she did as he directed, and he leaned over her, hands on the headboard, watching as she took him as deep as she could, until the head bumped up against her throat. *Fucking hell...* "Emma... Babe."

"Mmm?"

The vibration of her lips against his shaft was nearly the end of him. Then she sucked on him and shattered any semblance of control he might've had. He came hard, and she was right there with him, never letting up until he was completely wrecked.

"Ah, fuck, Emma," he gasped when he'd caught his breath. The sight of her swollen lips, flushed cheeks and satisfied smirk started the fire burning all over again. "That was... God, I can't even tell you..."

Her husky, sexy laugh was his new favorite sound. "Did I do it right?"

"You couldn't tell by the way I completely lost it?"

"Just making sure. I'm not very experienced in these things, so you have to tell me if I do it wrong."

He stretched out next to her and gathered her into his arms. "There is nothing you could do where I'm concerned that would be wrong."

"So the next time I do that, teeth would be okay?"

"Ahh…"

She laughed. "Didn't think so."

He cupped her breast and rolled her nipple between his fingers, watching with fascination as it hardened. Moving so he was between her legs, he bent to take that hard tip into his mouth.

Her fingers in his hair kept him anchored to her chest.

"You are so sweet and so soft and so sexy," he said as he kissed a path to her belly. "I'm completely addicted to you." With his hands on her thighs, he pushed her legs apart and dipped his tongue into her heat.

She moaned and raised her hips in encouragement.

Grasping her bottom with both hands, he feasted on her, sucking her clit into his mouth and drawing a screaming orgasm from her. He pressed two fingers into her to ride the waves of her release and triggered a second wave when he pushed a wet finger into her anus. He kept his finger buried deep inside her as he drove his cock into her, filling her from both sides as one orgasm rolled into another. He loved the sounds she made, the gasps, the moans and the way she gave him everything she had every time they made love. Her every thought and emotion was on full display. With his Emma, there was no artifice, only truth.

He rocked into her from the front and the back, and when he dropped his head to suck on her nipple, she exploded all over again, her muscles clamping down so hard on his cock and finger that he came, too, rocking into her again and again, lost in the purest bliss he'd ever experienced.

She clung to him, their bodies damp with sweat, both of them breathing hard.

He needed to withdraw from her, to get up, to clean up, but he couldn't seem to get the message from his brain to muscles gone lax with satisfaction.

Emma held him close and ran her fingers through his hair, even as her body continued to throb.

Gray couldn't believe it when he felt himself begin to harden again inside her.

She groaned when she felt it, too. "You're going to be the death of me."

Chuckling, he withdrew from her slowly, going for maximum effect and loving the way she quivered from the aftershocks. He placed a kiss on her soft belly. "Don't move. I'll be right back."

"I couldn't move if I had to."

He went into the bathroom, washed up and brought a warm washcloth back to bed for her. When she would've taken it from him, he said, "Let me." He eased her legs apart and pressed the warm cloth to her sensitive flesh, loving the flush that overtook her body when he touched her so intimately.

"I had all these plans for tonight," he said. "We were going to get dressed up and dance and have dinner, and then I was going to sweet-talk you into bed."

"You started with the sweet talk, and look at where we ended up."

"I can't help it if I'm powerless to resist you."

"Likewise."

"Simone told me to order shrimp pad Thai from the place down the block if I wanted to make you happy."

"My daughter knows me very well."

"It'll be here in about twenty minutes."

"Mmm, perfect. Best New Year's Eve ever."

"Is it? You wouldn't rather be dressed up and out dancing somewhere?"

"There's nowhere I'd rather be than right here with you."

"Me, too, honey."

After getting up to eat the dinner he'd ordered, they spent the rest of the night in her bed, where they watched the revelry in Time's Square on television. As the clock ticked toward midnight, Gray rolled her under him and was deep inside her as one year rolled into the next.

"I want to begin every year for the rest of my life just like this," she said.

"Yes," he whispered. "Let's do it."

Emma ran her hands over his back and down to grip his muscular ass as he pumped into her.

They were awake all night. At three o'clock, he introduced her to the finer delights of shower sex, and at five thirty, he took her from behind. This was utter insanity, she thought, as the sun began to peek through the blinds. Curled up to him, she hoped her dad would take Simone to brunch the way he often did when she spent Saturday nights with him.

That was the last thought she had before a ringing phone in the other room woke her hours later.

"That's me," Grayson said, disentangling from her to answer it.

Facedown in bed, Emma was on her way back to sleep when she tuned in to the tense tone of his voice.

"Are you sure?" After a long pause, he said, "Well, yes, I guess I can do that. Wednesday at ten. I'll be there."

Emma waited for him to come back to bed, but when he didn't, she got up to check on him. She put on a robe and tied it around her waist. "Gray? Is everything okay?"

When he looked up at her, she could see that he was upset.

She sat next to him on the sofa. "What is it? What's wrong?"

"I'm a match for my dad. An almost perfect match, the doctor said."

She took his hand and held it between both of hers. "They called you on a holiday to tell you that?"

Nodding, he said, "Apparently, his situation is somewhat precarious. They want to do it right away, and they need to harvest the actual marrow, which is a surgical procedure."

"What does that entail? How long does it take to recover?"

"They're going to talk to me about the details on Wednesday. This means I have to go back to Vermont Tuesday night."

"Of course. You have to do this."

"I want to be here with you."

"I'm not going anywhere. I'll be right here waiting for you to come back to me." As she spoke the words, though, she wondered if there might be a way for her to be there for him when he had the surgery. Her dad could stay with Simone for a couple of days, and Emma had personal time she could take. She hoarded her time off so she could attend functions at Simone's school and take her to doctors' appointments, but she'd gladly make the sacrifice for Grayson.

He put his arm around her and leaned into her. "Let's go back to bed for a while."

She went with him, but Emma couldn't sleep. She looked over to find him staring up at the ceiling, too. "What're you thinking?"

"I'm pondering the humor of it all."

"What do you mean?"

"My father left our family twenty years ago, forcing me to step up for my mother and siblings, and now he's asking me to step up again. History is repeating itself."

"And you find that funny?"

"I find it ridiculous. If I don't laugh, I might scream."

She reached for him and drew him into her embrace. "Don't scream. Hold on to me."

He put his arm around her and rested his head on her chest.

"You'll do what you need to do to be able to live with yourself," she said, running her fingers through his hair. She didn't mention that she was going to try to be there until she knew for certain that she could make it happen. "And then you'll come back to me knowing you're a far better man than your father will ever be."

"Keep telling me that, will you?"

"Any time you need to hear it."

CHAPTER 28

The best thing to hold onto in life is each other.
—Audrey Hepburn

Grayson flew home to Vermont Tuesday night and called Emma as he drove from the airport in Burlington to his aunt and uncle's home by the lake, where he'd spend the night. In the morning, he would meet with doctors at the University of Vermont Cancer Center to see about getting it done so he could get back to Emma as soon as possible. He missed her like he hadn't seen her in a year rather than a couple of hours.

"How was the flight?" she asked.

"Bumpy the whole way. I hope that isn't a metaphor."

"I read through the info they sent you about the bone marrow harvest."

"And?"

"It sounds awful."

"They say it doesn't hurt at all until afterward. I'll be out cold. I won't feel a thing."

"Have you talked to your siblings?"

"Just by text. They're being supportive, even if I'm sure some of them don't think I ought to have to go through this to save him. They'd never say so now that it's happening."

"It's the right thing to do. You're not capable of letting someone die, even someone who's hurt you the way he has, if there's something you can do about it."

"I wish I was more of an asshole," he said with a sigh. "That would be easier."

"I love you just the way you are."

"I miss you like crazy, and I just left you a little while ago."

"I miss you, too, and so does Simone. She was out of sorts tonight after you left—or maybe I was and she picked up on it."

"A few days, and I'll be back. I've got some work to get done while I'm up here, so I'll be all yours when I get back."

"All mine. I love the sound of that."

"Me, too. Thanks for the best weekend." They'd had dinner at Ray's on Sunday and spent the last day of Simone's winter break playing tourist in the city. In addition to visiting the top of the Empire State Building, they'd watched the ice skaters at Rockefeller Plaza and went to see the movie *Sing*, which Simone had loved.

"It was the best weekend ever."

"Yes, it was." It'd been nice to feel like a family for a few days, and he was counting the minutes until he could be with them again.

"Are you going to be able to sleep tonight?"

"I hope so. I need to catch up on my sleep while I can. My girlfriend has been messing with my sleep lately."

"Right," she said, laughing. "It's all my fault."

"You can't keep your hands off me."

"I admit it."

"I seem to have the same problem where you're concerned."

"That's one problem we don't need to solve."

Laughing at her witty reply, Grayson pulled into the driveway at the lake house and cut the engine. "I'm at the house. Talk to you in the morning?"

"Call me after the appointment."

"You'll be at work."

"I'll be waiting for your call."

"I'll call you as soon as I can."

"Try to get some sleep."

"You, too. I love you, Emma."

"I love you, too."

He ended the call with her and sat in the darkness, staring at the vastness of Lake Champlain, feeling more unsettled than he had in a long time at the prospect of having to do this huge thing for his father. His phone rang, and he saw his mother's number on the caller ID. He hadn't talked to her since finding out he was a match.

"Hi, Mom."

"Grayson… Are you still in the city?"

"No, I'm in Burlington. I flew home tonight."

"You're not really going to do this, are you?"

"Yes," he said with a sigh, "I really am, and I don't want to fight about it."

"I'm so sorry he's put you in this position."

"He's sick, Mom. He didn't set out to corner me into doing something for him. It's a medical procedure. I'll do it and be done with it. I'll hope it works and that he regains his health. That'll be the end of it for me."

"Do you have to see him?"

"I don't think so."

"I really hope not."

"Look, Mom, I know you're understandably wound up about this, but I don't want you to worry. It's a two-hour procedure for me, and that's that. I'll go on with my life without having to feel guilty that I let someone die when I could've done something about it."

"I've been reading about it, and you'll need to take it easy for a week afterward. You should come home. I'll look after you."

"Thanks, but I'm going back to New York as soon as I can."

After a long pause, she said, "Okay, then."

"I'll let you know what's going on after the meeting tomorrow."

"I'll speak to you then. Grayson…"

"Yeah?"

"You're a good man, a better man than he'll ever be. Even though I wish you didn't have to do this, I admire you for being willing."

"Thanks, Mom. Love you."

"Love you, too. Sleep well."

After ending the call, Grayson got out of the car and retrieved his suitcase from the trunk. At the front door, he punched in his aunt and uncle's anniversary and gained admission to the house. He'd talked to his uncle earlier, and Linc had told him to make himself at home at the lake house for however long he needed to be in Burlington.

Grayson empathized with his mom in this situation. In her shoes, he'd feel the same way about a child of his doing something to save the life of the parent who'd abandoned him. She had every good reason to be upset, but that wouldn't stop him from doing the right thing and then getting back to Emma as soon as he could.

Emma flew to Burlington on Friday morning. She'd timed her arrival to coincide with Grayson's procedure so she could be there when it was over. He'd called her early that morning, and she could tell he was nervous, even if he tried to hide that from her by repeatedly telling her it was no big deal and she shouldn't worry about him.

Her dad had been happy to stay with Simone for the weekend, and they had a list of plans that would keep them busy. Over the last year, Ray had been sharing his love of cooking with Simone, teaching her the basics and gradually introducing new concepts. In his retirement, he'd taken some cooking classes, and Simone loved spending time with him in the kitchen.

This weekend, they were planning to make pasta from scratch, and they were trying out the new bread maker Emma and Simone had gotten him for Christmas. The two of them shared a very special bond, and it was one that Emma couldn't and wouldn't break by moving her daughter away from her dad. She owed Linc Abbott a phone call and would take care of that after she got Grayson through today's procedure.

The ninety-minute flight seemed to take forever, and by the time the wheels touched down in Burlington, Emma was more than ready to get off the plane. She grabbed a cab and arrived at the University of Vermont Cancer Center just after ten. If he'd gone in at eight as planned, he ought to be in recovery soon.

Upon entering the surgical waiting room, she stopped short at the sight of Hannah Coleman, who looked up from her magazine, seeming equally surprised to see Emma. Dragging her suitcase behind her, Emma took the seat next to Hannah's. "Have you heard anything?"

"Not yet. Any time now." After a long pause, Hannah said, "It's good of you to come."

"I love him," Emma said without taking even a second to contemplate whether she should say that to his mother. It was the truth. Why not say so?

"He's one of the best men I know."

"I agree. What he's doing today is further proof of that."

"I... I'm sorry if I've given you the impression that I don't like you. That's not true. I have... at times... projected my past experiences on to people who don't deserve it."

"I understand completely. I've done the same at times by suspecting that all men are like the bad one I had the misfortune of knowing when I was younger. Gray is the first man I've dated since my daughter's father." Emma watched as her meaning registered with Hannah.

"We have more in common than I thought," Hannah said.

"Yes, we do, including our love for Grayson. Like you, I want the best for him, and if we can figure out the logistics, I want to try to make him happy."

"You do make him happy. I've never seen him so gone over any woman the way he is with you."

Emma smiled at her. "The feeling is entirely mutual."

"That's good," Hannah said with a sigh. "He certainly deserves to be happy after everything he's done for others from the time he was far too young for the responsibility that was put on him."

"On that we agree."

A short time later, a nurse came into the waiting room. "Family of Grayson Coleman?"

Hannah jumped up, but Emma hung back, intending to take her cues from Hannah.

"Are you coming?" Hannah asked, waiting for Emma before she followed the nurse.

"Yes," Emma said, elated to have had this unexpected chance to talk to Gray's mother and to clear the air with her. "I'm coming."

Grayson came awake in a brightly lit room, and for a minute, he couldn't figure out where he was. At the sight of a nurse looking down at him, the story came flooding back to him. His father. Bone marrow. Surgery.

"How're you feeling?" the nurse asked.

"Fine." That much was true, and they'd told him to expect to feel fine until the pain block wore off. Then he would be achy and sore and probably fatigued for a few days before he bounced back. No biggie, he'd thought then, and now he was glad it was over. He was eager to get back to New York, to be with Emma and Simone and to figure out a way to be with them all the time. "It went well?"

"The doctor said it was textbook. He'll be in to talk to you shortly. You have some visitors. You feel up to seeing them?"

"Yeah, sure." His mom had told him she'd be coming. Izzy or Noah must've come with her.

"I'll go get them."

Grayson thought his eyes were deceiving him when his mom walked in with Emma. "Where'd you come from?" He held out the hand that wasn't tethered to IVs and monitors.

She took his hand and bent over the bed to kiss him. "All the way from New York."

"You've been keeping secrets from me."

"Only the good kind."

He was so damned happy to see her.

"How're you feeling?" his mom asked, her face pinched with concern.

"Fine. Just groggy from the drugs." He returned his gaze to Emma, unable to look anywhere but at her when he'd been missing her so much since leaving her three long days ago. "I can't believe you're here. Where's Simone?"

"In school at the moment, and then hanging out with my dad for the weekend."

"We've got the whole weekend?" Grayson asked, feeling better by the minute to know she was here for a few days.

"We sure do."

"My own private-duty nurse," he said with a teasing smile, loving the way her face lit up with embarrassment.

"Not in front of your mother," she said sternly.

"Yes, Grayson," Hannah said with unusual amusement. "Not in front of your mother."

Eager to be alone with her, he gave Emma's hand a squeeze and said to the nurse, "When can I get out of here?"

They released him at five o'clock with orders to stay local until his follow-up appointment Tuesday morning, when he would hopefully be cleared to resume normal activities. Emma drove him to his aunt and uncle's lakeside home, where they would spend the weekend taking it easy as directed.

Since he was in good hands with Emma, his mother had gone home to Butler with promises to check in later. Emma was glad to have him all to herself for a few days. She was due to fly home Sunday night, but that was forty-eight hours from now, and she planned to enjoy every second of the time they had together.

"Is it wishful thinking or have you and my mom had some sort of breakthrough?" he asked on the short ride to the house.

"We had a good talk in the waiting room. I think we're on the same page now."

"And what page is that?"

"The we-love-Grayson-and-want-the-best-for-him page."

"You told her you love me?"

She glanced over at him. "I figured it couldn't hurt my case for her to know that."

A smile lit up his handsome face. "Well played, my love. You handled her just right."

"I hoped so. I think it meant a lot to her that I came up to be with you."

"It means a lot to both of us." He brought her hand to his lips and kissed her palm.

She tugged at her hand, but he didn't let go. "Don't do that while I'm driving. I hardly ever drive, and I don't need any distractions."

"I should've asked if you had a license before I let you drive my car."

"I have one, but it rarely gets used in the city."

He directed her to the Abbotts' home, which was off a dirt road that led right to the shore of the vast lake.

"This is beautiful," Emma said when she brought the car to a stop in the driveway.

"Isn't it? I love it here. It was a foreclosure sale years ago, and my aunt and uncle jumped on it. Lots of good times at the lake since then. This is where Hannah and Nolan got married last summer."

Emma got out of the car and went around to the passenger side to help him out. As the day had gone on, he'd had some pain in his lower back.

With her arm around him, he walked slowly toward the door and landed on the sofa in the living room, grimacing as his back made contact with the cushion.

"I'll get you a pain pill," she said, heading for the kitchen to get him some water.

He gratefully took the pill from her and washed it down, closing his eyes against the gnawing ache in his back. It was exactly what he'd been told to expect and wasn't so bad that he couldn't handle it, but bad enough that he wasn't about to say no to taking the edge off.

"What else can I do for you?" Emma asked.

He held out his arms to her. "Come lie with me."

"I don't want to hurt you."

"You'll hurt me more if you don't."

What could she say to that? She curled up to him on the sofa, putting her arm across his waist as he wrapped both of his around her.

"This day turned out way better than expected. I thought I'd have to spend a long boring weekend here by myself."

"Good surprise?"

"The best. But I have to remember you've got this sneaky side to you. I talked to you this morning, and you never told me you were on your way."

She laughed. "I was already at LaGuardia when I talked to you."

"*Very* sneaky."

"You'll discover that's about the extent of my sneakiness."

"It means so much to me that you came, that you took time off work, that you had to arrange coverage for Simone, that—"

Emma kissed him. "I couldn't stay away."

He cupped her face and kissed her back. "Love you, sweetheart."

"Love you, too. I'm so glad this is over and done with for you."

"So am I."

"Close your eyes and get some rest."

"Only if you stay right here with me."

"I'm not going anywhere."

He released a deep breath and tightened his hold on her before dozing off.

Emma didn't expect to sleep, but the late nights on the phone with him and the early morning trek to the airport had her closing her eyes.

His ringing cell phone interrupted their nap.

He woke with a groan and released Emma so she could retrieve the phone from his coat pocket.

She handed it to him.

"I don't recognize the number. Probably the hospital checking on me." He took the call and then went totally still. "Yes, it's me."

Emma sat next to him, wondering who was on the phone.

He took hold of her hand and mouthed the words *my father* to her. "It was no big deal," he said. "I hope it helps."

Emma could barely breathe as she held his hand.

He tipped the phone so she could hear both sides of the conversation.

She heard his father say "more than I deserve." On that they agreed.

"I just wanted to say thank you, Grayson," his father said. "Thank you very much."

"You're welcome. I'm going to go. Take care."

"You, too, son."

Grayson put the phone on the coffee table. "That's the first time I've talked to him in nearly twenty years."

Emma leaned her head on his shoulder, wishing there was something she could say or do to provide comfort.

"He sounds exactly the same. The doctors told me he's going through an intensive round of chemo ahead of the transplant next week." He gazed down at her. "I'm really glad you're here. If he'd called me when I was alone, that might've taken me back to a time and place I never want to visit again."

"You did the right thing today, and now you should put it all behind you and look forward, not back."

"I like the view in front of me," he said, smiling at her. "I like it very much."

CHAPTER 29

True love stories never have endings.
—Richard Bach

After a relaxing two days tending to his every need—except the sexual ones, which she'd refused to tend to until after he saw the doctor on Tuesday—Emma flew home to New York on Sunday night, more in love with him than she'd been before, if that was possible.

They'd done nothing but lie around, cook the food he'd bought before the surgery, watch movies, sleep, make out a little and talk. Like they had from the beginning, they talked about big things, little things and everything in between. He promised to catch the first flight he could get out of Burlington on Tuesday after his appointment.

Emma arrived to snow falling at LaGuardia and indulged in a rare splurge on a cab ride home, pulling up to her building just after seven o'clock. She ran up the stairs, eager to see Simone after two days apart. They'd FaceTimed on Saturday, and Grayson had answered her many questions about the operation he'd had and how his donation could save his father's life. Simone had found the entire thing fascinating, and he'd been endlessly patient in explaining it all to her.

The smell of garlic met Emma in the hallway, making her mouth water for whatever her dad and daughter had made for dinner. She used her key in the door and stepped into her cozy apartment.

"Mom! You're back!"

"Get over here and hug me."

Simone came running across the small room and into her mother's outstretched arms. "How's the elbow?" The orthopedic doctor had taken a look at it earlier in the week and determined it was healing well.

"Hardly hurts anymore." Simone bent her arm a few times to demonstrate and then tugged on Emma's hand to drag her toward the kitchen. "Come see what Pop and I made for dinner."

"Whatever it is smells amazing."

"It's homemade pasta with our own meatballs and sauce. We made it all from scratch. And bread from the new bread maker."

"Wow, I'm impressed, and I'm starving." She gave her dad a kiss on the cheek. "Hi there."

"Welcome home, sweetheart."

"Thanks, and thank you for making it possible for me to go."

"We had a great time. How's the patient?"

"Sore and achy, and yesterday he had a bad headache that's one of the possible side effects. But he was better today."

"That's good. Quite a thing he did for his father."

"Yes, it was, especially under the circumstances."

"I know. I talked to his mother last night. She's having a real hard time with her ex-husband asking the kids to be tested in the first place, not to mention what Grayson did."

Emma was still stuck on the words *I talked to his mother last night*.

"Don't look at me like that," Ray said, flushing with exasperation. "We exchanged numbers after we talked on Christmas. We're just friends. It's no big deal."

Emma couldn't wait to talk to Grayson later to tell him this news. "If you say so." She'd never known her father to call any woman since her mother died, so it was, in fact, a big deal to hear he'd called Hannah Coleman.

They ate the delicious dinner and worked together to clean up the kitchen before Emma sent Simone off to shower and get ready for bed.

"How about a beer for the road?" Emma asked her dad.

"I won't say no to that."

She opened two bottles and handed one to him. "Thank you for all the time you give Simone. She loves every second you spend together."

"So do I. She's a natural in the kitchen. Pays attention to the details. I like that."

"Did you hear her quizzing Gray about the transplant yesterday? He says she's a sponge when it comes to learning new things."

"That's a very good word for it." Her dad sat on the sofa and patted the seat next to him. "I got a very strange call earlier today from Linc Abbott."

"What did he want?" she asked, wondering if he'd called Ray to plead her case.

"He told me about the job he offered you."

"Oh," Emma said on a long exhale.

"He said he realized you'd never take the offer if it meant leaving me here by my lonesome, so he offered me a job, too."

"He did *what*?"

"He asked if I might be interested in serving as the general contractor on the construction of their new warehouse."

Emma was so shocked, she could barely breathe, let alone speak. "But... You... You're retired!"

"And bored out of my mind most of the time."

"Wait... You're actually *interested* in the job?"

"Only if you're interested in the one he offered you."

And then, like puzzle pieces slipping into place, the picture became clear to Emma, and she began to laugh. She laughed so hard that tears spilled down her cheeks.

"Are you going to tell me what the heck is so funny?"

After she laughed some more at the priceless expression on his face, she said, "Lincoln Abbott is funny."

"Because he offered us jobs?"

"Because he and his father-in-law are master matchmakers." Emma told him about the lengths Linc and Elmer had gone to pair Will with Cameron, Colton with Lucy, Nolan with Hannah, Charley with Tyler, Hunter with Megan and Gavin with Ella, although Ella had done most of the heavy lifting in their case. "He wants me with Grayson and has thought of every possible detail that could stand in the way of me accepting the job offer and moving to Vermont to be with him."

"Huh, wow. Are you saying we're being played?"

"In the best possible way. They may be shameless, but their hearts are in the right place."

"Do you want the job that Linc offered you?"

"I think I do," Emma said, free to admit as much to herself as well as him now that she knew he had options. "It's a really great offer—more money, full health coverage for me and Simone, cheaper cost of living and a new challenge in a town Simone and I both love. Lucy is there more often than not these days, and…"

"Grayson is there."

Emma's face felt hot as she said, "Grayson is there."

"And you love him."

"I really do. But the only way we're moving is if you come with us."

"I made a big mistake when Lucy first fell for Colton. I let her think I disapproved of her moving away from me, and that hurt her. I like to think I've learned my lesson. I want to be wherever my girls are. If my ladies want to be in Vermont, I'll move to Vermont."

Emma smiled at him, filled with euphoria that what had seemed so impossible only that morning might not be impossible after all. "I can't imagine you anywhere but Queens."

"It'll be an adjustment for all of us, but what matters is that we'll be together, not where we are."

"Troy is going to kill me."

"He'll get over it. He loves you, and he wants you to be happy. He might have his nose out of joint over it at first, but after he has time to get used to it, he'll be fine. Maybe we can fix him up with one of Gray's sisters, and he'll find his own way to the Green Mountain State."

"I'll suggest that to Linc and Elmer, the experts."

"Are we really going to do this?"

"I suppose we ought to ask Simone what she thinks."

"About what?" Simone asked as she came into the room wearing pajamas, her hair wet from the shower.

Emma held out her arms to bring her daughter onto her lap, even though she was getting too big for Emma's lap. "What would you think about possibly moving to Vermont?" While she waited for Simone to reply, Emma held her breath.

"Like *forever*?"

"Pretty much."

Simone thought about that for a minute. "Would we live with Grayson?"

"Umm…"

Ray smirked at Emma. "Yes, Emma, I'd like to know that, too."

"Probably?" Emma's voice was a high squeak that made her dad laugh.

"That'd be okay," Simone said.

"You'd have to change schools and leave your friends." Emma wanted there to be no ambiguity about what Simone would be agreeing to.

"Could we come back and visit sometime?"

"Of course."

"And could I text them and FaceTime?"

"Absolutely."

"What about Pop? We can't leave him here by himself."

"I'd go with you," Ray said.

Simone's eyes got very big. "*You* would move to Vermont, too?"

"That's right. I want to be wherever you, your mommy and Auntie Lu are."

"Then I guess it would be okay. I like it there. It's fun. There's always stuff to do, and Auntie Lu is there, and I want to ski some more. When would we go?"

"I'm not sure yet. I'll have to figure that out, but it'd probably be soon."

"Can I bring all my toys?"

"Only the ones you still play with. The rest we could donate to kids who aren't as lucky as you are."

"Okay."

"Okay what?" Emma asked.

"We can move."

"Are you sure? Our whole lives would change, and you need to be all right with that."

"Would Grayson be my dad when we move?"

Emma glanced at Ray, who looked away when his eyes filled. "I'm sure he'd love that. He already adores you."

"I like him, too, and he makes you smile a lot."

"Yes, he does." Emma hugged her daughter as tightly as she had in years. "Love you, Pooh."

"Love you, too."

"Give your Pop a kiss and get in bed."

Simone hugged and kissed Ray. "Thanks for a fun time this weekend."

"I had a blast, sweetheart. Thank *you*."

Simone scampered off to her room.

Emma looked at her dad. "So…"

"So… What d'you say we move to Vermont?"

Emma felt like she was on the precipice of jumping off the high dive for the first time in her life. "I say let's do it."

By the time Grayson called at nine, Emma was about to spontaneously combust from excitement. Before he could even say hello, she said, "You aren't going to believe it! Your uncle offered my dad a job helping to build the warehouse, and he's actually *interested*. We talked to Simone, and she's all for it, and… I think we're going to do it."

"Are you saying what I think you are?"

"We're going to move, Gray. We're all going to move! And Simone… She asked if you would be her dad if we lived with you, and I hope it's okay that I told her you'd probably like that."

"God, Emma, of course I would. Am I having some sort of post-bone-marrow-donation dream or something?"

"No," she said, laughing. "Your matchmaking uncle has made us offers we can't possibly refuse."

"I love him so much. Almost as much as I love you."

"It's not the job that's taking me to Vermont, Gray," she said softly. "You know that, don't you?"

"It's not? What else could it be?"

She smiled. "There's this guy, you see. He's wonderful to my daughter and sweet and sexy, and I can talk to him about anything, and when he touches me…"

"What happens when he touches you?" he asked gruffly.

"*Everything* happens. I love him so much. I had no idea this kind of love even existed in the real world."

"He didn't know either, baby. It's the best thing to ever happen to him. And to know he gets to have forever with you…"

"Is that what he wants? Forever?"

"That won't be long enough for him."

Emma sighed with contentment. For once, everything was absolutely perfect and about to get even more so. "Are you still coming on Tuesday?"

"I'll be on a plane the second I can, babe. I'll be there on Tuesday and every single day from now on."

"I can't wait for Tuesday and every day afterward."

"That makes two of us."

"Well, three actually…"

His low chuckle made her smile. "To start with."

The possibility of having more kids with him made her feel giddy rather than overwhelmed. "Guess what else I found out?"

"What's that?"

"My dad called your mom to check on her about you donating for your dad."

"Is that right? Maybe he has more than one reason to move to Vermont, too."

"Wouldn't that be something?" After a pause, Emma said, "I haven't even asked how you're feeling."

"I have never, in my entire life, felt better than I do right now."

EPILOGUE

Elmer was already at their usual table in the diner when Lincoln came in wearing a smug smile. "You're looking far too pleased with yourself, my boy," Elmer said to his son-in-law.

"With very good reason."

"I gotta give you credit," Elmer said begrudgingly. "Offering Ray a job was a nice touch."

"It was the only way Emma was going to accept the offer I made her, and it's not like we don't need someone with Ray's experience to oversee the warehouse project. It's a win-win all around. Orders are through the roof since the website went live, and our foot traffic in the store is up by ten percent in *January*."

Linc didn't have to tell Elmer that January was usually one of the slowest months of the year in the store. "Great news all around."

"We've got Charley moving in with Tyler and now Grayson looking for a place big enough for three as well as in-law lodging for Ray. Lucy is over the moon that her family is moving north, she and Colton are finally planning their wedding, and baby Callie is getting stronger every day." Linc rubbed his hands together gleefully. "It's all coming together. And, in other news, my very talented nephew and your grandson has made Ed Sheeran and his pointless complaint go away."

"Did he now?"

"Yep. He dropped the complaint after Gray talked to his attorney and made him see he doesn't have a leg to stand on."

"Hot damn. That is good news."

"Everything's going our way, my friend."

"So it seems. Have you heard any more about why Mary is leaving the company?"

"Nothing yet, but I'm working on that. I've got Cameron talking to Patrick to see if he can shed any light."

"There's a story to be had there. Mark my words."

"Oh, I know it."

"What're you hearing about Coleman?" Elmer asked, scowling.

"Grayson heard from the doctors that he had the transplant. I guess it's a waiting game now."

Elmer grunted in response. "Still can't get over the gall of that guy coming to kids he abandoned, looking for one of them to save his life."

"Desperate times, I suppose."

Elmer scowled at that. "Anyway," he said, "since the last time we talked about our little project, I've done some digging into the situation our friend Wade finds himself in with a woman he wants but can't have." Elmer withdrew sheets of paper from an envelope and placed them on the table in front of Linc. On the pages were copies of newspaper articles about a huge heroin bust that had gone down in Caledonia County. It had been all over the news for days now.

"What the heck does that have to do with Wade?" Lincoln asked as he scanned the headlines.

"I have reason to believe that the woman our Wade has set his sights on is mixed up with this guy." He pointed to the photo of a man identified as the ringleader of the drug operation.

"How do you know?"

"The day Caden was born, Wade drove me to Burlington. He told me just enough to give me the gist. I put the rest of it together on my own. The question now is *what're we going to do* about it?"

"We're not doing anything. I don't want my son mixed up in something like this."

"I hate to tell you, but he's already mixed up in it. The boy is miserable, wondering if the woman he cares about is safe. He's been even more withdrawn than usual lately, and that's saying something where he's concerned."

"Yeah, it's true. He has been." Linc leaned in, lowering his voice. "Look, this has been fun, helping the kids along to happily ever after, but I won't have my son involved in anything dangerous or illegal."

"We're talking about *true love* here, Linc. Doesn't he at least deserve a chance to find out if she's suddenly single?"

"What if she's mixed up in it?" Linc asked, gesturing to the newspaper articles.

"There's no mention of a woman named Mia anywhere in the documents relating to the case. I read every article that's been printed about the bust, as well as the police reports and the indictment. She's not involved."

"I don't know about this one, Elmer. I've got a bad feeling about it."

"I'll confess that I'm not entirely comfortable with it myself. What do you say we keep an eye on the situation?"

"I could live with that."

"Then that's what we'll do."

AUTHOR'S NOTE

Thank you for reading *Every Little Thing*! I hope you loved Grayson and Emma's story as much as I enjoyed writing it. It's always so fun to return to Butler and revisit the Abbotts, the Colemans and, of course, Elmer and Fred the moose! Much more to come from Vermont! The next full-length book will feature Wade Abbott, but I hope to sneak in a novella called *Can't Buy Me Love*, about Patrick and Mary, before Wade's book, which will be called *Here Comes the Sun*. Make sure you're on my newsletter mailing list at http://marieforce.com to keep up with all the news from Vermont.

When you finish reading *Every Little Thing*, join the Every Little Thing Reader Group at www.facebook.com/groups/Every-LittleThing1/ to talk about the book with spoilers allowed. Make sure you're also a member of the Green Mountain Reader Group at www.facebook.com/groups/GreenMountainSeries/ to keep up on news about the series. Some of you have asked if the group name will change to reflect the new Butler, Vermont series name, and the answer is no, because Facebook doesn't allow us to change the name of groups with a membership as big as we have in the GM group. So the group name will remain the same even as the series shifts toward Butler, Vermont.

A big thank you to my HTJB team, Julie Cupp, Lisa Cafferty, Holly Sullivan, Isabel Sullivan, Nikki Colquhoun, Cheryl Serra, Ashley Lopez and Courtney Lopes, as well as my beta readers, Anne Woodall and Kara Conrad, and my editorial team of Linda Ingmanson and Joyce Lamb. I so appreciate everything you all do to keep things running smoothly while I write the books. Thank you as always to Sarah Spate Morrison, Family Nurse Practitioner, for her help with all things medical—dislocated elbows and premature babies and bone marrow transplants—oh my!

And to my readers, thank you for following me from Green Mountain to Butler. I promise we're just getting started with this series, and there is a lot more to look forward to from Vermont. I always love to hear from you. Get in touch any time at marie@marieforce.com.

xoxo

Marie

OTHER TITLES BY MARIE FORCE

Other Contemporary Romances Available from Marie Force:

The Gansett Island Series

Book 1: Maid for Love

Book 2: Fool for Love

Book 3: Ready for Love

Book 4: Falling for Love

Book 5: Hoping for Love

Book 6: Season for Love

Book 7: Longing for Love

Book 8: Waiting for Love

Book 9: Time for Love

Book 10: Meant for Love

Book 10.5: Chance for Love, *A Gansett Island Novella*

Book 11: Gansett After Dark

Book 12: Kisses After Dark

Book 13: Love After Dark

Book 14: Celebration After Dark

Book 15: Desire After Dark

Book 16: Light After Dark

Gansett Island Episodes: Season 1, Episode 1

The Butler Vermont Series
Book 1: Every Little Thing

The Green Mountain Series
Book 1: All You Need Is Love
Book 2: I Want to Hold Your Hand
Book 4: And I Love Her
Novella: You'll Be Mine
Book 5: It's Only Love
Book 6: Ain't She Sweet

The Treading Water Series
Book 1: Treading Water
Book 2: Marking Time
Book 3: Starting Over
Book 4: Coming Home

Single Titles
Sex Machine
Georgia on My Mind
True North
The Fall
Everyone Loves a Hero
Love at First Flight
Line of Scrimmage

Books from M. S. Force
The Erotic Quantum Trilogy
Book 1: Virtuous
Book 2: Valorous
Book 3: Victorious

Book 4: Rapturous
Book 5: Ravenous
Book 6: Delirious

Romantic Suspense Novels Available from Marie Force:
The Fatal Series
One Night With You, *A Fatal Series Prequel Novella*
Book 1: Fatal Affair
Book 2: Fatal Justice
Book 3: Fatal Consequences
Book 3.5: Fatal Destiny, *the Wedding Novella*
Book 4: Fatal Flaw
Book 5: Fatal Deception
Book 6: Fatal Mistake
Book 7: Fatal Jeopardy
Book 8: Fatal Scandal
Book 9: Fatal Frenzy
Book 10: Fatal Identity
Book 11: Fatal Threat

Single Title
The Wreck

About the Author

Marie Force is the New York Times bestselling author of more than 50 contemporary romances, including the Gansett Island Series, which has sold nearly 3 million books, and the Fatal Series from Harlequin Books, which has sold 1.5 million books. In addition, she is the author of the Butler, Vermont Series, the Green Mountain Series and the erotic romance Quantum Series, written under the slightly modified name of M.S. Force. All together, her books have sold more than 5.5 million copies worldwide!

Her goals in life are simple—to finish raising two happy, healthy, productive young adults, to keep writing books for as long as she possibly can and to never be on a flight that makes the news.

Join Marie's mailing list for news about new books and upcoming appearances in your area. Follow her on Facebook at https://www.facebook.com/MarieForceAuthor, Twitter @marieforce and on Instagram at https://instagram.com/marieforceauthor/. Join one of Marie's many reader groups. Contact Marie at *marie@marieforce.com*.